GW00503415

SONGS OF THE ABYSS

ROBERT J. BRADSHAW

Songs of The Abyss

Second Edition

Copyright © 2022 by Robert J. Bradshaw

All rights reserved.

No part of this book may be reproduced in any form or by any electronic or mechanical means, including information storage and retrieval systems, without written permission from the author, except for the use of brief quotations in a book review.

This is a work of fiction. Names, characters, businesses, places, events, and incidents are either the products of the author's imagination or used in a fictitious manner. Any resemblance to actual persons, living or dead, or actual events, is purely coincidental.

First Edition: October 2020

ISBN-13: 978-1-7773763-0-7

Dedicated To My Parents:
Who have eternally been my number one fans.

———

CONTENTS

SIDE ONE

THE ROAD LESS TRAVELLED

The buckshot-riddled *DEER CROSSING* sign waved as Mike's Ford Escape S.U.V. rumbled down the dirt road. There was nothing to see but trees, ditches, and the occasional squirrel. It had been like that for hours. A lone farm house here, an abandoned gas station there. The scenery had swapped from trees to open fields seemingly at random.

Mike had been forced to drive. His girlfriend, Shelly, didn't feel comfortable driving long distances; a convenient excuse if he'd ever heard one. Mike wasn't fond of long drives either, for that matter, but Shelly was his high school sweetheart. He could never turn her down.

Penny and Carlos, sitting in the back seat, had been arguing since Mike and Shelly had picked them up. They were quiet for now, but only because they were asleep. The incessant banter would resume the moment one of them opened their eyes, Mike was sure of it. This cottage trip was supposed to be a fun getaway, but so far, it had been nothing but a headache. They were coming up on the five-hour mark of a seven-hour drive. Mike gripped the steering wheel harder in an attempt to relieve some of his pent-up frustrations.

Up ahead, Mike saw the first sign that wasn't, *WATCH FOR*

WILD LIFE or *PREVENTING FOREST FIRES IS EVERYONE'S RESPONSI-BILITY.* This break in the usual signage was a welcoming sight. The white letters on the green background read, SAINT TERESA, TAKE NEXT LEFT IN ONE MILE. Mike glanced down at his gas gauge and realized he would need to fill up, and soon. He looked over at Shelly, who was deeply engrossed in a show she had downloaded on her phone. Her blonde hair shone in the sunlight that emanated through the trees. She was growing more gorgeous every day.

I hope the drive isn't much longer; my back is killing me from sitting so long, Shelly thought as the credits rolled across her screen. *I would offer to drive but its going to get dark soon.*

Mike looked back to the road and put the turn indicator on as he pulled over to the unpaved shoulder.

"What's wrong?" Shelly asked, taking her eyes from her phone and looking to the road ahead.

"Nothing," he assured her. "We're low on gas. Just seeing how far the next town is. The Saint Teresa turn-off is less then a mile away, but the GPS says to keep going straight and to bypass it."

"We should follow the GPS," Shelly replied, turning her attention back to her phone as she selected a new episode to watch.

"Right," Mike responded as he looked at the digital map.

Shelly shrugged. *He's not listening again,* she thought and shook her head.

Mike was fiddling with the GPS map in an attempt to un-zoom and see the area around them. By his estimate, it would be another hour before they reached the next town using the GPS's route. Saint Teresa was less than twenty minutes away from this left turn coming up. No way they could go an hour and not tank up.

Mike had an idea. He dragged his finger across the GPS map and set it to go through Saint Teresa instead. The route recalculated. The estimated time of arrival switched from

9:15PM to *8:12PM*. Mike smiled; this new route would save them an hour. They could get gas and arrive sooner. *A win-win scenario if I'd ever seen one,* Mike thought as a boyish grin appeared on his face.

He pulled off the dirt shoulder of the rural highway and began to drive down the unevenly paved road. He drove for a minute before turning on his indicator, signalling that he was turning left.

As he made the turn down the road that led to Saint Teresa, Shelly asked, "Where are we going?"

"The lovely town of Saint Teresa to get some gas. GPS says going this way is going to save us an hour." Mike almost sang the words, still flying high from his discovery.

"We should just stay on the GPS's original route. They put it that way for a reason," Shelly said, her eyes wide as she cocked her head. *I've never heard of Saint Teresa, doesn't sound like a great place. I'm sure gas is way overpriced, always is in these small-town communities.*

Mike glanced at her and noticed she was doing her puppy dog pout. *She thinks she's going to convince me to keep going and by pass this town. That face she does always works, but not this time. This time I know I'm right.* He adjusted his hands on the steering wheel before saying, "The GPS just sets it that way to make us stop in more towns so we spend more money. Besides, we need gas. We won't make it to the next town if we follow its original route."

"Are we there yet?" Penny's voice sounded from the back. She was awake and Mike bit his lip, letting out a quiet sigh as he did so. *She's up, oh joy.*

Penny stretched her arms and thought, *If I have to sit in this car any longer, I'm going to literally scream!*

"If we *were* there, Mike wouldn't still be driving," Carlos said, as he looked out the window.

Mike watched as Penny gave Carlos the finger and then put her earphones in. Mike shook his head and was glad the cabin they rented had two separate bedrooms with thick wooden doors. Not that Mike wanted to stay inside all week. No, he planned to sit on the porch and watch the lake ripple in the wind, maybe go kayaking. He wasn't sure; he just needed to relax.

This past year had been especially hard. Being a minimum-wage security guard at the Kaluvalley Mall wasn't the easiest of gigs. He'd been applying to police jobs all over the state for a solid eight months now and had heard nothing back —with the exception of two rejection letters. He needed a win and this cottage trip would be it. The hardest decision he wanted to make this week was what type of beer he would drink on what particular day. He needed this vacation and Penny and Carlos' drama wasn't going to ruin it.

He headed down the dirt road and felt the wheel jerk in his hand, this section of roadway was much bumpier. While the previous rural highway hadn't been smooth by any stretch of the imagination, this was more noticeable. The road continued like this for a few minutes before seeming to even out.

"You should get a Terrain or Acadia. G.M. makes the best S.U.V.s," Carlos said from the back seat. "I can get you a deal. Forget employee pricing. How about the family discount?" he added after a second when Mike had failed to respond.

"Noted," Mike said. *Is this guy really still trying to sell me a car while I'm on vacation? These sales types just don't quit. How many times so far today? Two? Three? Take a hint man.* After a moment of realizing how rude he sounded, he then added, "Thanks, I'll—I'll try to keep that in mind. I like this, though."

Carlos made it no secret that he worked as a car salesman at the biggest GM dealer in the city. Every opportunity he had he flaunted this trait about himself. Mike had tried to be nice, but found Carlos to be a little snotty and uptight. Perfect for Penny.

Shelly and Penny had been friends since college. Penny

was a nice enough girl with a good fashion sense and was easy on the eyes, but had problems holding onto a man. Carlos was heads and tails above the last few guys she'd been seeing. At least Carlos worked.

Carlos patted Mike on the shoulder and said, "Just think about it." He leaned back in his seat and thought, *If the guys from the dealer saw me in a Ford, I'd be a laughing stalk. Gotta keep up the pressure, I'll get him eventually.* He looked out the window and watched the trees as they passed by. He clicked his tongue as the dullness of the trip set in once again, *this drive is killing me.*

Penny took an earphone out and started talking to Shelly about some work drama she'd been dealing with. Mike could see Carlos rolling his eyes and pushing himself farther back in his seat. He looked like he couldn't be more bored if he tried.

By the time they reached the town, the sun was disappearing behind the trees. It would be dark soon. Saint Teresa itself wasn't much to look at, and consisted of just a main street with several roads that forked off to either side. In the distance, past the main strip of the town, lay a large body of clear water. Small islands sat scattered in the middle of the lake adding touches of green and brown to the sight. The Ford Escape turned and headed down the hill that lead into town.

"It's beautiful," Shelly said as she marvelled at the pristine waters. She raised her phone and took a few photos.

"We should have gotten a cottage here," Penny added.

She sounded innocent enough, but the comment had dug its way under Mike's skin, *you picked the spot we are going too. It took you days to decide, now after seeing one lake you change your mind?* He thought as he bit his lip, eyes wide.

Shelly seemed to sense this and said, "Don't be silly. The one on Nectar Lake is way nicer. You said you loved the pictures you saw. And, it's much more private." She looked into the back seat at Penny as she spoke, while also touching Mike's knee.

"Hear that, hun? More private," Penny said as she ran a finger along Carlos' arm.

"Ya, real pretty," Carlos responded, completely disinterested.

"Why do you gotta be such a stick in the mud? They won't want to hang out with us anymore," Penny snapped.

Mike sighed. The ceasefire between them had ended and their eternal war had begun again. Shelly adjusted her hair in the sun visor mirror as she thought, *here they go again. Hopefully they settle down when we get there.*

The main drag was empty of pedestrians, though a few trucks were parked neatly along the side of the street. Each had faded paint and caked-on mud sprayed across their wheel wells, adding to their overall aging appearance. Mike's S.U.V. passed a small family-owned pharmacy on the right. Looking in as they drove by, he saw a red-haired girl standing behind the counter explaining something to an elderly gentleman.

The girl looked up from the bottle she held and did a double take as the dark blue Ford Escape passed by. The elderly customer noticed that she was staring out the window and turned around to look as well. His eyes studied the S.U.V. just as it finished moving across the wide windows of the pharmacy.

Mike looked forward to the road once again.

"That was ominous," Shelly said, as she turned her attention back to the setting sun. She noticed the strange looks they received as well.

"Maybe they just liked the car, eh Carlos?" Mike said, chuckling to himself.

He looked in the rear-view mirror and saw that Carlos couldn't have cared less. He was too busy flicking the window control button on his arm rest in an attempt to occupy himself.

As the S.U.V. rumbled through the small town, Mike noticed that all the stores appeared to be closed or very close to closing. His spirits lifted when he saw a gas station at the end of the main drag, right by the lake. Its lights were still on and the rusted pricing sign was backlit, displaying quite an inflated price for gas.

The Ford Escape pulled up to the pumps just as the sun set behind the trees on the far side of the lake. A calm darkness swept over the town. Mike got out of the vehicle and unscrewed the gas cap. He pressed the button on the pump and heard a beep coming from inside the building. The sound slipped through the two dusty glass entrance doors that watched over the station.

Mike waited patiently for the cashier to activate the pumps. He waited, and waited, then waited some more. The insistent beeping continued. The attendant never came. Mike sighed, removed his hand from the nozzle and walked over to the glass doors.

Stuck to the glass on the right was a sign that displayed store hours. Everyday the times were the same: *7AM UNTIL SUNSET*.

Mike looked at the now dark sky, "Great," he said to no one in particular.

Mike pulled on the door handle, but it refused to budge. The station was already closed for the night. Despite the locked door, a *COME IN, WE'RE OPEN* sign hung on the left glass panel. The sign depicted a jolly little blue mechanic who stood underneath the welcoming words of the sign. Directly beside him was a tow truck in the same shade of blue. The mechanic held a wrench in his hand and wore a grin on his face, clearly depicting a man who enjoyed his work.

Mike took his eyes off the sign and grounded his teeth, trying to figure out what he was going to do next. *Maybe there's another gas station in this one-horse town?* The wind began to pick up behind him, but he didn't pay it any mind.

He was about to walk away when he saw a pudgy, balding man in an oil stained golf shirt approach the counter from the back room. The station attendant headed over to the beeping computer and held his hand over the button when he saw Mike's face in the glass. The attendant's brown eyes widened and his enormous lips parted in a slack jawed expression. He looked around his empty gas station, sweat appearing on his wrinkly forehead. The attendant raised a fat finger and started to yell for Mike to leave. He gestured a few times by waving his hand in the air, the universal sign for "get lost."

Seeing that Mike was not budging, the greasy man came around the counter and walked towards the glass doors. Mike took a precautionary step backwards and clenched his fists. The attendant came up to the glass and Mike could see the attendant was out of breath from the short walk over from the counter.

"Get the fuck out of here. We're closed," the attendant said, the heavy smell of bourbon slipping through the cracked seal between the glass doors.

"Look man, I just need some gas. I'll slip in an extra twenty just for your time," Mike said as he rubbed his head thinking, *I can't believe I'm going to give this trailer trash asshole more money! But I need the gas.*

"We're closed." The man grabbed the OPEN sign and flipped it.

The happy little blue mechanic was swapped for a red version of himself driving home for the night in his matching red tow truck. The words CLOSED, PLEASE CALL AGAIN, hung over the scene.

The attendant walked to the register, grabbed the key from the closed tray and turned off the lights inside. He waddled to the back room and Mike lost sight of him.

"Douche," Mike spat between the glass doors. The words echoed off the walls of the now dark building.

Now what? Mike thought, as he stood under the overhead lights of the station. The yellow bulbs buzzed angrily as flies zipped around them. A cool breeze ran up the street causing the trees to sway. That early September weather had arrived and it was even colder up here, five hours north of home.

Mike walked to the car and stepped into the driver's side.

"What was that about?" Shelly asked, flicking a strand of hair from her eye.

"Some hick who won't sell us gas," Mike said as he started the engine.

"Well, what now?" Carlos asked from the back, looking out the rear window as he spoke.

"Um—well," Mike sputtered trying to come up with a plan. He had to remain in control. *If I can't keep this simple situation in hand how can I ever hope to be an officer?* He cleared his throat and continued. "This town's gotta have *someone* who keeps a jerry can or something around. Let's head down that side road there and see if there's a mechanic or police station or something," Mike said, speaking the only plan that came to mind.

"I don't know, Mike. Let's get out of here," Shelly said, her voice trembling. She tugged on her sweater as she thought, *these 'northerners' are weird. I don't like this. Mom always said so too, and now I get why.*

"We don't have a choice. We won't make it to the next town if we go the way the GPS originally wanted us to," Mike replied as he chewed on his fingernails, thinking *I knew we should have stopped for gas in Whitevale, an hour and a half back, but we were making such good time.* He was kicking himself now.

"Let me see that," Shelly leaned over and grabbed the GPS from the windshield, pulling it to her lap. She moved her finger around the map. "There," she added after a few seconds. "There's another town on this route, maybe like half an hour away. We can still stay on this route. No back tracking, and still get to the cottage earlier than we thought. Markov's Point, it sounds nice. Please, Mike. I don't like it here."

"Ya Mike," Penny chimed in from the back seat, "Let's go

to Markov's Point. It must have a gas station, probably nicer people too."

"Let's try my plan for a minute," Mike said as he looked at the gas gauge again. The low fuel light hadn't come on yet, but it would soon. He didn't think they had enough gas to make it another half hour, especially on these dark dirt roads.

The Ford Escape was silent, but Mike could tell Shelly hated this idea. She sat with her arms folded across her purple Nike sweater. At least Carlos and Penny were quiet for once. The S.U.V. pulled out of the gas station and moved to a street directly across. The lake came into view immediately on their right side. A few houses sat directly along the coast, their private docks jostling against the tide. Mike looked over just in time to see a shooting star headed over the mountain range on the far side of the clear water.

The girls marvelled at the rippling water, serving as a nice distraction from the present situation. Carlos, though, couldn't have cared less. If it wasn't a product owned by General Motors, it wouldn't hold his attention. Despite his total lack of interest, however, it was Carlos who pointed out the objects a moment later.

"What's that?" he said as he gestured to the sky directly above the lake.

Three lights floated in a triangle, small dots hundreds of feet in the air.

"Must be a constellation," Mike said. He took his eyes from the road to study the orbs over the lake before adding, "Remember there is a lot less light pollution here. More stars for us to see." He focused on the road once again and continued to drive down the side street across from the gas station.

"Three of them in a pyramid? That bright? I have never seen stars like that," Carlos said as he sat back in his seat and looked out to the dark tree line.

"And what? You've seen every constellation, have you?"

Penny said as she folded her arms. "I didn't know you were Mr. Astronomer all of a sudden."

Carlos didn't say anything to defend himself. He just sat there thinking, *Why does she have to give me a hard time constantly? I wonder how deep that lake is? And I wonder if she knows how to swim.*

The side street had a few houses dotted along it, each sitting on enormous lots that were much bigger than anything you would find in the city. Every property was lit up, their owners already home for the night, and Mike could see people moving around inside. Some were eating dinner, some watching TV; everyone seemed pretty normal. He licked his lips and thought, *must have just been that one Neanderthal at the gas station. No reason to condemn this entire town.*

A few people looked up from their meals and watched his S.U.V. drive by. Their eyes followed the vehicle as it moved down the road, unblinking. Mike shivered as they stared at him.

Penny noticed the peculiar looks as well and said, "I'm starting to think we aren't welcome up here."

Mike looked to the end of the road and saw a sign that read, ACE'S REPAIR AND TIRE DEPOT. He looked over to Shelly, his face already lighting up. "See," he said proudly.

He stepped on the gas and accelerated. Despite his calm exterior he wanted to get out of this town as well, preferably as quickly as possible.

Mike pulled up the gravel drive-way of the repair shop. Several small windows in the garage doors revealed that a few lights remained on inside the vehicle bay. A single illuminated bulb sat over the main door, but it was relatively dim. As the vehicle approached the aging building, the Ford's headlights picked up someone just as they walked behind the building, disappearing from sight.

"Someone's still here," Mike's voice cracked as he spoke. He pulled up to the front door, turned off the engine, and exited the vehicle.

"You're not going by yourself, are you?" Shelly asked, her eyes were wide.

"Well ya, I—" Mike replied, as he leaned over and looked through the open driver side door.

"No, you ain't. We're all coming," Shelly insisted as she looked back at Penny and Carlos. "Right guys?" she added after a second of silence filled the Ford Escape.

Carlos sighed, and Penny looked around the backseat dumfounded, like Shelly was talking to someone else all of a sudden. She unbuckled her seatbelt as she thought, *she wants us to go into that creepy repair shop?*

Mike moved his head so he could look in the back seat. "Well, since you're coming, Carlos, pass me that flashlight in the front pocket of the bag beside you." As he spoke, he pointed to Carlos' right shoulder.

Carlos did what he was told but couldn't resist saying, "Just use the app on your phone. What do you need a flashlight for?"

Mike shrugged and grabbed the cheaply assembled torch that Carlos retrieved from the bag. Carlos wiped his nose and adjusted his short, gelled hair before opening his door and exiting the Escape. Penny was last; she took her time putting on a pair of pink gloves and a yellow wool hat. *God forbid she catches a chill,* Mike thought as he felt his back tense with impatience.

The group trotted along the gravel driveway and walked around the back of the building where the person had last been seen. Carlos had taken his own advice and was using his phone as a flashlight. He was hovering behind the group and kicking stones as he walked. *Christ, he's a slow walker,* Mike thought.

They rounded the building and Mike's flashlight picked up no one at all. A pile of tires, some scrap metal, and a rusted out 1987 Honda Civic sitting on blocks were all that was present. The cool breeze flicked off the lake and caused the un-mowed grass to sway against the shins of his jeans.

Mike looked out at the lake and noticed the pyramid of lights had disappeared from the sky. He made a mental note of this and took a few steps towards the ratty Honda.

"Let's get out of here guys," Penny said, clutching her arms. Her beige autumn vest and thin white long sleeve shirt offered her little warmth against the wind.

A flapping of wings caused the group to turn their attention to the roof. A flock of at least a dozen crows took flight into the sky. The gigantic, plump, mangy looking things cawed as they ascended. Mike turned his attention forward as he heard the trees and bushes sway in the wind. A distant splash in the lake caused Penny to yelp, putting Mike on edge.

"Did anyone else notice that those crows were the only animals we've heard since being in this town?" Shelly said, as she clutched Mike's arm. "No crickets. No chipmunks. No cats. Not even a dog barking."

Mike *hadn't* noticed. He was too busy thinking about his vehicle and its lack of fuel. But now that Shelly had pointed it out, she was right. This town was eerily quiet and completely devoid of wildlife with the exception of those crows, which were gone now, too.

"I hate to be a broken record, but let's get out of here," Penny said, her voice shaking as she spoke. *Can't we just get gas somewhere else. Literally anywhere else?* she thought as she listened to the sounds of the lake.

"Right," Mike replied. He turned around and noticed that the group now consisted of three. Carlos was nowhere to be seen. "Where—where's Carlos?" he asked, trying to sound innocent so as to not scare Penny. He didn't want to have a repeat of the ski trip two years prior when Earl, the unemployed wreck of a man that Penny was dating at the time, had vanished in a drug induced stupor.

"What?" Penny shrieked. Her eyes widened and she scanned the various piles of junk behind her.

"Do you think he's screwing around?" Shelly asked, her nails burrowing into Mike's blue Adidas sweater.

"No. I—I don't think he is," Mike replied as he pulled Shelly behind him and slowly approached Penny.

The poor girl's eyes were filling with tears. She took a few steps forward and flinched when Mike put an arm around her. "Carlos?" Penny called into the cold night.

The only reply was the slight breeze over the lake. "Carlos?" Mike called out, even louder than Penny's little voice.

The wind was picking up by the second. The trees in front of the group swayed violently in the breeze. The water rippled against the rocks down the hill from the repair shop. Mike looked to the tree line, and that's when he saw the figure standing there, looming.

It was perfectly still. He thought his eyes were playing tricks on him at first and he squinted, but it changed nothing. Someone was there, and he was sure it was no illusion.

"Carlos?" Mike's voice quivered as the word came out. Mike raised his flashlight to the figure. The bulb shattered the moment the light illuminated its black spindly chest. Glass rained down on the dew-covered long grass. Penny screamed.

The figure staggered forward towards the group.

Mike didn't dare stay put. He dropped the flashlight to the ground and screamed at Shelly to move before pulling her behind him. Penny screamed again as the figure continued to trudge forward, aiming for her.

Disproportionate, lanky black arms were coming out of the tree line. Mushy, moist footsteps sounded off in the soggy dirt under the trees. Mike adjusted his grip and grabbed Penny by the vest, pulling her along with his left hand. Shelly was gripped tightly in his right. Penny snapped out of her screaming trance and followed.

The group ran toward the far side of the shop, the opposite way they had come. They rounded the corner and headed toward the gravel parking lot where Mike's Ford was waiting to take them to safety. The wind was ripping through the trees beside them, and the footsteps continued behind. Slow and monotonous.

It was coming.

They reached the end of the garage and came out onto the gravel lot. Mike's beautiful blue vehicle was still parked. But there was something else. Something that stopped them dead in their tracks.

A second figure. Dark as the night that shrouded them, it stood at the driver's side door of the Escape.

A misshapen hand ran along the hood of the car. Mike shrieked and the figure looked to the group. It moved from the far side of the hood and came at them. The way it moved, so unnatural and clumsy. Penny wailed and both girls broke free from Mike's trembling hands. Penny ran into the trees behind them, her cries echoing off the old and silent branches. Shelly took off to the left and sprinted down the street, giving the advancing figure a wide berth.

Mike panicked and pivoted as he decided to follow Penny instead. Her screams of terror would give away her position and she would get herself caught. Mike also knew he could at least catch up to her. Shelly had been a track and field champion her whole life, and there was no way he would reach her.

Mike ran into the tree line, branches and leaves hitting his face. He could feel blood forming at a fresh cut below his right eye. Twigs behind him snapped as he moved deeper into the woods.

It was coming.

Shelly ran down the road yelling out for help. The repair station was a good stretch behind her, but she didn't dare look back. *Don't you dare look behind you. Keep running! Keep running!* She thought and focused on a house that sat on the right side of the road. The porch light was on, a white picket fence surrounding the property, and a tire swing hung from a twisted tree on the front lawn. *They must have children. They will help*, she thought, hoping and praying they would.

Shelly ran up the drive way, but just as she was about to enter the cobble stone path, the porch light turned out. Immediately, it was followed by the warm indoor lights going dark as well.

"No! No! No!" she screamed. "Help, I need help!"

She reached the maroon painted door and slammed her fists on it. She punched it; the wood made her hand ache. No answer. She turned around and looked towards the repair shop. One of them was gliding down the road after her, the moonlight offering little illumination to its finer details.

Its backward legs were like nothing she had ever seen, nor would she ever care to describe them. It looked like a man, but its arms were long and jagged. Its legs warped and twisted. The spectre's head was an empty pit of darkness that consisted of no features one could recognized as human. The figure bobbed up and down as it moved along the road toward her.

Shelly let go of the doorknob and ran across the front lawn. She leapt over the picket fence and moved up the road. Another home sat peacefully on the left, a short distance ahead. The porch light was on as well, and she could see lights illuminating the main room. She ran across the road and straight up to the window.

A man sat on a grey recliner, drinking a Coors Light from a can as an 80's action film played on the T.V. in front of him. Shelly hammered on the glass and called out for help. She knew the man could hear her, as he had jumped slightly in his recliner as she hit the window. But he did not turn his head, or get up to assist this woman who was pounding at his window. He just stayed there, studying the television.

Shelly could tell he was watching her in his peripherals, pretending not to notice. The man grabbed the remote from the wobbly wooden end table beside him and turned up the volume to *First Blood*. She slammed on the glass again, but realized what he was doing. Drowning her out, muffling her cries. She turned around and looked down the road.

It was coming.

Shelly took off behind the house. It was almost at the front lawn. It would catch her if she headed down the road again and she was getting tired. Her heart felt like it was going to beat out of her chest. She ran through the back yard, the grass swaying in the night breeze. There was a single shed sitting in front of the tree line behind the house. She moved toward it, hoping to lose her pursuer in the dark forest.

Shelly turned the corner of the shed and ran face first into a figure. She screamed but the figure covered her mouth to muffle the sound. She raised her hands and went to claw at the attacker when she noticed the blue Adidas sweater the figure was wearing and looked up. It was Mike with his freckled face and short brown hair. There was a cut just under his right eye.

Mike saw Shelly's eyes recognize him and let go of her mouth. Penny was clutching onto his left arm, her small fist cocked back to defend herself.

"Go. We gotta go!" Shelly cried. "It's right behind me."

Mike grabbed her by the arm and as the group ran into the woods Mike said, "There's a path. We lost the thing from the tire place in the trees back here. If we keep following this trail it looks like it will take us to the main street. Maybe we can find help."

"No one will help. I called and called," Shelly said, hardly able to speak the words.

The three of them ran up the forest path and turned right. Shelly could see the lights of the main drag that Mike had mentioned. She wasn't sure how they were going to get back to the Escape but this felt much safer.

They charged through the woods and were almost at the road when Mike saw movement in front of them. Something ran from the main street and entered into the tree line ahead, heading toward them. This figure moved with a more natural gait and was shorter than the others. Mike grabbed Penny and Shelly and forced them to stop.

The group stood still and in silence, watching as the figure stopped on the path ahead a moment later. It was dark, almost impossible to see, but Mike could tell this figure was a person, specifically a man by the way it carried itself. He appeared to be wearing clothing, something the other figures lacked entirely.

"Come here," the stranger whispered.

Shelly stepped forward.

"No, Shelly, he might be one of them," Penny said, her voice on the verge of tears.

She had called out louder than she should have. If any of them were nearby they would hear her.

Shelly took another step forward thinking, *its okay, its okay. Finally, someone who will help.*

"Shelly," Mike said.

"I promise you, I'm not with them," the man's voice cut through the darkness in a low whisper. "But if you don't let me help you, I will leave."

Mike could see the man was holding a shotgun. If he wanted to kill them, he would have done so already.

Mike followed Shelly's lead and Penny reluctantly joined them. The man gestured down to a ditch beside the trail and slid into it. Shelly followed without hesitation. *She's always so trusting,* Mike thought as he squinted, trying to see if the ditch was safe to enter. Shelly motioned for him to follow and he did so a moment later. Penny jumped down last.

"They don't move so good in the woods," the man said,

pointing his shotgun to the top of the ditch. "I couldn't stand by and let them take more. Not after the last time. I heard your screams. I had to act."

"Why doesn't anyone else help?" Shelly asked, trembling.

"What are those things?" Penny squeaked as she clutched onto Mike.

The man ignored Penny and directed his answer to Shelly. "They don't take anyone from town. They only take visitors and passers by. I don't know why that is, but that's all they want. The only residences to go missing are those that help the ones already marked. Giving them shelter, a ride out of here. Anything that interferes with their plans. I'm putting myself at risk now just talking to you."

"So, they don't take anyone from town who doesn't help. Just visitors?" Shelly asked.

"Right." The man adjusted the grip on his shotgun. "And they only come out at night."

"Why haven't you people moved if you knew about these things?" Mike asked, his voice a mix of horror and disgust.

"Some folks did. That population sign used to be a whole lot bigger. But within three weeks or so of moving away, they all disappeared. And I mean gone. We're talking people moving cities and, in some cases, states. Hundreds of miles. They would move in, unpack, then disappear. Whole families, never found. These beings are keeping us controlled like a little play house or science experiment. We play by their rules and we don't get hurt."

"How long has this gone on for?" Shelly asked.

"Too long. Too many people taken. But long enough that—"

A twig snapped in the distance. The stranger gritted his teeth, and ceased speaking, he eyes searching the dark trees all around.

The group sat, silent, in the muddy ditch for a long time. Only the sound of rustling leaves could be heard.

The stranger took a deep breath and broke the silence. "Look, you kids gotta go. I have some fireworks in my house. I'll get them and set 'em off in the old camp ground up the block. When they go off, get to your car. The fireworks should distract them long enough for you to get out."

He stood up and went to exit the ditch but stopped for a moment. He turned and said, "Last thing. Whatever you do, do not stop in Markov's Point for any reason. And remember, if you see the crows, it's too late."

He got up, checked both directions of the path, and was off into the night towards the main strip.

"What now?" Penny asked.

"Didn't you hear him? We wait for the fireworks," Mike said through gritted teeth.

"Don't snap at her," Shelly bit back. "She's just scared. Just like you." She stroked Penny's long brunette hair as she thought, *I have to keep her calm, if she gets hysterical, they'll find us.*

The three of them waited for a long time. Penny asked a couple times about Carlos, but every time Mike and Shelly dodged the question. The woods were silent with only the occasional howl of wind and branches crashing against one another. At one point, a car alarm on the main drag sounded off. Its loud beeping raised everyone's already-high adrenaline levels, until the owner switched it off a few moments later from the safety of their living room. The noise ceased and the remnants of the alarm trickled off into the lake, fading into the night.

Mike was just about to give up hope on the stranger when he heard the screeching of a firework as it flew up into the air and exploded. The trees blocked the sight but Mike knew the signal when he heard it.

Shelly stood up first. "Come on, come on. That's it."

Mike charged up the slope of the ditch and scanned the trail. No movement, just blackness. Shelly and Penny followed behind as the group ran toward the Ford. The echoes of

Roman Candles, Screaming Mimi's, and Dancing Dragons, sounded off behind them. The woods were still; even the wind had died down. Mike and Penny tripped many times in the dark but Shelly maintained her footing.

They came to the end of the path and saw that it overlooked the repair shop. Mike's S.U.V. was visible, sitting quietly in the stone drive way. The coast looked clear. Mike could see on the horizon to his left, the last of the fireworks exploding, a green flash of light, and a single crack, followed by silence. They didn't have much time.

The group ran across the long grass and came to Mike's vehicle. The Ford beeped as he unlocked the doors and the three of them jumped inside.

Mike started the engine and the fuel warning indicator illuminated in an instant. His eyes widened at the orange glow of the light but he quickly pushed the thought to the back of his mind. His priority was getting far away from this lake-side town. Mike set the car to drive and stepped on the gas.

Rocks flew from under the tires. He turned the wheel and swung the S.U.V. around. The vehicle motored up the street, the CAUTION! WATCH SPEED, CHILDREN AT PLAY signs were for decoration. There was only one speed, and that was get-the-hell-out-of-there.

Mike could have sworn people were watching them from the safety of their homes, but he didn't dare look. The Ford came up to the main drag and turned right, the tires squealing as he took the corner and blew through the stop sign.

"We're going back the way we came, right? Out of this town?" Shelly asked but it sounded more like an order.

"Absofuckinglutely!" Mike yelled as he straightened up the vehicle to get it back to the right side of the road, narrowly avoiding crashing into a parked and rusting Dodge Truck.

Penny was crying in the backseat, either about Carlos or about the beings, but a combination of both was most likely. Mike raced through the main road and up the hill that overlooked the sleepy town. Upon reaching the top, the Ford made a quick right leaving Saint Teresa behind. The sounds of their exhaust echoed off the still water.

The Ford thundered down the road that led home. "Too fast, Mike! We'll go into the ditch. Slow——"

Shelly was cut off as two figures stood in the middle of the road a little under a hundred meters away. They were guarding the exit back to safety.

Mike swore and slammed on the breaks.

"Run them down, run them down!" Penny screamed, her voice full of hysterics.

"Penny, shut up!" Shelly yelled back.

The figures watched the vehicle come to a screeching halt. They stared at the Ford for a moment before both taking a synchronized step forward. The moment their legs hit the ground Mike's radio sprang to life. It fluctuated between John Denver, Van Halen, and A Flock of Seagulls before resting on an aggressive, ear-piercing static that sounded like a distant wailing. It was a static that would burrow into your skull and never depart.

The lights on Mike's dashboard started to fade along with his headlights. The beings wobbled towards the car and the headlights turned to black. A perfect way to mask the intruders' approach.

"Fuck this!" Mike yelled as he slammed the Ford into reverse. Luckily, the ol' girl still had some life in her.

He accelerated and looked out the rear window behind him. His view was blocked mostly by copious amounts of luggage, beer cases, and coolers, but he could see just enough to not steer into a tree. The radio turned back to music as some old Johnny Cash song began to play and his dashboard lit up, followed by his headlights. He came to a bend in the road and put the car in drive, immediately pulling a U-turn. The vehicle accelerated and the tires wailed against the dirt as the S.U.V. flew past the scenic view of Saint Teresa.

Mike was watching the road but Shelly chanced a look at the street leading into town. She could see four more figures walking the lane; they hadn't started up the hill yet, but they would no doubt reach the top in no time. She looked to the lake and saw that the lights had returned to the sky. Six of them this time, they were even lower and brighter than before. Her view was cut off as the tree line filled the driver-side windows. Shelly decided she wouldn't say anything. It would just scare the others, especially Penny.

Before long, they passed a sign that displayed: MARKOV'S POINT, 30 MILES. Mike knew there was little chance they would be able to make it past the town with the gas light already on, but he kept this to himself. He would drive until they had no more fuel. He didn't want to scare the others, especially Shelly.

The road to Markov's Point was full of bends and twists that seemed to occur at random. The asphalt was poorly maintained and overgrown. It looked like it had been years since someone had driven down it. Leaves and branches littered the highway from various storms. No one had bothered to clean them up. It was apparent even the locals didn't like to come this way. A disconcerting thought. The words the stranger had said echoed around Mike's skull, haunting him, *"Whatever you do, do not stop in Markov's Point for any reason."*

Multiple miles passed by before Shelly said something under her breath. It was distant but the fear in her voice was clear. "What the hell is that?"

Mike scanned the road ahead: just sticks and leaves. Then he looked to the escarpment, the same escarpment that started to box the road in on either side. A person, a man by the looks of it, stood in the tree line on the top of the cliff. He was naked and watched the S.U.V. drive by. A toothy grin was plastered on his face. Mike stepped on the gas and swerved around a fallen tree, swearing as he did so.

Mike looked in the rear-view mirror and saw that Penny

was in a deep, stress induced sleep. She hadn't seen the man, which he was thankful for. She would have yelled and put the other two in an even higher state of alert. *The adrenaline and the stress knocked her right out,* Mike thought. Shelly looked to Mike and pulled on his sleeve. He looked at her and followed her finger as she pointed up the road.

A group of people stood on the right side of the escarpment. Four of them, men and women. All clothed this time. The women had smiles etched on their faces, but the men, they frowned. Their expressions looked so unnatural and cartoon like, so exaggerated in their presentation. The people stood and watched the vehicle go by. Their torn up and ratty overalls clung to their bodies.

That was the last of the people they saw for a few miles, at least the ones that Mike reported to Shelly. He had seen one more person just as the escarpment eased down and flattened out. A woman in the forest to his left. As he looked at her, she turned and sprinted farther into the woods. She was naked and ran like no one he had ever seen. She took long, clumsy strides like someone who had only watched a person sprint from afar and was unsure of how to replicate it convincingly. He shuttered just thinking about it.

A few miles after Mike saw the woman, they passed a sign that read, WELCOME TO SUNNY MARKOV'S POINT. YOUR ESCAPE TO NATURE SINCE 1890.

As they passed the sign, Mike saw something moving in the distance. The vehicle's headlights illuminated a naked man, walking down the side of the road away from the vehicle. As the S.U.V. got closer to him, Shelly gasped.

"Carlos!" Penny yelled.

Mike slammed on the brakes and felt the vehicle come to a skidding halt. "No Penny. Don't—" Shelly called out.

She tried to grab her friend's shirt but it was too late. The overhead lights came on as Penny flung open her door and went out into the night. She ran up to Carlos and hugged him. Carlos stopped walking and glanced down at her.

Mike saw something in the left corner of his eye and looked over. A black oval bobbed up and down in the tree line as a mangled, three-fingered hand wrapped around the trunk of a tree.

Mike went to call out to Penny, to scream her name, but when he looked to the field on the right, he saw them.

Ten people. Some were naked, some were clothed, but all were smiling, sprinting at full speed, charging through the field. They would be at the car in a matter of seconds. Mike stepped on the gas and the tires squealed.

"No Mike! Don't leave her. Mike! Don't!" Shelly yelled. She tried to seize the steering wheel but he grabbed her hand and pinned it to her body. Mike looked in the rear-view mirror and watched as Carlos started to shake violently. Penny separated herself from him and took a step back.

His arms broke first, followed by his spine. He wretched forward but continued to stand. Then his neck snapped. Mike could tell Penny was screaming but the engine silenced her cries. She turned to run away just as Carlos' legs broke. Then Carlos wasn't Carlos anymore. Mike looked away as Penny was pulled backwards into the night.

Shelly sobbed. At first it was because Mike had left Penny behind, but then it was because of the images burned in her brain. She had seen how Carlos changed into something— something unspeakable. How her friend had been ripped away like that. The people. Their exaggerated faces. The same fate would have awaited Mike and herself if they had stayed.

The car died less than ten minutes later. It lurched forward several times before sputtering as it sucked up the last of the fuel. Mike guided it to the side of the road and coasted it until it came to a stop. He slammed his head against the steering wheel and held it there.

Shelly put her hand out to comfort him. When she turned to look over his arched back, she saw they had stopped directly in front of a T-intersection. The blood left her face as she realized they were sitting directly in front of a town.

Markov's Point.

She could see what looked like a school, a gas station, a super market, a fast food joint. All right where they should be, but not a single light was on in the entire town.

Mike sensed Shelly was staring at something and followed her line of sight.

"Shit," he said. "The one place he said not to stop."

Shelly rubbed his back and said, "There is no way we are going into that town. Not to look for gas. Not for nothing," her voice was commanding and stern.

"Ya, no way," Mike answered, still staring into the town. "What if we stay here 'til morning, maybe—"

"With those grinning freaks running around?" Shelly said, cutting Mike off mid-sentence. "No way. I am *not* staying here. They could control your car again, remember. Like the radio and the lights. They could just do that with the locks or smash your windows. No way, Mike."

"Well, what do we do then?"

"We run. As fast as we can, making as little noise as possible." As she spoke, she pointed up the road ahead of them. "At least we might have a chance. Did you pack any weapons? A knife, something? Your dad hunts."

"You said the cottage was fully furnished with a complete kitchen," Mike responded as he looked into the backseat of the vehicle, praying he would find some sort of sharp object sitting under the seat. "I didn't think—"

"Not even a Swiss army knife?" Shelly asked rhetorically, already knowing the answer.

Shelly double knotted her shoes, zipped up her sweater and watched as Mike did the same. They looked at each other and Shelly nodded. They opened up the car doors and the overhead lights came on. Mike quickly turned them off hoping not to give away their position but realized the headlights of the car had probably already done that. He turned off the vehicle and pocketed the keys, hoping they would find some gas and be back tomorrow. Hopefully, with a sheriff or someone with a *very* large gun.

Shelly moved to the front of the Ford and Mike joined her. She reached out for his hand and they jogged down the road.

They ran a mile before Mike insisted they slow down. Shelly wanted to keep going but Mike was out of breath, having had too many Miller Lites that summer. They walked for another mile before Mike saw a farm house sitting on the right side of the road. A single porch light was on over the front door.

Mike looked at Shelly and was about to speak, when she cut him off. "No! No, No, No. Not a goddamn chance. We keep walking. He told us to not stop for any reason."

"I was just gonna look quick for a gas can or—"

"I am not waiting for you. You go in there, and I'm gone. This is what they want. For us to go in there. Maybe there is some gas, maybe there isn't. But they've found the car by now either way. They'll be waiting."

Mike went to argue but held his tongue. Something was off with how dark the rest of the farm house looked. Only the one porch light was on, no other signs of life. It was suspicious, and the old barn that loomed behind it looked like something out of a horror movie Mike had seen as a child. A barn full of human skin and loud farm equipment caked in blood.

Mike and Shelly walked down the road in front of the silent farm house. They didn't utter a word and watched it cautiously as they passed by. No movement, just a still house with one porch light on. Mike breathed a sigh of relief when they managed to get down the road and were almost completely past the house. Then, he heard it.

The flapping of wings.

Mike looked to the barn and saw a flock of crows take flight. The sound was immediately followed by the slow creek of a barn door. Shelly looked behind her and felt a cool breeze running across the untamed wheat fields. She watched as the barn door swung open.

They were coming.

BRITANNIA'S HUNG IN BLACK

"Papers, Miss. Papers. Stop!" the Gestapo officer yelled at me as I walked from the parked car. It was of course in German but I translated. That was my job after all. I complied and felt the sweat forming on my back. I had forgotten about this checkpoint; I was too focused on my task.

These officers were always here, always lurking by the car park. They weren't very good at hiding, but then again, I think they wanted to be seen, to let the people know that they were patrolling the road up to Blenheim Palace.

He approached me from my right, slipping out of the shadows of a parked truck. He was clothed in a black trench coat, cold leather gloves, and had a clean-shaven face. The ideal man, according to someone's ideology anyway.

"Papers," he said again, this time with more venom on his lips.

I handed him the documents from my purse with my free hand. The bag was in my left and it was getting heavy. He looked them over and stiffened up upon recognizing my name. I'd come to this palace enough bleeding times in the past six months, I would have been more surprised if he hadn't. He spoke again and I understood it was a half-hearted apology.

He handed me back my papers and looked down the road at the car that delivered me this evening. The agent waved a hand at the driver, signalling him to leave. The driver nodded, and turned the vehicle around. The Gestapo didn't recognize him. Excellent, my driver was the newest member of our group.

Two officers approached from the left and smiled at me as I glanced at them, their MP 40 sub machine guns out, in plain sight. I knew they fancied me, always staring when I was around.

I thanked the guard with a simple, "danke" and returned the papers to my purse. I wished the other men a goodnight and as I did so, touched the lead officer's arm gingerly. He swallowed; he was married, but she was far away in Berlin. Oh yes, our little group had done its research on everyone who would be guarding the palace tonight.

I walked up the path and could hear the two guards talking about me, comparing me to a few other aides and secretaries that had gone up to the palace earlier that night. One of them thought I was the best looking, while the other said he preferred another, a blonde woman. How typical.

The walk up to the palace seemed longer than usual. I had never been this nervous, had never attended a meeting this important. A squad of Messerschmitt fighters raged overhead, startling me. No doubt a personal touch by Herr Goering as a show of force to both the locals and the other officers in attendance. He was always quick to flaunt his air power. After all, it had been the Luftwaffe that had won the battle of Britain and paved the way for the invasion.

I had received the guest list two days ago. All the top Nazi brass would be in attendance: Von Rundstedt, von Leeb, Hitler, Himmler, Goering, von Bock, Keitel, all of them. Being the secretary to a general who was also a Nazi sympathizer had its perks. Even though I despised the man, I appreciated the access it granted me; I was privy to confidential documents, schedules, meeting notes, all of it.

The red Nazi flags clung to the walls of the castle like a type of cancer. Beams of light shot up at the tapestries from fixtures in the garden to illuminate the black swastikas etched upon them. I missed seeing the once proud Union Jack sway in the wind, but it had not flown since October of 1940.

It was April now, and Britain had endured six months of Nazi tyranny. I was confident that tonight all that would change. Tonight would be the last night that monstrous flag would fly, the end of The Third Reich and the rebirth of Great Britain.

The guard detail at the main gate was heavy this evening, and rightly so. Even if there had been no signs of resistance in nearly three months, they weren't taking any chances. Not today, not with a meeting this important. A few anti-Nazi rumblings had sprung up in Bristol and Manchester a while back, but Franz Six had added a few extra hundred names to his black book and his death squads acted accordingly. They were highly potent and never asked a single question. The resistance took refuge in Glasgow for a time, but ever since the monarchy and remnants of the Home Fleet had fled to the colonies, the entire movement had never been the same.

I approached the checkpoint, my papers already visible. The two machine gun nests on either side of the gate were imposing, but the guards behind them were casually smoking. The watch towers had their spotlights pointed at the tree lines and I could see a group of soldiers patrolling the perimeter. *Calm breaths. Calm breaths,* I thought, controlling my breathing. *You belong here remember.*

"Ah, Miss Bennett. I thought we would not see you tonight," a corporal said, his English being rather poor and with a thick accent to boot.

I smiled and handed the SS guard my papers. His brown

eyes scanned the documents out of habit, but I could tell he wasn't really looking at them.

He turned his attention to the case in my left hand. "They still make you bring that?"

I nodded. "Every time, unfortunately. The amount of times I've asked for a new one is getting ridiculous."

"I will have to check it," he said, and held his hand out to receive the case.

I complied, trying not to hesitate. They had searched this bag at least ten times, every time I've come. This guard in particular had been on duty seven of those times. "Try not to break this one or else I will have to use the rubbish one inside. The keys stick you know. Bothersome little bugger that it is," I said as calmly as I could, though a sheen of sweat had formed under my blouse.

He nodded and sighed as he placed the case on the wooden inspection table beside the gate. Two other guards gathered around, Kar 98k rifles gleaming in the moon light. Those SS lapels stared at me. My pulse elevated as they approached, but I tried to keep it under control.

McDowall, my resistance contact, said they had hidden it inside perfectly, making it impossible to spot the modifications to the untrained eye. The car ride over to the palace was full of debriefings, pliers crushing acid filled blast capsules, plastique, and hastily shoving the primed bombs into the hidden compartment on the bottom side of the typewriter.

The guard pulled the modified typewriter out of the case, looking at it for a second, turning it in his hands. My heart was pounding in my ears. To my surprise, he slid it aside and instead inspected the bag itself. The two guards behind him mumbled something in German and then laughed. It was some old joke that didn't translate well. Some slapstick mongrel humour.

After removing some papers, the guard picked up the bag

and shook it. Satisfied it was empty, he placed the typewriter back in the case and handed it to me.

Before releasing the grip of the handle, he said, "Something bothers me."

My hand froze as I grabbed the case. "Oh? Something wrong?" I replied. A cold wind had begun to pick up and blew past my exposed legs. My skirt rumpled in the breeze. My long coat did almost nothing to shelter me from the chill.

"You secretaries. You don't type in meetings. You——" He gestured with his hand in the motion of someone writing.

"We short hand?" I replied.

"Yes. That," he said. "Why do you always bring this, then?"

"To type out the notes and speeches later. I have two dogs at home. I prefer the quietness of the palace. Besides, the architecture is quite breathtaking, wouldn't you say?"

He nodded. I could tell he was struggling with a few of the words I had said. He let go of the case. I heard dogs barking in the distance and I couldn't tell if they were coming from the castle or the woods beside it. The main gate always echoed in a peculiar way.

I nodded at the guard and went to walk past the checkpoint when he said, "One more thing." I stood up straight and ceased moving as he continued, "Why is it that——"

"Corporal," a voice from my left rang out, cutting him off.

The guard snapped to.

A thin man with a field cap and piercing blue eyes marched over. The SS Totenkopf—Death's head—was dead center on his cap. I recognized this man as Sergeant Wilhelm Mentz. He had assisted in rounding up many an undesirable in London and was infamous for loving his work a little too much.

Mentz spoke to the corporal quietly, his harsh tone making me glad he wasn't talking to me in this way. He asked the guard if there was a problem as he was to report to another posting for the remainder of the night. The meeting was about to begin.

The guard stated that there was no issues and the sergeant turned his attention to me. His English was much better. "Ms. Bennett. Aren't you going to be late?"

"Well, I *had* budgeted enough time. But between car trouble and your guard here asking about the finer details of secretary work, well, who can account for that? Perhaps he is eager for a career change. If he would like, I can put in a good word with General Corrin on his behalf?"

The corporal turned a shade of red and looked at his sergeant. I could tell he wanted to be a million miles away from Britain and Wilhelm Mentz.

The sergeant beamed at the guard and muttered something along the lines of, "We will talk about this later."

Mentz nodded at me and adjusted his field cap. "That won't be necessary, Ms. Bennett. Have a good night." That skull on his field cap still stared down at me.

I headed up the walkway and could hear the sergeant berating the corporal. Judging by the words used, this soldier made a habit of chatting up pretty secretaries. The bag dug into my palm.

The guards on the roof top were out in force. Snipers sat in windows along the spires and multiple machine gun nests were scattered across the roof. There were more tonight than there had been for the meeting held a month ago. Of course, the guest list for the previous assembly was a third of what it was this evening. The tops of multiple anti-aircraft guns could be seen as well, but I knew they were more for decoration. It had been nearly four months since the last R.A.F. plane had taken to the skies.

Just as I approached the front door of the palace, two German Shepherds turned the corner to the left of the building. They smelled the air and pivoted towards me. My hands trembled. The two brooding handlers that gripped their leather leashes looked more fearsome than the dogs. I entered the building and hoped they didn't find my quickened pace suspicious. But why would they? I was running late for a meeting where the Fuhrer himself would be in attendance. I'm sure a great many people had been scurrying about the palace.

A doorman took my coat, his accent telling me he was British, but whether he was a true sympathizer, it would be impossible to know. He put my jacket on a hook and I noticed many other secretaries' coats hung beside it. I nodded at the doorman and looked down at my white blouse. That red arm band with the black swastika glared up at me.

I walked around a patrol of soldiers and up the stairs. As I rounded the corner, I passed by a small meeting room where Field Marshals von Rundstedt and von Bock were talking casually with a few subordinates. A wall of cigarette smoke fluttered about the room and out the open windows behind the field marshals. I clenched my jaw as I glanced at the medals that clung to their perfectly pressed uniforms.

These were the men responsible for decimating our entire expeditionary force at Dunkirk. *How many of those ribbons were graced upon them by the Fuhrer for killing Britannia's children?* I thought as I continued to walk down the hall. At least the guest list was looking accurate so far.

I entered the main meeting room. Generals von Manstein and Marcks were present at the front, addressing their aides and pointing to a series of papers and file folders. General Halder was also accounted for, but he and a junior officer stood quietly off to the right of the room. The general looked annoyed, as per usual.

I saw General Corrin seated eight chairs from the front, his lieutenant aide seated next to him. Many other officers floated in and out of the room, some British, but most were German. I looked at the table and saw a large map of Europe displayed upon it. It was clearly new as it showed Britain with a swastika carved into its center.

I walked past the table to stand behind General Corrin. He waved vaguely at me as his aide spoke into his ear. I was his favourite, his longest serving secretary, and was no doubt pleased I had made it to the meeting on time.

The Nazis were originally hesitant to use me, but secretaries that spoke German and were willing to cooperate were few and far between. Most that had spoke the language, lied and destroyed their files during the invasion, before the Wehrmacht could seize them. The thought of helping the enemy, even with the simple act of translating documents made them ill.

I was a trusted candidate. Not only was I already a secretary to a general who defected and was a Nazi-sympathizer, I also had Aryan lineage that was easily traceable. Many a SS officer had made passes at me the moment they found out that detail. They wanted to keep Himmler and his little blood line agenda happy. Why wouldn't they trust me? I spoke the language, wore the arm band, Seig Heiled when I was supposed to, and was not linked to any resistance member that Franz Six could find. I was the perfect infiltrator.

I knelt down and placed my case underneath the table, right where Hitler traditionally liked to stand. I knew he would pace around, but he usually started and ended the meetings in the same spot. I stood up and was startled when I nearly bumped my nose into Colonel Lehmann's chest. He was a tall man with a menacing smile pressed firmly on his ghostly white skin.

"Where will you be sitting?" the chief of Hitler's security asked, his high-pitched voice sounding like broken glass.

I pointed to the chair next to the wall beside a few other secretaries. "Here, let me take that for you," he said, and went to reach for the bag.

I swallowed and replied, "Colonel, I don't wish to be a

bother, but the room I usually store my things in—" I stopped and he stared at me until I continued. "Well, it's currently occupied by Field Marshals von Rundtedt and von Bock. Their meeting sounded important and there are no other spots for me to use at the moment."

Colonel Lehmann loosened his grip on the bag. I knew he was intimidated by the mere mention of von Rundstedt. The two had a slew of run-ins in the past.

He cleared his throat. "Perhaps another room then?"

"I'm afraid it will get lost. So many guards, so much shuffling. Besides, it has important files for General Corrin in it. You know how he gets when his things are moved. He may wish to refer to them in the middle of the meeting, and you know how he hates clutter. But if you think it should be moved?"

"No, I'm sure it will be fine. Just place it underneath your chair. I would hate for von Rundstedt to trip on it." I could hear the distain in his voice.

He moved my bag and placed it under the seat, a courteous smile as he did so. I was sweating but I hid it well as I adjusted my skirt. The bomb was farther away than it should have been. The meeting room was full of windows and wouldn't contain the explosion. I was still close to the meeting table, though. The bomb would kill them. It would work, it had to.

I sat down on my chair and watched as Lehmann shook hands with a colonel a few seats down. I nudged the bag with my foot to ensure it hadn't moved in the past five seconds. A few of the secretaries were murmuring to each other, but I wasn't listening. The meeting would start soon but all I could think about was the ticking time bomb underneath me. The acid silently melting through the wire that held back the firing pin.

The seat next to me became occupied and I stiffened up. I looked over and saw it was Ellaine Adwell, a secretary for

Major Wolfgang von Hagen. The young major was an up and comer in the German Administrative Regions of Great Britain. While he worked under General Corrin in the British-Axis forces, he reported all of Corrin's orders to his superiors in Berlin.

The fascists wished to ensure the good general was as loyal to the new regime as he swore he was. Ellaine was a bit of a ditz but she typed well and was something to look at. Von Hagen kept her around for her blonde hair and sense of humor, I think.

Ellaine looked at me and smiled. Her swastika arm-band mocked me as she displayed it proudly. She brought up the weather, but I wasn't really listening, frightfully aware that the timer under my seat was counting down.

The first half of the delegation entered after what seemed like an eternity. Generals von Kleist, von Brauchitsch and Model in the lead. They were immediately followed by Field Marshals Keitel, von Greim, von Leeb, von Bock and von Rundstedt. A moment passed before a great number of officers I didn't recognize entered the room as well, all generals and their aides. Some of their faces looked familiar but I couldn't quite place them. The original guest list I had received just two days ago appeared to be quite incorrect. There seemed to be more officers present than we could have ever hoped for. This was excellent news.

Reich Marshal Goering entered last, behind the group of officers. He waddled over to my side of the room, that white uniform standing out from the sea of grey. He approached General Corrin and the two shook hands. Goering and Corrin had become quite chummy since the occupation. *The ace and the defector, what a piss take this is*, I thought, watching Goering utter a few words to the general before he continued towards the head of the table.

He started to pass me but stopped after a quick glance in my direction. "Good evening, Miss Bennett, Miss Adwell," he said. This was not the first time he had stopped to talk to us before a meeting.

I reciprocated the pleasantries. I had seen a lot of Goering, in particular these last few months, as he was always around the palace reminding everyone how it was *his* Luftwaffe who crushed the R.A.F., as well as the Home Fleet. *His* Luftwaffe who now patrolled the skies of cities like London, Oxford, Liverpool, and Glasgow.

Goering left us and took his place at the front of the table, looking proudly at the freshly made map. A moment passed and the chatter ceased as everyone stood up. Goering looked to the door.

The Fuhrer entered, followed by Himmler and a few other SS commanders. My pulse started to race and I could feel myself getting light headed. *Why am I so bloody nervous? I've seen Hitler before, even been in the same room as him. He's been to the palace loads of times,* I thought as I focused on my breathing.

At first, Hitler would visit the country just to admire his conquered land but his appearances became more frequent when former King Edward VIII declined his invitation to return to the throne. After that, the Fuhrer took a keen interest in the operation of Axis occupied Great Britain. I think he liked hosting meetings here as a way of showing the naysayers in his general staff just how wrong they were. They'd said an invasion of Britain would be a mistake, that Operation Sealion was bound to fail. These same officers had also said France would not be so easy to eliminate. Look what happened to them. The French folded like a house of cards— not that we fared much better, of course.

The Fuhrer stood at the front of the map, running a finger across the oak table. He mumbled something to Goering and Keitel before looking around the room at all in attendance. Everyone had their arm extended towards him in a heil. All the aides and secretaries returned to their seats after he flicked his hand in a half-hearted salute, indicating that he received their gesture. The officers at the front studied the map, intrigued by the positions of the wooden pieces that littered the surface, each representing a division of either infantry, armour, or aircraft respectively.

Hitler looked over to General Halder and nodded.

Halder cleared his throat and addressed the room, "Good evening members of the Third Reich. Tonight, General Marcks and myself will unveil our plan to remove Communism and the tyrant Stalin. We will liberate them from Bolshevism and bestow National Socialism upon them. Only when this is accomplished, can the Fuhrer's dream of Lebensraum be accomplished. Now, with the Fuhrer's blessing we will unveil Operation Barbarossa."

The Fuhrer nodded and began to pace around the head of the table. He watched as Generals Marcks and Halder began moving the small wooden pieces around the eastern edge of German occupied Poland. Hitler eventually stopped pacing and stood to the right of the table, which was the farthest possible spot from the case under my chair. Von Leeb stood closest to me with his back turned. As Halder and Marcks talked about the operation, they would move different pieces from all around the map. Goering would usually add something soon after, gesturing a fat hand at certain areas of interest. Halder stiffened up each time.

I knew I only had a few short minutes left until I was out of time. I had maybe a minute or two if I wished to make my exit. My plan was to reach into my case, grab the documents and hand them to General Corrin. He of course wouldn't read them as he would be too busy listening to the briefing and the translator that spoke through the headset into his ear.

I would then excuse myself and hopefully be by the north entrance when the bomb went off. In the chaos, I would slip away. But I was running out of time. If I didn't leave soon, this would be a one-way trip.

An aide entered the room and walked over to my side of

the table. He approached a general who's name I didn't know and whispered something. This general was never mentioned in any of the resistance briefings, so I wasn't too hard on myself for not knowing the name. The general nodded his head and moved over to Field Marshal von Bock. I couldn't hear what they were saying, but von Bock shook his head in annoyance before the two of them turned and left the room. I noticed that the general had left his bag behind, no doubt planning to return to the meeting shortly. Lehmann watched them depart. I could tell he was irritated that someone would leave during such an important meeting.

I watched as a young lieutenant entered the room only a few moments after von Bock and the other general had disappeared through the doorway. The lieutenant moved over to Lehmann and asked him something. The chief of security nodded and gestured for someone in the hallway to enter. A German Shepherd pulled its way into the room. The handler behind it was one of the same men I had seen previously patrolling the grounds of the palace.

Lehmann pointed around the table and the sergeant pulled the dog along as it sniffed at people's boots and bags. Several officers looked down at the dog in disgust and were annoyed that their concentration was broken. Himmler glanced down at the animal and nodded in approval. Hitler, however, was so focused on the map that he didn't even seem aware of the dog moving around the room. The Fuhrer's eyes probed Moscow and then moved to the oil fields in the Ukraine. He was too focused on Lebensraum—living space.

How could we have been so stupid? Of course the Fuhrer was paranoid and would think of this. The attack in November of '39, Georg Elser's bomb, the same bomb that had hideously scarred Hitler in Munich as he was leaving the assembly. He had never been the same since, thinking spies and assassins were everywhere, his mind clouded with the fog of painkillers.

He had hired Lehmann as his head of security less than a month after. Lehmann had made it his personal mission to let nothing happen to his beloved Fuhrer again. This dog, and others like it, were no doubt a testament to months of hard work to achieve such goals. Lehmann was attempting to demonstrate to the Fuhrer just how safe it was and to ease some of his anxieties.

I tried to keep a generic expression on my face as I wrote notes into the book on my lap, but the voice inside my skull was screaming in panic. *Run, make up an excuse, anything.* I tensed my hands and swallowed a lump in my throat, *It's hidden perfectly. It won't be found. The dog won't notice, just stay calm. Do not draw attention to yourself!*

Despite my calming breaths, my mind raced as to why the dogs hadn't been stationed at the main gates of the palace. Perhaps they had been, but my lateness was a stroke of good fortune. In any case, whatever luck I'd had, was running out. The dog was smelling each bag, then moving onto the next—moving quickly towards mine.

I glanced at the Fuhrer; he had now looked up. He turned to Himmler and the two gestured towards the dog as it searched bags. Hitler nodded and then continued to listen to General Marcks. Lehmann glowed with pride.

The dog came up to Ellaine's purse and smelled it quickly. Its ears perked up and it stuck its nose under my chair. It smelled around my shoes and then forced its nose into my case. I looked at the sergeant, expecting him to be staring down at me, but he wasn't paying attention. He was watching the Fuhrer and the wooden pieces moving around the board. The sergeant had never been this close to the Fuhrer before, let alone witnessed a plan of this scope being discussed.

"Looks like you've made a friend Cathy," Ellaine whispered, as she looked down at the dog and rubbed its head.

The sergeant heard her and turned his head to me. I was shaking but attempted to look inconspicuous, hoping the dog would leave, praying it would. The sergeant pointed at me and said something my brain couldn't translate. I was too stressed.

I looked at Hitler. He was still studying the map, all the officers were. All except Himmler. His eyes fixated on me, arms folded. His Totenkopf cap badge smiling at me.

Lehmann briskly walked over and whispered, "You. Up. Stand up. Your bag. Let me see it."

His voice was quieter than I had expected, as he was trying not to disrupt the meeting in case this was a false alarm. I knew the dog was right. I cursed it and the trainers who had taught it so well.

"It's just a typewriter," I said, my voice trembling.

He refused to listen and grabbed the case from under my seat, pushing the dog out of the way.

"Nein!" I yelled.

The Fuhrer looked up.

As Lehmann moved to open the bag, something new caught the dog's attention. The shepherd cocked its head and sniffed the air. It spun in a circle before pulling the handler over to von Leeb and stuck its nose to the Field Marshal's boots. The sudden jerk of the animal caused the handler to bump into Lehmann and almost pulled the sergeant's shoulder out of place. Von Leeb moved aside and stared at the handler, his look was clear: *control your hound, boy.*

General Halder tried to get the meeting back on track and Goering concurred. The dog stuck its nose into a black bag beside von Leeb's freshly polished boots. The field marshal whispered to the handler and turned behind him to look at Lehmann who still stood over me, my case still in hand. Von Leeb spoke and clarified to both the handler and Lehmann that the bag in question was not his own and belonged to someone else.

Lehmann's eyes widened as the dog sat down beside the black bag, its tail wagging vigorously. Lehmann dropped my case and it clattered to the ground. I flinched as it hit the hard wood floor with a heavy thud. To my thanks it didn't detonate, not yet anyways.

I watched as Lehmann jogged over to the black bag and von Leeb backed away. *A stroke of good luck,* was all I could think as a soothing calm washed over me. I had never felt so thankful in my life. The mission still would succeed as planned. As I watched the animal I thought, *I need to leave. But how can I now? How will it look if I get up after the hound showed me so much interest?*

The dog sitting was the indication that it smelled something. Lehmann clenched his jaw as he picked up the bag gingerly. While he had his back turned, I leaned forward and pushed my case under my chair, as far from that infernal dog as possible. Lehmann stood up and held the bag at chest level.

He studied it for a moment before turning to von Leeb and said, "It's General Tresckow's bag."

The general from before? The one that left? I thought, as Von Leeb turned and looked at von Rundstedt. Himmler moved from around the table to get closer to Lehmann. Von Manstein whispered something to the Fuhrer while Keitel leaned in and listened as well. Lehmann looked around the room in a panic and placed the bag on the table. The dog looked up at the bag, panting heavily. Droplets of drool flicked off its tongue and landed on the hardwood floor. It had done its job and now wanted recognition.

Lehmann opened General von Tresckow's bag and pulled out a series of papers. He looked inside it and cocked his head. He then pulled out a wooden box of Cointreau brand alcohol. The bottle inside rattled against the wooden interior. I looked at the box and wondered, *why in the bloody hell would a general bring a bottle of booze to a meeting?* Judging by Lehmann's expression, he was thinking the same thing.

Lehmann gently removed the wooden lid and glanced inside. He turned to the sergeant and said, "It's just a bottle."

I could tell he was embarrassed. The dog had made him

look like a fool in front of his peers, and the Fuhrer. More importantly he had just interrupted one of the most significant briefings of the war with this charade. Surely, he would never—

There was a flash as the box exploded in Lehmann's hands.

SOLAR FLARES OFF THE STARBOARD BOW

I stood there, looking at the view screen and my heart filled with dread. The situation was dire and we were heading straight for it—The Calypso Pass, the lightning and ion storms that had raged for a millennium. We were hopelessly off course and those solar flares had fried our systems. Waters, our navigator, had attempted to plot a course around but we were already too close. The Calypso Pass' mystical gravity had us in her clutches.

No ship had ever made it through before.

The Pass was thought to hold hundreds of black holes and at least seven solar systems were circling the drain to immediate extinction inside her depths.

Once inside the Calypso Pass, the closest system would be the Magnacarta Straight, with its two suns orbiting each other into oblivion. It would be impossible to escape their grasp. Waters advised me that our only chance of survival would be to enter an orbit with the Magnacarta Straight's larger sun, Phoenix, and attempt a sling shot manoeuvre. He said the odds of survival were slim, but at least they were calculable. If we went any deeper into the Pass, we would never make it through.

Our Communications Officer, Mason, was attempting to send an SOS but he said there was too much interference, and the solar flares had damaged our long-range dish. No one knew where we were and I could feel the stress building. We were all alone with our valuable cargo.

We were a transport crew and I'd been in this profession for the better part of twenty years. But this haul was different. I should have known something was up when the scientists payed us triple the asking price. I should have turned them down, but I needed the money. I had too many debts to pay, too many luxurious tastes. A crippling drug habit was an expensive hobby.

These scientists had contacted me directly and the job sounded easy enough: move a cell block from one system to another, and whatever we did, we weren't to open Cell E under any circumstances.

When we arrived at the research base, they moved the concrete bunker into my cargo bay. I was informed that the other six cells were empty and only Cell E was active. No one would tell me what was inside it though, just kept saying it was classified.

The most I could find was one mercenary who said he was at that base the day it opened. He wouldn't say much more than that at first, but then I found out he had an expensive pallet like mine. I sold him the finest the Skilie Edge could offer and he loosened his tongue a little bit. He was paranoid, but that probably had to do with his hobbies. He said that our cargo was alive, but of course, I already figured that out for myself.

After selling him another round, he added that the scientists didn't dare take it out of its cell, and that's why they were shipping the entire block. The only other thing he'd mentioned before he drifted off into a stupor, was what frightened me the most.

He said our guest knew when it was being watched and hated it.

The scientists had tied the cell block controls into our ship. They advised us repeatedly not to tamper with the life support setting they had set up inside the holding pen as, "That would anger it."

I snuck a peek at the temperature inside Cell E as a technician completed his last round of checks. It was colder than Pluto in there. One of the scientists, a skinny, balding man, made a comment about there once being two cameras in the cell, but they were long gone.

The first thing I did when his back was turned was check the inputs to the camera feeds. Both screens were black, no data to receive. That mercenary had told the truth—this thing did not want to be watched.

Shortly before takeoff the science team handed us a crate of weapons. These things had a long and technical sounding name, but the gist was that they would freeze living tissue down at the atomic level. I vividly remember the look on the last scientist's face as he closed the crate. His eyes suggested that he had seen something no mortal man was meant to see.

Just before he turned to leave, he said, "If that thing gets out, well, these are the only things that will stop it."

It was at that moment that I began to worry about this mission. His eyes betrayed him, looking like he wanted to warn us, to tell us not to take this contract. Of course, that could have been my imagination, or the side effect of the Talkian Crystals I'd been slamming back for the better part of two years.

There was a sharp crack as the bridge of our vessel shook, snapping me from my daze and surprising me more than anyone else. Multiple alarms blared.

Chief Engineer Gilmore looked at a view screen and said, "Seismic blast, radiation increasing drastically. Ion strike, direct hit."

"We have officially entered the Pass, gentlemen," Waters replied as he typed a series of commands into the console in front of him.

I looked at Gilmore, the newest member of our crew. He was supposedly the best technical officer in known space—his price tag certainly agreed with such a statement. Mason had recommended him after our ship had taken some damage on our last mission. The ship was getting old but Mason insisted that Gilmore could keep it together.

As I watched him, he seemed unfazed by the ion blasts. He typed a command into his console and the alarms ceased.

Wright, our weapons specialist, did not look so calm. He stood directly behind Gilmore, and a thick layer of sweat poured down his face. Wright had repelled at least a dozen boarding crafts in his time on my crew, but these storms upset him more than any pirate raid ever had.

Our command deck was dark, just the way we liked it. The only source of light came from a barrage of brilliant purples and blues, and yellows and reds that danced across the main view screen. The Calypso Pass' beauty was matched only by its danger.

Another ion blast hit our hull. The alarm blared, but Gilmore switched it off with quick fingers. A moment passed before the bridge shook again. Another blast. This one was bigger than the last, much bigger.

A few sparks flew from a console near Mason. He jumped from his flight seat and grabbed a nearby fire extinguisher to put out the flames that hovered over the aging console.

Gilmour's head shot up from his monitors, swearing silently. "Those solar flares that hit us did more damage than I originally thought," he said.

"What's the problem?" I answered, trying to keep my composure. I was coming down from my high and I could feel the shakes coming. My body was jonesing for another hit of that Skilie White.

"That last ion blast went right through our storm shields, and a power surge knocked out electrical in Sections Three through Eight," Gilmour continued as a map of the ship filled his monitor.

More than half our vessel was flashing red.

"These old shields only have to last another forty minutes and we'll be completing our sling shot around the sun," Waters said, sounding almost bored by this inconvenience of shield failure.

"Wait," Wright spoke rather abruptly. He turned around to look at Gilmore. His eyes widened. He was clearly frightened. "You said we lost power in Sections Three through Eight?"

"Yeah, why?" Gilmore replied, studying his screen for a moment before turning around to see what the matter was.

"Goddamn it," Mason said. "Section Eight is cargo. Or am I the only one who hasn't forgotten that?"

It took me a moment to realize why Mason was so flustered, why his face had turned a ghostly white. Then it came to me, the crushing notion that sent dread coursing through my body. *If it's broken free—while we're in the Pass—* My thoughts were disjointed and broken as my mind raced in an attempt to sober up.

I ran over to the main view screen, pushing Waters out of my way. I keyed in a few commands and watched as the screen switched from the vibrant colours of the Pass to a black screen. I typed in another command and turned on the reserve power to all sections effected by the blast.

The reserves wouldn't do much, but it would at least keep life support and the doors operating. The only thing I really cared about though, was the camera feeds. I started with Section One, our command deck. Next were Sections Two, Three and Four; all were transmitting a grainy image. It wasn't until I got to the feed of Section Eight that there was a problem.

The view screen stayed blank and never received a picture. Only the words *NO SIGNAL* were displayed. We all stood in silence as we stared at the black screen, hoping, pleading, a picture would appear.

After a moment of no change, Wright started to pace, and Mason broke the silence as he swore and rubbed some sweat away.

I pressed the "next" key and the view screen switched to Section Nine, a black and white feed of our engine coolant deck. I had been meaning to fix the colour on that deck for years, but who had the time? This hardly seemed like the moment to focus on such trivial matters, however. I shook my head and switched the feed to Section Ten. Again, everything was fine. Only Section Eight was giving us problems.

"Don't panic," Gilmore said as Wright and Mason continued to sweat profusely. "It could just be an issue because of the power surge."

"Only in that sector, David? Give me a break!" Wright shouted as he clutched his sidearm, knuckles white with stress.

"I agree with Gilmore," I said, trying to sound as relaxed as possible. However, I felt like Mason had seen through my facade. "It's just an issue from the storm. We don't even know the last time those cameras worked. They could have been out for months. When was the last time anyone had a need to check them?"

"Check Section Seven again," Wright said as he moved closer to the main view screen.

"I hardly think that—"

"Just do it!" Wright ordered, cutting me off.

I had never seen him this upset. I glanced at Mason and he looked equally concerned. I did as was requested and reset the camera feeds. I cycled through all the decks: One, Two, Three, Four, all normal. Five, Six, Seven—

The feed from Seven was now black.

Wright gasped and Mason shot out of his chair. "It's

loose," Wright decreed. His voice was distant as he stared hopelessly at the black view screen.

Gilmore swung around and typed a string of prompts into his console.

Wright turned and asked, "What are you doing?"

"Initiating a ship-wide lockdown. These doors can now only be opened with our palm prints."

There was a collective sigh of relief just as the ship shuttered once again. Another ion blast had detonated a few kilometers off the bow.

The crew was silent until Mason spoke up. "Okay, we stopped it, but it's still loose, what are we going to do now?" he asked.

"We will just have to put it back, wont we," I said and looked at the crate of weapons the scientists had brought us. My mind was finally knocking loose the cloudy residue the plagued my consciousness. I was amazed by just how confident I sounded, no trace of the fear that flooded through me was present in my tone. "Put it back where it belongs," I added after a moment in an attempt to calm my own nerves.

"Why?" Waters replied, his voice carrying with it a hostile edge. "Let the mercenary guys waiting for it at the other end deal with it." That was out of character for him, having never backed down from a fight before.

"If this thing is as aggressive as that mercenary implied, we can't risk it wandering around and giving it free reign of Section Seven," I answered, my lips dry and aching for a drink. "It's just a matter of time before it rips its way through the door, or worse, the hull. Then what? Explosive decompression in the Calypso Pass while completing a sling shot maneuver around a star? Sounds like an awful way to go," I said as I scanned each one of my crew's faces.

"We don't know anything about it. Maybe it isn't that much of a threat? Besides, you are underestimating the thickness of those blast doors," Gilmore said. I wasn't sure if he was trying to convince me or himself.

"Those scientists were terrified of it," Mason chimed in. "They said that even messing with the temperature would anger it. Right, Captain?"

I nodded and thought, *how much did they know about this thing? How long did they have it sealed away?* Mason saw my expression change as the thoughts mulled around in my head.

He continued as he tugged at his flight suit collar, "See, that tells me they weren't even confident that a concrete bunker would hold it. They were right to doubt that because look, it got out. Last I checked, Section Seven wasn't as cold as its cell, so its going to get aggravated, quick! We need to take care of this thing."

"I'll go," Gilmore said after a long silence. "I was in wild life protection on the reserve worlds in my early twenties. I know how to deal with a loose animal. Wright, you're coming with me."

"Why me? There are three others you could have picked!" Wright yelled, his voice cracking.

"You are the weapons specialist, are you not? You're the only one with military training here," Gilmore replied. Already in his first mission out, he was taking command.

Gilmore moved over to the weapons crate and opened it. He pulled out a slender black rifle with a grey tank jutting down from the center of it. Warning labels littered almost every free inch of the canister. Gilmore felt the weight of it in his hands and handed it to Wright who looked at me for reassurance. I nodded and he gingerly accepted the weapon. Gilmore grabbed one for himself and checked the pressure gauge. He was satisfied it was in working order.

"I'll turn the microphones on in each section so we can communicate with you and vice versa," I said.

The two men nodded and left the room. Waters switched the view screen to that of Section Two and watched them move through the living quarters. I walked over to the command terminal and switched on the internal speaker system.

I selected Section Two and said into the microphone, "How are we sounding, gentlemen?"

"Loud and clear," Gilmore replied, his voice much shakier then it had been just a few moments ago.

I switched the speaker system to Section Seven and listened. A sound of shuffling filled the speakers of the command deck. It was distant, on the far side of the section, near the blast door to Section Six. Sounds of smashing glass, followed by a thump as something hit the steel floor. My imagination ran wild as I pictured this thing getting into the power junctions and causing a fire. Then we heard the breathing, deep, throaty and ragged. It sounded like no animal I had ever heard.

Mason let out a whimper and I stiffened up. The microphone on our command deck was transmitting to the speakers in that sector as well. I hadn't remembered to switch it off. The breathing stopped. The sound of rustling continued for a moment before erupting into a thundering bass that filled the speakers. It continued to get louder and louder, until it was right on top of the microphone.

I jumped back as the screeching sound of feedback filled the command deck. The microphone in Section Seven had been ripped out of the wall. Waters swore and I tried to swallow the lump in my throat. My mouth was so damn dry and my heart was beating rapidly. I looked at Mason who was hovering over my shoulder. His face was pale, almost ghostly white. He was trembling.

I switched back to Section Two's speaker system and Gilmore's voice filled the loud speakers. "Can you hear me?"

"Yes." My voice cracked. I coughed to try and mask it. "We can hear you."

"We are entering Section Three now," Gilmore said and I

could hear the sound of blast doors opening followed by a whoosh of air.

Wright and Gilmore ventured through the different sections, until they came to the end of Section Six. Gilmore hesitated as he stood at the door leading to Section Seven. Wright stood behind him, constantly shifting his weight, wiping sweat from his palms onto his dusty flight suit as he balanced the weapon between his hands. Gilmore stood still, staring at the door's control panel. He let out a deep exhale and nodded to Wright that it was time to open the door.

Wright moved back and took cover behind a cargo crate. He positioned his weapon against its steel frame and steadied his sights. The scientists at the base had informed us that the weapons were incredibly easy to handle. The rifles had no recoil and pin point accuracy. They assured us that no training was necessary.

Gilmore scanned his palm print on the reader and watched as the panel turned bright green. The lock down was released in that sector. There was a loud click as the mechanism spun inwards. Gilmore backpedaled rapidly, moving to the other side of the room across from Wright.

The door slid open and only darkness could be seen within Section Seven, no emergency lights, nothing. The two men stood a great distance away from the opening, waiting. But the darkness persisted. It stayed that way for what felt like an eternity. Then I saw a slight flicker in the abyss of the doorway. A whisk of movement, a lumbering yet shapeless mass. Gilmour saw it too, and yelled out for Wright to fire.

Wright screamed and I watched as the two men held down the triggers of their weapons. A spark of blue, crystalline light arced from the muzzles of each rifle and collided with the darkness. The lurching figure from the void moved forward and the cameras lost connection. I punched the screen and shook it attempting to get the image back, but the familiar words *NO SIGNAL*, appeared.

That's when I heard the wailing. There was no image to associate what was happening but I had never heard a man scream like that. At first it was both of them, but Wright stopped first, suddenly. There was a sound of footsteps, crates being tossed aside. Then the weapons fire stopped entirely. Gilmour's screams became louder and more blood curdling.

Then, a horrible, gut wrenching sound filled the speakers. It sounded like he was being boiled alive from the inside. The sound of flesh being incinerated, the water in his pores evaporating, teeth exploding.

Then silence.

Mason, Waters, and I listened from the safety of the command deck, the hum of the engines was the only audible sound. Then the raspy breathing started once more. The microphone picked up an item as it clattered to the floor. I shrieked, but covered my mouth to mask the sound. The item sounded heavy and metallic, most likely one of the rifles.

Then a moist sound followed, no doubt the remains of Gilmore as he was tossed aside like a rag doll of skin and dried organs. Something moved past the microphone and then the sounds of bootsteps were heard, slow and unorganized at first, but quickly picking up their pace. That wasn't what disturbed me the most, though.

It was the slithering sound behind them that made my skin crawl. The shambling boots moved away from the microphone and towards the entrance to Section Five. I looked at my crew mates. Shock and panic filled their eyes. Mason's mouth was open, the pen in his right-hand shaking.

Waters wiped the sweat from his face and gestured for me to cut the microphone's feed. I complied and he said, "We still have it trapped. It can't get out of Section Six. David locked the doors behind him as they moved through." He paused and sipped the four-hour old coffee by his terminal. I knew from his taste in addictions that it contained more booze than actual coffee, but if it calmed him down, so be it. Besides, I was the last person who should be judging someone for their substance abuse problems.

He put the mug down and continued, "We can still put it down. They said the cool keeps it docile right? So, I say we vent the heat in that section, that should—"

Waters was cut off as the console beside him glowed bright green. The three of us turned and looked at the messages being displayed: LOCKDOWN LIFTED IN SECTOR FIVE. MANUAL OVERRIDE ACCEPTED.

"That's not possible," Waters protested as he stared, dumbfounded, at the screen.

Mason muttered something similar as I punched up the camera feed to Section Five. The blast door leading to Section Six was open. Wright stood in the opening but I knew it wasn't really him. Just a soulless husk with his dead flesh as a disguise.

The corpse shuffled forward through the door, its feet dragging with each step. Blood covered his yellow flight suit. The camera picked up the details of his eyes, lifeless and empty, almost all black. The pupils were wide open, viewing everything, but seeing nothing at the same time.

Wright moved through the room and out of the camera's gaze. I saw movement in the open door once again. The black shimmer was moving. I stepped back as the camera caught one detail before the feed was cut. A silver bloated tentacle slithering across the ground into the sector.

"It must be using Richard to lift the lock down," Waters said.

"Well that's it then, we're done for," Mason said as he paced around the terminals. He shook his head for a moment and then continued, "What about venting the atmosphere? The idea you had before?"

"Won't work," Waters replied as he took another sip of his coffee, the liquid rippling in the mug as his hands shook. He wiped his mouth before continuing, "Richard—or what's left of him—will just keep opening the doors. We will end up sucking out all the air in the entire ship."

"Why didn't you think of that idea before Gilmore and Wright left!" Mason screamed, as he continued to pace frantically around the command deck.

"I did. But I didn't think disabling our life support in key areas of the ship while we were about to sling shot around an unstable star in the most dangerous sector of known space was a good idea. I only suggested it now because it's the only idea I got left, isn't it."

Mason stopped pacing. "So, if we kill Richard, we can trap it again. Then you can vent just the sector it's in, right?"

"In theory, but we will still have the problem we had before. An aggressive creature loose on our ship. It will just be more docile than before," Waters replied.

"That's a chance I'm willing to take," Mason said, before turning to me and continuing, "Barret, can you weigh in on this?"

I sighed and tried to calm my rapid breathing. "We vent the section. I know its not the best idea to screw around with life support while in the Pass, but we are out of options."

"Good. I'll take care of Wright and then you vent that sector," Mason said.

"Wait, you're going?" I said in shock as Mason rolled up the sleeves of his orange flight suit.

"Someone has to try. We're all dead if I don't." He grabbed his revolver from the drawer next to his terminal. Eight bullets were loaded, but I prayed he would only need one.

"Let me go with you," I called as he moved toward the door.

"No, you two need to say and pilot the ship. You don't need the radio operator for that. Besides, I'm the fastest one here and a much better shot than both of you. I'll head this thing off in Section Three. We saw on the cameras that it lets

Wright walk ahead by a considerable distance. I'll ambush him and shoot—" he paused, the idea of shooting his friend clearly troubling him. "Shoot whatever is left of him. Right in the head. Bullets still work, right? This thing can't control him if there's no brain left. Then I'll run back into Section Two and lock it in Section Three."

He moved to the door before either of us could say anything. Either he didn't want us to poke holes in his plan, or he didn't want to think much about it himself. Before he left the command deck, he shot me a glance. A look of dread I never wanted to see again.

We watched him move through the ship on the cameras and heard his breathing through the microphone. He reached Section Three long before Wright and his puppet master did. Mason stood in the brightly lit recreation sector, having made the pool table into a makeshift firing position. He stood around the corner from the door to Section Four. I assumed he was hoping to catch Wright's shambling corpse off guard and then sprint back to safety.

We waited for five minutes, sweating, hearts racing, no movement through the door to Section Four. I switched camera feeds and attempted to look into the sector in question but, of course, there was no signal. I heard the door open over the speakers and switched back to Section Three. Wright entered, a thin train of blood trailing behind him. In the lights of the recreation area, I could see just how fast he was deteriorating. His neck was ripped open and one of his legs appeared to be broken, but he walked as if feeling no pain. The bicep on his right arm was missing and the remainder of the limb hung by his side, twitching. He shambled forward and turned the corner.

The camera feed went out immediately.

A moment of silence and then a gunshot, then another. The sounds of a struggle followed. Grunting and then nothing. Not a single scream. Not even a whimper. Just silence, like Mason had just disappeared off the ship.

Waters turned from the blank screen and looked to me, "Now what?" His face covered in a cold sweat.

I grabbed the 9mm pistol from my hip and walked up to the door controls. I fired four rounds into the palm reader. I hoped such damage would ensure that the door would stay sealed, even if the person on the other side had access. The ship wouldn't risk causing a short circuit or the fire that would likely result. I regretted that I only thought of this now. We could have tried that in Section Three to trap it there and Mason could have lived. These accursed narcotics. My hobbies were getting the better of me, slowing my thoughts, sapping me of my creativity and drive. How could I be so foolish?

I gritted my teeth as a sudden urge to drown my sorrows with Felium Gel overcame me like a wave at high tide. Just the thought of the drugs made me want to consume them, and their call was tempting. My mouth salivated at the prospect of its sweet nectar. I bit my tongue to snap myself out of this downwards spiral.

I turned to Waters and yelled, "Vent all sectors!"

I knew we were trapped and the chances of us starving to death before reaching our destination were likely but we were out of options. Our chances of survival were dropping exponentially by the second.

"Right—Um. It will take a few minutes," Waters mumbled, as he pressed the commands on his console.

It took four minutes for the last of the heat and air to exit all sections of the ship, save for Section One. We waited in silence for another six minutes. I attempted to check the cameras in Section Two but they were out. I couldn't tell if the creature was still moving or hibernating. I wished it was dead but I knew that wasn't the case. I wasn't that lucky.

Waters stared at me, waiting for orders, but I had no idea

what to say. We listened to the microphones in Sector Two, but quickly realized without any air there would be no sound to hear.

A scratch on the door behind me. My blood turned to ice. It was faint but none-the-less terrifying. The scratching was followed by a thud. A moment passed and the thudding was followed by a deafening boom. Something was battering the door.

A third thud occurred and this one was strong enough to dent the door. The noise was becoming louder and louder, almost deafening. The door was now severely indented and the steel had moved into the room by a solid two inches. A few more hits and the bulkhead would give way. Solid steel battered in like it was nothing. I wasn't sure what would kill us first, the lack of oxygen and heat when the door came crashing down, or that thing boiling our blood the same way it did to Gilmore. Both sounded awful.

Another thud, the loudest one yet echoed around the command deck.

I looked at Waters and said, "We can't let this thing get out."

Waters nodded and aborted the flight plan that had the ship set to complete the slingshot. I heard the steel behind me start to give in with a creaking of twisting metal. I took a deep breath knowing the writing was on the wall. I looked over to Waters' console and saw we were less than five minutes from entering our slingshot maneuver. So close to turning around and being back on the correct bearing.

Alas, you have to play the hand you're dealt. I knew we needed to act. We had to kill it.

I grabbed Waters' shoulder and said, "Send us into the heart of the sun."

N.G.M.S.

The mangled wreck of Pearcy Baldwoods' motorbike sits peacefully beside its rider's corpse. The poor bastard is still smeared across the track from two laps ago. Going four hundred miles an hour makes it hard to view the finer details, but I'd recognize that red jump suit and yellow paint job anywhere.

He had slammed into the wall, going faster than I was now. Normally, his motorcycle's shields would have caused him to bounce off, but after taking that much fire power from Cyclone, well, his shields were long gone. Cyclone is quite the force to be reckoned with. He's Norway's meanest racer and the nastiest competitor in the entire championship.

I pass the fiery wreck of Baldwoods' crash and turn the corner. Nile and that silver bike of hers are far ahead of me, but I'll catch up. Her bike is slow. Her motorcycle manufacturer is Raven, a second-rate company if there ever was one. This is only their third year in the championships.

Bloodsport Bikes holds the distinction of being the second newest, but their chances of winning went up in smoke along with Baldwoods. Raven's engines are shoddy old tech that the little Chinese manufacturer had bought from Soko Solutions, a Japanese powerhouse who had been selling off old patents. What Raven lacks in engine power they make up for in shielding and weapons. There is a reason I am behind Nile; you'd be crazy to get in front of her with that arsenal of Valkyrie missiles.

Nile is a good racer, hoping to win it all this year. Getting the gold in her third outing? Talk about cocky. She was dropped by her previous sponsor and manufacturer Orion during the offseason, which is why she finds her self racing with the hacks at Raven. Nile has many flaws, the most damaging of which is her inability to keep her mouth shut. Some attribute this to her young age. Combine that with her addiction to social media and you have a recipe for self sabotage.

In my humble opinion, she should just stick to being a swim suit model in the offseason. That's why her accounts have so many followers, not because the people need to know what Nile, a.k.a. Jenna Cristalli, is thinking at a particular moment in time.

She had blamed Orion for chinsing out on the coolant for her ion engine, saying that was the reason for her "pathetic placing" last year. The suits at Orion didn't like that one bit and within twenty-four hours they had dropped her contract. Hell, I don't know what Nile's complaining about. It took me more than four championships to get any higher than twelfth place. Seventh in your second year? That's unheard of; talk about a racing prodigy.

I see her tail lights go over the bend and know the Valley Drop is coming up. I prepare myself. This is the biggest descent out of any of the five tracks of the championship. I follow Nile's lead and head over the hill. We both plummet straight down and I can see the Martian landscape all around. Red dust, craters, mountain ranges, a real welcoming environment. You couldn't even tell that they had terraformed it.

The downward turn presses me against my handle bars as

I approach a speed of eight hundred miles per hour. The crack of thunder from behind informs me I've broken the sound barrier. I have full confidence in my Wraith manufactured gravity locked wheels, the N.G.M.S. really upping everyone's safety requirements on gravity tech recently.

Three years ago, on the Antarctic course, the two lead bikes suffered a malfunction as they went onto a downward 90-degree slope. They lost all traction and left the track, plummeting to the pavement below. There is a picture of the resulting fireball in the N.G.M.S. museum. Biggest pileup in the company's explosive history. Terrible for the six riders that lost their lives as a result, but great for the ratings and a massive spike in viewership. Still, even with that accident in Season Twenty-Five, this year has turned out to be the bloodiest one yet.

Critics say the high destruction count can be attributed to the addition of a fifth race in the series, the Martian track. But this logic is flawed, with more heads rolling in the previous four races to easily bump this championship over the past twenty-seven seasons.

"Weapons lock. Danger. Weapons lock," Anastasia, my bike's A.I. informs me.

Her cool, sexy accent is ever present. Wraith spent good money hooking me up to all sorts of sensors to see what style of voice I would respond best to. Their research and development team figured I would listen to the guidance of my A.I. more often if I was attracted to it.

I look into my mirrors, and see Drax, with his deep blue styled motorbike. Marauder spares no expense when it comes to their fan favourite rider, making them a killing every year in endorsements alone. I'm not all that worried, though. Despite having a name like Marauder, their weapons systems are nothing to be afraid of.

I feel my bike lurch forward as a few high explosive rounds from his blaster cannons slam into my tail fins. My shields absorb it easily enough. I look down at the corresponding gage, noting hardly a dent. He fires another salvo of explosive tipped rounds; I lurch forward in my seat. Now he's beginning to annoy me.

I begin to steer around in an unpredictable fashion, trying to shake the lock on. The track becomes much wider as we hit the bottom of the drop, making it easier for me to move around. Despite my best efforts, I can't shake him. His weapons might be underpowered but that lock-on technology he's got is top notch. Better than mine, I'm afraid to say. No wonder Marauder has more championship wins than any other manufacturer.

My shield gage has dropped to half at this point. I take a sudden bend in the track and break the lock on. Drax's shots fly off wildly over my canopy, crashing into the mountains to my left. He's right on my tail and Anastasia thoughtfully informs me that he has another weapons lock.

"That's it," I say, my voice echoing around the airtight cockpit.

I slam on the brakes and wait for Drax to go flying past me. His bike streaks by in a flash of blue. My Wraith manu-factured cycle has the best acceleration in the whole N.G.M.S. championship and as such, I catch up in a matter of seconds. However, I need to get closer for a lock-on.

My weapon system of choice is a set of grenade launchers and, while powerful, their range is limited. I need to finish him off before we go over *Helix's Climax*, knowing the infamous inverted portion of the track will screw with my grenades targeting like it had in the previous laps. The mix of gravity and speed will cause them to fly off wild and plummet to the Martian surface below.

I close the gap and hear my favourite words in the English language, "Target Locked."

I fire. Two white projectiles spiral out of my side mounted cannons and crash on either side of Drax. His shields glow white. He's fully charged. I fire again and these shells hit his canopy directly as he attempts to swerve out of the way of the incoming salvo. His shields are still glowing white. *I've got to get me a shield generator like this guy,* I say to myself.

I squeeze the trigger on my handle bars, but my launchers click. They are dry and my AI companion utters, "Reload."

Damn it! I think as I press the flashing red button. I know I have about four seconds until I can fire again. I look ahead and can see *Helix's Climax* sitting peacefully ahead, its ominous inverted skyway watches us fast approaching. We will hit it soon and then I'll lose my chance to knock him out of the race for a while.

I smile as Anastasia says, "Weapons ready. Knock 'em dead handsome." I asked Wraith to add that line in special.

Drax has been competing in this sport a long time and begins to swerve about frantically, knowing I must be reloading. I lose lock on momentarily but a simple course correction fixes that little problem. I fire another salvo. His shields glow blue. He's in trouble and he knows it. Drax slams on his breaks but I am lined up right behind him. His tail fins collide with my front wheel. I lurch forward and see that my shields have dropped down to half from the collision. Our shields' kinetic energy repels us from one another and I am forced backwards while Drax is pushed forward down the track. I see his shields flash from blue to a ruby red. He's done for.

I fire again just before his shields start their recharge cycle. The grenade rounds explode and Drax experiences a total shield failure. The red tinted barriers flicker and die. His shields don't absorb all of the blast and smoke begins to pour out of his tail fins. It looks like the cannon on his right side is damaged as well. I fire one last time. Goodbye, Drax.

His front wheel flies off and the chassis of his bike slams into the concrete. His motorcycle flips forward turning end over end. I watch in my rear-view as the remains of his bike go for a slide down the race way and collide with the guard rail, finally coming to a rest. I hope he lives; Drax was always a worthy opponent.

I come up to *Helix's Climax* and enter the corkscrew that will end with me inverted. I look up through the glass of my cock pit and see Nile is already racing across the skyway.

The corkscrew is over quickly and I enter the climax for myself. The mountains and concrete of the track are far "above" me now as my entire world is flipped upside down. I look up and see flashes of blues, purples, blacks, greens, from all the different riders who are far behind me. These guys and gals haven't even taken the turn that claimed Baldwoods' life.

This race has been a particularly nasty one and I'm sure the executives at N.G.M.S. are loving every second of it. The first time the Martian track is used and it results in such a high destruction count. The mining operation had originally been weary of hosting the championships here, but then the N.G.M.S. showed them those briefcases full of money, and that weariness turned into a loving embrace.

All the mining company had to do was secure land for N.G.M.S. to build the track, which was easy enough on a planet like Mars. They had even signed in the contract that if the race destroyed any of the mining equipment or facilities, N.G.M.S. would pay for the damages in full. It was a win-win situation for everyone involved. The mining company got paid and N.G.M.S. got to add a fifth race to their championship, and on an exhilarating new locale to boot.

The in-person attendance for this race was sold out. Every seat filled, standing room cramped to capacity. N.G.M.S. of course offered packages to have the fans transported from Earth to the red planet. They had even built luxury hotels for this event. The suits were making a killing.

Of the eleven crashes so far in this race, I had contributed to only two, including Drax. Nile was the leader in terms of kills, four in this race alone. That's how she managed to become one of the leaders despite having a much slower bike, those Valkyrie missiles are no slouch. She planned on winning by sheer force, not with speed.

My H.U.D. indicates I am in fourth place with Nile sitting in a comfortable third. I'm not sure who is ahead of us but I can make an educated guess. If I was a betting man, I would put my money on Alberto Castillo Cabrera—who adopted the first of his last names, as his official racing moniker—in the lead with Svetlana Kravchenko in a close second.

This is Castillo's seventh championship and before he ever put tread to the track, he was something of a celebrity. Prior to joining the N.G.M.S., he spent four seasons as the lead striker for Real Madrid C.F. During the offseason he realized he had a gift for racing and could make a lot more money breaking the sound barrier than kicking a football. Sure, racing is a hell of a lot more dangerous than his previous profession, but Castillo likes the challenge. God knows he doesn't need the money anymore. While he has never won a championship, he is a sponsor magnet. He is also doing tremendously well this year, placing top five in every race this season so far.

I finish with the inverted climax on the skyway and enter the exit corkscrew that will take me back down to the Martian surface. I see several explosions in my rear-view mirror. I look just in time to see the purple remains of a bike go flying off the Climax and plummet to the surface below. *There goes somebody,* I think.

I am not too concerned about the riders entering the climax now, as I am several kilometers ahead of them at this point. Coming out of the corkscrew, I see Nile, almost right in front of me, as her bike slows and her engine starts to give out after twenty-three laps of maximum red line.

I fire a salvo and Nile's shields flicker from white to blue. Her shield technology isn't supposed to be this weak. I would know, I'd been shooting at her the entire race prior and only knocked out her shields once. She must be over clocking her power cell in an attempt to catch the leaders. I fire again but she zips around the bend causing my grenades to explode on the concrete blast rail.

I come around the bend and see that Nile has stopped. My reaction time is not as good as it should be and I race past her. *I'm getting too arrogant,* I think as Anastasia instantly informs me that Nile has weapons lock. I feel the explosions before my A.I. even finishes the sentence. My shields drop down to below half. One more volley like that and they will be scraping me off the Martian surface with a spatula. I know if I step on the brakes, I will end up like Drax. Out-running her also isn't an option, as her missiles have too great a range.

I look in my rear-view mirror and see the flash as she fires again. I decide to do what they tell you never to do, drop the bike. I push the cycle to the track and slide across the concrete as the salvo of missiles race over me. All I can see is the pavement and the yellow contrails from their engines as they zoom ahead of me. Confused by their sudden loss of target, they spin around and crash into the road and guard rail farther down the track.

Nile is surprised by that maneuver and cruises by me. She probably assumes I have just given up on the race and will be stuck on my side until it is all over. She no doubt imagines me needing the crew chiefs in the red jumpsuits to bail me out. One less rider in her way to achieving a top three spot in the championship. She is still a novice, even with three years in, I can tell.

I fire my grenade launchers into the ground beside me. My shields flashed to red but the explosion was powerful enough to get my right side off the ground. I accelerate and shift my weight to the left. My bike straightens and I am back on two wheels. I thunder ahead and wait for my shields to fully recharge before I start closing the gap with Nile.

My shield gauge signals I am green across the board and I speed up. I'm on her in a matter of seconds. I fire another volley and her shields flash to blue. Another round of grenades, her shields flicker to red.

We both crossed the lap line and my A.I. announces, "Lap Twenty-Four. Start."

Even at this speed I can hear the crowd cheering. Hundreds of thousands of people fill the stands around the lap line and continue off into the distance for what seems like forever. I go to fire again but watch as Nile takes a sudden right and enters the pit lane. The entire maintenance area along with the grandstands are shielded. Firing at her now will be a waste of ammo, and a breach of the rules.

I pass the pits and look over. I see that she is giving me the finger. Classic Nile, the spoiled princess that she is. She's gone in a flash as I race away, leaving her in the pit lanes with her maintenance crew. Nile would be out of the race for a while as she had her coolant drained and replaced along with her shield motors. Better that and live to fight another day, than to be blown to bits by me. Besides, the girl has enough points from the last four races to still finish in six or seventh place in the championship, depending on how the other riders fare today.

I see the communications light blink on my H.U.D. but ignore it. It is flashing yellow which means my coach wants to speak with me. He knows I go radio silent during a race, the talking distracts me, so I don't know why he's bothering. If it flashes again, that means is an emergency, and I'll answer it then.

The straight-away that is the audience section comes to an end with a sudden left turn. I go around it and enter the bumpy Martian surface. This is my least favorite part of the track. It's four kilometers of open terrain that has been flattened out to the best of N.G.M.S.'s ability. I think they want this to be an area for passing and a shooting gallery of sorts but with the number of bumps, it makes going for a weapon lock much trickier. My bike really struggles in this area and it doesn't handle the best on this dirt terrain. I decelerate drastically.

I pass the remains of Ottello Nacksar's motorcycle and a few seconds later I see his blue parachute off to the side. The guy had been shot up badly on Lap Twenty and needed to eject. He is alive, from what I figure, which I'm sure the people of Nigeria are happy to hear. For his first year out and the first Nigerian to participate in the championship, he has the whole country behind him.

The open dirt portion ends and I hit the concrete. Next comes a series of twists causing me to decelerate even more. The moment I come to the end of the turns I am welcomed by a hail of blaster fire from behind. I look into my rear-view mirror and see Arisaka is right on me. The amount of gunfire I am receiving this race doesn't surprise me. I know exactly why all the racers are so hostile to me, more so than usual anyways.

It's due to my actions in the race prior. I had been in second place just behind the reigning champion Jaspreet "Jazz" Khatri. This guy had been the champ for three years in a row, participated in nine seasons and was the fan favorite to say the least. His company, Mirage, had made a lot of money due to his talents.

Well, Jazz's biggest problem was he didn't know when to quit, even when taking continuous fire from me; he refused to give up first place. That race was the fourth one of the series and was located on the Pacific Track, off the coast of Japan. Over ninety percent of the track is under the ocean encased in a concrete tunnel system.

We had come to the part in the race where the tunnel changes to glass, allowing one to admire the ocean floor. I knew there was a section of track up ahead that was cracked when a rookie racer went colliding into it headfirst on an earlier lap. Must have been quite the crash to crack the pressure proof glass.

When we came up to this area I fired at the damaged wall and it exploded. Seawater came rushing in and Jazz lost control of his bike. His wheels washed out from under him and he slid into the wall. The track's steel water shutters came down and blocked the breach but enough water had already poured in. Since Jazz's shield generator had already experienced so much damage, the collision with the wall crippled his bike and caused his cockpit to shatter. He was knocked unconscious from the crash and was unable to exit his bike as the water rushed in. He drowned in his own cockpit.

I became a villain of the N.G.M.S. in seconds and Mirage put a bounty on my head. I had killed their championship winning horse and they wanted revenge. The bounty is simple enough to collect. The rider to kill me gets it all, but they will have to catch me first.

For the record, I feel terrible about it. I didn't want the guy to die, I just wanted to win. I never thought shooting the glass would kill him, I just thought he would go for a slide down the pavement. I assumed he would lose control and that would be it; I didn't think he would drown.

I've built up a reputation of being a ravenous murder machine in this championship, a title I loath. Every year prior, I've been something of an underdog, but this season the fans are asking for me to fail.

It all started in the Detroit Turnpike race, the first of the championship. The course was straight-forward enough: race around the abandoned Detroit and Dearborn highway systems. It's the oldest track of the N.G.M.S.

In the off season, a rider named Harvey "Widow Maker" MacArthur had been bashing me along with Wraith. I chirped back on social media and in numerous interviews. As fate would have it, I found myself behind him in Detroit. I had knocked out his shields pretty quickly and his bike was starting to smoke. Despite this, he kept up his speed, even continuing to take shots at the rider in front of him, who at that time was Pearcy Baldwoods. I had no choice, so I fired again. MacArthur's obsolete plasma engine casing cracked. I had never seen an explosion like that before, a ball of blue and orange.

The press played it up that I went out of my way to target this guy. They said I showed no mercy even when his bike was crippled and there was no way for him to win the race. I was an undisciplined animal according to the media.

In the next two races, I took out Hector "Falcon" Borjas, Ernst Stengel, Mathew Smith and Natalie Devin. Mathew and Natalie survived but still the press depicted me as ruthless. I preferred to take out untrained rookies apparently, which was news to me. Due to slander like that, I decided to take it easy in Race Four. I was careful not to disable a single bike for over ninety percent of the event. I used my speed and reflexes to get ahead of everyone. Despite my best efforts, none of that mattered. My reputation was sealed in those last few laps when Jazz perished.

With Mirage putting that bounty out on me and the media constantly saying how bloodthirsty I was, I decided that for Race Five I would just embrace the monikers and eliminate anyone who got in my way. That's what the news outlets said I did anyway, right?

Arisaka's blaster fire is an annoyance to be sure and forces me to concentrate and let go of the past. This little runt honestly thinks he can take me out? I think about doing the brake and fire trick, but I know the canals are coming up. I will lose him in there. Arisaka is a coward and won't risk entering the glaciers, which are much too dangerous for him.

The road ahead forks while my shields flash red.

"Shields compromised," Anastasia informs me.

I steer to the left fork and head into the canals. I watch in my mirrors as Arisaka takes the track to the right. My shields are still flashing, but I know the ice canals will be sparsely populated of racers. My shields should have plenty of time to recharge. The canals are about the same length as the regular track but have a great deal more twists and turns. No one wants to risk the added danger when they don't need to. That is, no one but me.

I jump out of my seat as a burst of minigun fire slams into my tail fins and fries my slowly regenerating shield. The last round pierces through the glass of my unshielded cockpit and exits the other side. A few inches to the left and my head would have been gone.

I look in my rear-view, and see Cyclone, aiming for his fourth kill of the race and to collect the bounty. I rip the throttle and go around the twists of the canals. Outracing him is my only option. If I try to brake, I'll be a sitting duck and he would ice me.

It's funny, Cyclone has always been a villain in the N.G.M.S., a title he relishes in. However, if he manages to take me out, many will see him as a hero. A vigilante and an avenger for the fallen defending champion.

I am able to get far enough ahead in the twists that my shields recharge. I pass a flaming wreck of a bike that has crashed into the cement barrier that separates the road from the wall of glaciers. The flaming debris belongs to Louis "Empire" Markee. I had seen him enter the canals in the second lap after taking fire from Cyclone. I just assumed he had fallen to the back of the formation, but now I guess I know what happened to him. The twists of the canals had claimed their first victim.

We enter a straight away and Cyclone is able to catch up and get a weapons lock. He fires his miniguns and my shields absorb the shots. The weapons are hopelessly out of date, but don't fix what isn't broken. At least, that is Cyclone's logic.

There is a pause in his firing and I assume it's time for the maniac to reload. As I glance to the walls of the canals, an idea occurs to me. Instead of braking and giving up precious time in the race, what if I eliminate him with the ice of the glaciers? *It might work, he would never expect it. God knows I wouldn't,* I think as I study the crystalline walls that jut up into the sky.

I aim my grenade launchers up as far as they can go and fire at the left ice wall. The grenades collide with the glacier and send ice chunks the size of boulders down to the track below. The first piece crashes in front of me and I swerve out of the way. The rest of the ice falls behind as I zip through the falling debris. I watch as Cyclone dodges the first few but once the larger chunks start to fall, he's in trouble. He veers to the far right and I see an explosion, but I don't get my hopes up. An orange parachute emerges from the flames. Cyclone will live to race another day.

I take the vertical road up the glacier wall and follow the path across the top of the summit. Overlooking a landscape of ice, in the distance I can see the spires of the northern mining compound. Billows of smoke swim in the sky above it.

My view is cut short as I go over the edge of the glacier and down the ramp. The sound barrier breaks and I can see in my rear-view that the track engineers have covered the side of the glacier in steel and concreate for a good five hundred meters on each side of the track. They don't want the sonic boom to cripple their precious glacier.

The slope evens out and I am free of the canals. There is a low steel guard rail beside me and I can see the rest of the track. The two roads merge together beside a series of observation posts and grandstand domes. While I can't hear the roar of the crowd over my engine, I can tell they are cheering. I figure they are cheering for me and a grin fills my face. I couldn't be more wrong.

There is a flash of white and purple accents. Fontaine "Fury" and his signature colour scheme overtakes me on my left. Fontaine is the international man of mystery. No one knows his last name or citizenship. The people—especially the women—love this about him. He is an introverted and nearly silent rider who rarely partakes in interviews. The small number of times when someone has managed to ask him a question that he bothers to answer, he replies in a different language, depending on the day. His accent is a peculiar one, and its origins are something the internet loves to argue about in depth.

His bike is absolutely massive and takes up a tremendous amount of my vision. It needs to be this size to accommodate his weapon of choice: A.T. mines. These explosives can only be dropped behind him which makes for a curious design choice. His racing strategy is cocky to say the least. He figures he will be in first place so often that he only needs rear facing weaponry. He came in thirteenth last year, but that did little to shake his confidence.

The blast is instantaneous as he drops a mine in front of me. I run right into it. The explosion is powerful enough to push him forward and for both of our shields to flash. Mine flickers to blue while Fontaine's glows white. I fire my grenade launchers and his shields change to blue.

I go to fire again but hear Anastasia say, "Reload."

I press the corresponding button just as he releases another mine. This time I manage to dodge it by swerving out of the way. Despite this I hear an explosion only a second later. I look behind me and see the blacked-out bike of Nancy "Sapphire" Zang. Her shield still flickering between blue and white.

The kill count for this race must be high if she's this far ahead. Sapphire is not thought of as a particularly good racer, and that's putting it nicely. In truth she's terrible. In her four seasons as a rider, she has been dropped by three different companies and has never even been in the top twenty of any championship.

Part of her issue is her choice in weaponry, which is exclusively lasers. A great toy in theory, but they do not preform well under the pressures of an average race. Going speeds upwards of six hundred miles an hour while getting shot at is not something the lasers were designed for. On paper the continuous flow light beams will bypass shielding entirely, which sounds like a revolutionary design. But the lasers require their mirrors and lenses to be aligned perfectly to magnify their output in such a way to pierce the shields. The constant explosions and rumblings of the track cause the lasers to misalign themselves, making them effectively useless.

To compensate for this, Sapphire put seven of the things on either side of her bike this year. Even still, they are usually misaligned by the end of each race. In the early stages of an event, she will manage to disable a rider or two. but by the end she is left with no way to defend herself. She is too stubborn to switch to a more conventional weapon system and honestly believes her laser technology is the future.

Fury drops another mine. I swerve once again and see in my rear-view that Sapphire did as well. I fire at Fury but he dodges my grenades.

"Incoming damage," Anastasia says causing me to look around my cockpit in surprise.

My shields shouldn't that low? I think as I check the corresponding gauge. It shows they are almost fully charged.

I glance at my rear-view, and see that Sapphire has one laser still operational. Its blue beam pierces my engine coolant tank. She was no doubt aiming for my rear tire but with only one of the fourteen lasers active, it will take a few seconds to adjust her angle on me.

I have an idea. I line up directly behind Fury and watch as Sapphire follows me, her beam cutting a hole in my exhaust vents. A few more seconds and she will cut my bike up really good. I wait for the exact moment the mine hatch on Fury's bike opens.

I see movement on Fury's bike and I veer dramatically to the left. Sapphire's laser continues straight and slices into Fury's activated mine just as its about to be dropped onto the track. The shockwave completely obliterates his shield generator and parts from his bike fly off in all directions. Through some miracle, he manages to stay on two wheels. His remaining taillight flashes red as he slams on the brakes.

Without a shield generator, Fury is out of this race. All he can do is pray that someone doesn't take a shot at him as he drives around defensively. His mines were tiresome, so I won't miss dodging those. Now it's time to deal with Sapphire.

I press on my brakes as we go around a turn and let her pass me. I fire at her once to keep her under stress and pull up beside her. I ram into her right side where her only active laser is located. I know her shield will block any damage but the sudden shoves are bound to mess up her alignment. I ram her three more times and see my shields are turning blue. That should be enough anyway. I pull forward, but Sapphire doesn't fire at me. Her offensive capabilities are completely gone and she will no doubt slink back and attempt to stay ahead of Fontaine. She will simply try to stay alive long enough to cross the finish line. A perfect summary of her entire career.

I look at my position counter which shows I'm still third. No one has passed me while I was in the canals. I take a few turns and pass another observation area. I squint as I see taillights, two sets of them in fact. The leaders? No, one set is moving much faster and flies by the other like it is standing still.

It doesn't take me long to come up to the second set of taillights for myself. I see the red and gold paint job of a rookie whose name I can't remember. Black smoke is billowing out of his engine, a tell-tale sign that he's in rough shape. His shield unit must be heavily damaged as it constantly flickers between red and blue. One shot from my launchers will take him out, I am sure of it. That's what the reporters and talk shows want me to do. In fact, they are probably coming up with headlines now.

But I know me. I'm not a savage. I still have honour. I move to the left of the rider and see his cockpit is cracked. We are all lapping this poor kid who can't be more than twenty-one years old. He takes his eyes off the track ahead and they immediately widen when he recognizes my signature black and green paint job. "The N.G.M.S. Devil" "Champion Killer" "Wraith's Executioner." He has no doubt heard about my reputation and all the nicknames the press has laid on me in the weeks leading up to this race. His mind's likely racing faster than his bike with the thoughts of all the articles he's read about me. Fabricated details such as how I specifically target rookies and am a completely merciless, motherless subhuman without a shred of remorse.

I look at him for a moment and wave. He hesitates, but after a second, he raises his hand to signal back, more out of surprise than anything. I give him a thumbs up and a nod before accelerating away, leaving the kid far behind. *Let's see the press try to spin that in a negative way,* I think as I study the track ahead.

I go over a hill and see the taillights again, the same ones who passed that rookie a minute ago. We enter another straight away and I gain speed. My superior acceleration allowing me to catch up to the rider ahead with little trouble. I recognize the white paint job immediately; it's Castillo. He's in second, which is surprising. Svetlana must be leading, which means I'm losing the bet I made with myself. Good thing I didn't put money on it.

I get up right behind the Spaniard and fire. His shields go down to blue instantly. He swerves and tries to shake me off, but Anastasia keeps weapons lock. I fire again and his shields flicker to red. We come up to a bend where the wall can be scaled and is easily ridable. Castillo drives up on the right catching me by surprise as I foolishly decide to stay on the main part of the track. Through a quick manoeuvre on his part, he ends up behind me and lets loose with those modified flack cannons of his. My shields are at three-quarters strength before I know it.

I swerve and manage to avoid another salvo but he keeps on firing. I slam on my brakes but he's ready for me. We bash into each other and my shields flicker to red. He suffers major damage as well and his shields flicker and die.

We both know I'm too close for him to fire. If he tries to take me out, he will kill himself from the resulting splash damage caused by his own weapons. I have to make this quick, before Castillo backs off and fires again. I open the fuse box by my right knee and grab the wires leading to the engine block under my body. I'm looking for a green wire.

I feel the wires in my gloved hand and yank on the one I figure to be right. My roll of the dice is correct and I see the green one in my fist. I move my hand up and press it to the shield generator fuses. The corresponding power gage fills to about half as I trick the engine into feeding the generator directly. I'll blow the shield motors if I hold it there any longer, so I remove the wire from its arcing position. I lower my grenade launchers to the pavement and fire.

The explosion knocks my shields to almost nothing but causes the unshielded Castillo to lose control. *Didn't see that one coming did ya, ace?* I think, as I count my blessings that I didn't blow my self to bits with such a dangerous stunt.

There is a shower of steel as pieces of his bike hit the track. Since I cut power to my engine, he goes flying past me as my motorcycle decelerates rapidly. His bike begins to smoke and his back tire is looking like it's hanging on by a thread. His motorbike noticeably begins to wobble as it limps down the track.

Castillo manages to keep his cycle steady and begins to flash his brake lights while swerving aggressively from side to side. The universal sign for a truce. The villain that I supposedly am should open fire anyway, God knows Cyclone would, but that isn't going to happen. I know I'm not what the press paints me out to be, despite their best efforts.

I reconnect the green wire to my engine block and see

more sparks fly. I can feel the heat against my thigh, and judging by the smell I've scorched my racing suit pretty good. My engine comes back to life in a roar and I catch up to Castillo's crippled bike. I roll up beside him and look over at his cockpit. He's clearly shaken by my dangerous manoeuvre and upon seeing me, salutes as a show of respect. I return the gesture just as he steps on the brakes, moving behind me. I'm certain he won't fire, Castillo knows when he's bested. He races with honour and is one hell of a good sport. He will respect the truce.

Castillo is hoping that he can float behind me by a fair clip and nab a respectable third place spot. We are so far ahead of the pack of other riders that it's a safe bet he will be able to do just that. As I go over the hill of the "Valley Drop", I can see Castillo's smoking wreck of a bike is already far on the horizon. The sound barrier breaks and I see my shields are almost fully charged.

It isn't until I exit the corkscrew and enter *Helix's Climax* that I can finally see Svetlana Kravchenko's taillights. She's ahead of me, but isn't as far as I expected her to be. No doubt her bike is feeling the wear from this long race as we near the end of the second-last lap. I mange to close some of the distance on her when we finish with the skyway and go into the exit corkscrew. Her engine might be better on the straightaways but in the "twisties," mine has the superior handling. We finish with the climax and I'm almost on her, but she continues to stay just out of range of my grenade launchers. She knows this.

I have a tremendous amount of respect for Svetlana as a racer. She entered the N.G.M.S. at the age of eighteen. Following in her father's footsteps, Alexander Kravchenko, who raced in the first three N.G.M.S. championships in his late twenties. He won the title in his second year and is considered one of the greats. While she herself does not hold a gold trophy, she has three silvers and a bronze to her name. Svetlana has raced in nine championships and if she races next season, she will hold the title for most seasons participated in.

I am unable to get any closer to her as she takes the curves with a finesse I have never seen. Her racing prowess is exquisite. It becomes apparent to me that she not only has the better bike but also more skill. I'm envious. All I can do is watch as she sits just out of weapons range and beats me. Not a damn thing I can do about it.

We cross the lap line and Anastasia announces, "Final Lap."

Svetlana raises her left hand to the crowd. I know exactly who she's waving to, previous champion Alexander Kravchenko, her father. I had heard he would be in attendance today and was also aware that his health was deteriorating rapidly. He'd been diagnosed with an extremely aggressive form of cancer and the doctors gave him six months to live. That prognosis was nine months ago.

While it was a miracle the man was able to come out in person and watch this race, it was very clear to everyone that this would be the last time he'd get to watch his daughter compete. His will to fight was formidable, but there was no doubt the cancer was winning. He was dangerously frail and could hardly stand. His doctors had forbidden him from making the journey to Mars, but Alexander Kravchenko had never been one to listen to rules. He wasn't going to let anything stand in the way of him seeing his little girl race one last time.

The cancer had made him almost unrecognizable, a sliver of his former self. Long gone was the weightlifting physique he had maintained throughout his tenure as a racer. He wanted to see his beautiful Svetlana win and she wanted nothing more in the world than to take that gold trophy home and give it to her father, so he could place it right beside his own.

I give my head a shake and force myself from the thoughts

I am conjuring up. I need to concentrate and wait for her to make a mistake so I can pass her. I will deal with those menacing flechette launchers later, when I am in first place.

But Svetlana never makes a mistake, not even once. She is good, very good. Halfway through the last lap I fire a volley of grenades just to let her know I am still on her tail. They crash to the ground well behind her. She doesn't swerve or do anything to acknowledge the shot. She's too focused on the road, on the trophy that lays ahead.

She goes into the corkscrew of *Helix's Climax* perfectly. She loses no speed and is clearly getting better with every lap, showing no signs of exhaustion. She is precise in all her movements, a true pro. Any speed I am able to gain due to my cycle's more flickable design, is gone the moment we enter the inverted skyway. She pulls ahead again and stays out of range.

We enter the final stage of the last lap and I have come to terms with placing second for this race. My quick mental arithmetic tells me that due to my points accumulated from the other four races, I'll manage to come in second for the championship. My first silver trophy, I should be proud, and in a few weeks I probably will be. But right now, I'm still immensely resentful. I want that gold.

Just as we both come up to the second-last turn of the race, a flash erupts from Svetlana's bike. Sparks from her engine block are immediately followed by a pillar of black smoke pouring from her exhaust vents. She begins to decelerate rapidly, but her brake lights aren't illuminated. Her motorcycle is losing power, fast.

"Weapons Lock," Anastasia states.

My finger instinctively goes to the trigger but I stop myself. I won't fire, that wouldn't be honourable. I close the distance on her and can see that gold trophy hovering in my mind's eye. I begin to pass Svetlana; the smoke continues to billow out of her bike.

My heart is pounding; if I win the race, I'll have enough

points to win the whole thing, the entire goddamn championship. I turn and look into her cockpit. Her blonde braided hair hangs out of her helmet, running in front of her right shoulder. Her black form fitted racing suit makes her look more imposing than her small athletic frame would suggest. I see her face through her helmet visor and her expression surprises me.

Her face isn't full of panic, or hate, or rage, but simply disappointment. Tears stream down her pale cheeks and I feel a heaviness in my stomach. She cries not because she will come in second place, but because she was so close to being able to hand that gold trophy to her father and pose with him. Two generations of champions side by side, right before he died in a matter of weeks. But that future was gone. Ripped away from her, seemingly at random.

I speed ahead as her bike continues to decelerate. My mind racing. The trophy, the press, the fans, the N.G.M.S., all of them want something different. But what do I want? My conscience sinking into my chest, I take a deep breath. Svetlana has raced flawlessly during the entire championship. It wouldn't be right for me to win. She was clearly the better racer.

She wasn't losing because of any fault of her own, but because a small part in her engine had malfunctioned. A gasket or tube or electrical cable. A ten-cent piece of equipment that contained a defect was bringing down her otherwise expertly crafted bike. She had come so close only for me to steal all of it away from her. The future isn't certain yet. It's what I do right now that could make a difference. I can still change it all.

I exhale and step on the brakes. Svetlana comes limping up beside me a second later. Her expression is now of fear. I'm sure her coach is in her headset, telling her all about my inglorious reputation, assuming she didn't know already.

I can see the headlines now: "Titan humiliates, and then

murders Svetlana Kravchenko as her father looks on in horror."

She passes by me and I go cruising straight behind her, the cloud of smoke filling my forward view. My communication light is flashing. It is alternating between yellow and green, my coach and my pit chief. Both are wondering if I've gone insane or am suffering some sort of stroke.

I rev the accelerator and come up right behind Svetlana's rear fins. I'm gentle with the throttle and nudge her slightly. I'm careful not to bump her too hard, as it might spook her or worse, cause her bike to malfunction even more.

Our bikes make contact and I twist the accelerator. My cycle begins to push hers forward, up the steep hill. I can see through her glass canopy that she is attempting to look behind her and see what I'm up to. After a few seconds she seems to understand that I'm not the monster the press says I am and twists her own accelerator on the dying bike.

I get her to the top of the hill and can see the lap line in the distance, its colour has changed to the checkered flag of the finish line. I continue to push her forward but am filled with dread the moment I see a head light closing the distance behind us. I panic. I know the other riders won't be as merciful and would love nothing more than to come in first on the inaugural race of the Martian track.

I rev my engine even higher but I know it won't do any good. I'm already red lining my speedometer and have changed gears accordingly. It didn't matter that her bike was made out of a lighter alloy, my cycle was not meant to push around an object that weighs nearly a ton.

The headlight is getting closer by the second and I watch as it comes up right behind us. Svetlana and I are in the home stretch, another minute is all I need but it won't matter. Whoever this mystery rider is will beat us, no doubt about it.

The unknown rider bumps into my tail fins, unexpectedly I look in my rear-view mirror and see the familiar white markings above the headlight. The colour of Castillo. It appears that he has managed to put out the fires on his crippled bike and stop the plumes of smoke. I look into his cockpit and can see him gesturing furiously behind him. I turn my attention to the track behind us and see multiple headlights coming over the hill. The surviving riders.

Castillo has figured out what I'm attempting to do, he knows honour in a rider when he sees it. He rips his accelerator and my bike lurches forward. We are moving much faster now with the help of Castillo's motor.

Castillo could have passed us and come in first place with no trouble. If he did so he would win the race and the championship. The three of us were neck and neck in the points. Whoever won this race would push that person over the edge. If he wanted to, he could win it all, just as I could have.

The headlights in the distance are closing in and I can see multiple explosions, signifying they are still fighting, vying for position, wanting to win. Even if that means coming in forth or fifth, they still haven't given up. No doubt their coaches are in their ears berating them to accelerate, over-clock their engines, beat the three of us.

Our three bikes are locked together. We are inches from the finish line. The entire crowd is on their feet. Pit crews are jumping up and down. The roar of the crowd is almost deafening and is even audible over the scream of our engines.

We cross the finish line, all three of us, mere milliseconds before the rest of the racers do. Their engines wiz by us, each of them more confused then the last, wondering why we would give up our winning slots to help the Russian Rebel.

"Weapons deactivated," Anastasia informs me. "Congratulations, you placed . . . Second."

I see my communications light is still blinking yellow. I ignore it again; I'll see him in the pit in a minute or two. He along with Wraith can fire me then.

Castillo and I push Svetlana's bike over to her pit crew. They are ecstatic.

I stand and look at the race results on the wall of Pit Lane Six. Some management suits from Wraith had already stopped by and spoke with me about what they deemed, "The Incident." Most of them shook their heads and yelled about how I'd gone soft. A few of them added the genius suggestion that I should have crossed the finish line first and then have gone back and gotten her, if I insisted on being a hero. They shouted until they were red in the face about how many millions of dollars I had just cost the company in advertising deals and contracts that traditionally get awarded to the winner of the championship.

That's always how it goes isn't it? People are so quick to critique, to add in their two cents. These men and women weren't there on the track with me and they certainly didn't think about anything other than money and status.

I shrugged it off. I knew I did the right thing, the human thing. Coach was proud of me, at least. He said I was the best rider he'd ever seen. I knew that wasn't true, Svetlana was the best, and that's why she had won today.

Before leaving me alone in the pit, coach said that I'd made history. He had no doubt in his mind this would go in the all-time N.G.M.S. highlight reel. He said I could retire tomorrow, never race again, and still make it into the hall of fame with that footage playing beside the statue of me. I liked the sound of that. I hoped that if they did add me into that hall some day, I could be standing right beside the statue of Svetlana and her father, that would be the real honour. I wanted nothing more than to be remembered, for my name to live on. But that's not why I did what I did today.

I collect myself and look to my tablet for the official rankings of the race. The stats were being displayed on screens all around the pits, with live commentary playing over loud speakers. I didn't care what any of those reporters had to say. I wanted to scroll through the race results at my own pace. I read the screen quietly as the sounds of cheers and power tools continued to fill the pit lanes:

NEXT GENERATION IN MOTOR SPORTS: SEASON TWENTY-EIGHT:
CHAMPIONSHIP RACE#5: HELIX MINING COLONY: MARTIAN TRACK
OFFICIAL RESULTS:
1ST SVETLANA KRAVCHENKO- NOVA MOTORSPORTS
2ND ADRIAN "TITAN" JACOBSON- WRAITH CYCLE SYSTEMS
3RD ALBERTO CASTILLO CABRERA- STAR BLITZ RACERS
4TH JAFARI "TIGER" ACHEBE- PACIFIC SPEED ASSOCIATION
5TH JACQUE "HOPPER" GOLSON- E.W.P. RACING
6TH KWAITO "ARISAKA" SAITO- HEXWAY BIKES
7TH ISHMAEL KOTH- LIGHTNING M.C.A.
8TH KRISTEN "AVENGER" SINGER- TURBO C.A.S. LIMITED
9TH TALLI "APACHE" DAWSON- N.A.R.A. MOTORCYCLES
10TH JENNA "NILE" CRISTELLI- RAVEN MOTORS

The rankings continue but I lose interest after the top ten. My mind isn't on the results, I'm looking at them more out of habit than anything. I am still thinking about the last minutes of that race. Svetlana's bike malfunction, the black smoke, Castillo assisting us when he could have easily won. I have a million thoughts on my mind but continued to scroll down to the part of the stats that display the riders who didn't make it to the finish line.

DID NOT FINISH RESULTS:
D.N.F. LOUIS "EMPIRE" MARQUEE- FORTIFIED SYSTEMS- K.I.A.
D.N.F. PEARCY BALDWOODS- BLOODSPORT BIKES- K.I.A.
D.N.F. MATHIAS "CYCLONE" JORIG- ORION MOTORSPORTS-
SURVIVED

D.N.F. ELENA ORTEGA- LATIN PROUD SPORT BIKES- K.I.A.
D.N.F. OTHELLO NACKSAR- BANE MOTORS- SURVIVED
D.N.F. VINCENT "DRAX" WINDSOR- MARAUDER MOTORCYCLES-
SURVIVED
D.N.F. HARVEY ALI- SKY LIMIT INDUSTRIES- K.I.A.

The list goes on and on. The amount of causalities for this race is enormous. The maiden race for the Martian track has been a bloody one and the crowd loved every second of it. I am happy to see that Drax survived.

I stand on the podium with the night sky behind me. The commissioners of the N.G.M.S. have already handed Castillo his bronze trophy and I grip my silver trophy firmly in hand. The crowd erupts in a fury of bliss as the officials announce Svetlana Kravchenko as the Grand Champion of Season Twenty-Eight. They hand her the gold trophy and she raises it in the air immediately. The spotlights are quick to pick up her tears as they pour down her face. She gently puts the trophy on the podium and grabs my left hand throwing it into the air. The crowd cheers and I smile. She hugs me and then turns to Castillo raising his hand as well. The crowd can hardly contain itself.

Svetlana picks up her trophy and runs over to the front row of the crowd. The guards move aside as she heads straight to her father. She embraces him in his wheel chair and the photographers are loving it. I can see the entire Kravchenko family is crying. She kisses her father on the cheek and puts the trophy on his lap. He admires it and looks to me and Castillo, gesturing for us to come over. We shake his hand and he thanks us for making an already proud father, even more so. After a few minutes, Castillo and I back away so that the photographers can take more photos of the newly founded Kravchenko dynasty.

I smile. I know that I've done a good thing. The unexpected thing. This is it; this is the day I will be remembered for. Not for how fast I can race or how many bikes I shoot up, but for giving joy to this family, to a father and to his little girl. This will be the highlight of my career, this race, that last lap, that one moment, and I am more than okay with that.

THE DOOR

Bernard Steinman stood there, dumbfounded, the cigarette burning a hole between his index and middle fingers. "Has this always been here?" he asked to the empty cellar in his suburban bungalow.

There it was, plain as day, an oak door in the center of his basement's northern facing wall. It sat next to the empty beer cases and cleaning supplies. He had lived in this house for years and had never noticed it.

"How's that possible?" he muttered to himself. Again, the basement didn't speak back, which was good, Bernard still had all of his marbles.

He noticed the burning in his hand and winced. The cigarette dropped onto the cold concrete with a small click. He picked it up and tossed it into the laundry sink to snuff it out. Bernard had been down to the cellar hundreds, if not thousands of times. He had been down there earlier that day, in fact, adding to his pile of beer bottles.

Bernard lived alone; he was a widower. At least that's what he told the few people that asked. In truth, his betrothed had run away with some 4-F slob who was deemed unfit to join the ranks of the military. He stayed stateside while Bernard was busy dodging MG 42 rounds in the hedgerows of France.

Bernard shook his head again. Thinking of Sharyl always left him feeling aggravated. He pulled another smoke out of his breast pocket and lit it with a match. He took a long drag before building up the courage to approach it, the ominous door. He took a step forward.

The first thing he noticed was the smell: heavy, musty, overpowering wood. It reminded him of the old pews in his church growing up.

He put a hand out and felt it. It was solid and cold to the touch, ice cold. He withdrew his hand and looked at the knob. Solid forged steel, no markings, just round and innocent. He extended his left hand and grabbed the knob gingerly, expecting it to be the same temperature as the door. To his surprise it was warm, just like the nice September day outside.

Bernard turned the handle and felt the mechanism click. He pulled on the knob and watched as the door swung open. What he saw made him drop the cigarette from his open mouth.

Before him was a forest, not unlike those he grew up with in northern Maine. The trees were wet with dew and a slight breeze ruffled his hair. He blinked and looked down to see that several leaves had blown by his feet and into his basement.

Bernard took a step forward then stopped himself. He realized at that moment he wasn't wearing shoes and only had his white socks on. He grabbed the handle once more and shut the door. He wasn't an idiot; leaving the door open for whatever was in this forest to get out would be foolish, fool-hardy even. He had seen enough movies at the downtown cinema house to know better.

Bernard ran upstairs to his bedroom and slipped on the pair of shoes he left beside his end table. He sat for a moment and thought about it. Yes, he would bring it. He raced over to his closet and retrieved his rifle. The M1 Garand, the same model of rifle he had stormed the beaches of Normandy with so many years ago. He could still hear the roar of the landing craft, the Krauts yelling from their bunkers, the cracks of their Kar 98k rifles as rounds blew past his ears. He could remember it like it was all yesterday. This rifle brought back his nightmares from Omaha, a beach he planned to never see again.

He loaded the rifle and felt the weight. The eyes of that German boy he had closed forever in the Ardennes still haunted him. He remembered the snow, the smell of the shot, the blood trickling down onto the fresh layer of white. He hadn't loaded this rifle in at least five years, and the eyes had met him then as well.

Every time he touched this cursed weapon, he saw the ghosts, some of which had been his friends, some his enemies. What bothered him the most was that if he hadn't been at war with the Germans, many of the boys he shot might have become friends as well. He kept this rifle because whether he liked it or not, it was a part of history. His history. It shaped him into the man he was today, for better of for worse.

Bernard hurried down to the main floor and stood at the top step of the stairs leading to the basement. He hesitated. His mind spoke loudly about the door. A thousand unanswered questions filled his brain, but none of them mattered. He thought briefly about shutting the door that lead down to basement and never opening it again. But he couldn't bring himself to do that, he needed to know what was in that forest.

Bernard moved down the steps and approached the oak door. The rifle was heavy in his hands. With his right hand he gripped the knob and opened the door once more. He stepped through the doorframe and heard the mud against his shoes. Bernard walked a few paces forward and scanned the empty tree line. All was still. No birds, no deer, not even the breeze that had blown around before. These woods looked familiar, too familiar. It took him a moment to place it. Then it came to him,

Dachau concentration camp.

These woods were the spitting image of the ones that sat around that horrific death site. While he had not seen the facility when it was full of the Germans' undesirables, he had heard what was said about such a wretched place. Bernard had passed by it mere days after the allies had moved everyone and cleared up the bodies. There was no wind in the trees that day either, only the smell of rot and decay. He could hardly take it. He was glad he wasn't part of the first units that found those people, the boys who discovered the camp. The starvation, the burned bodies, the shallow graves.

Bernard made it thirty paces before he looked back. The door was still open, his basement still visible. He wanted to go back but something was pulling him forward, a need to explore. With every step forward the woods came to look like the ones of Germany in 1945.

Bernard reached a clearing about two hundred paces from the door. The grass was still and he could hear the sound of running water in the distance, the only sound he had heard in these woods since entering. He stepped into the clearing and the smell of Omaha filled his nostrils. The salty water, the smell of iron from the blood that painted the sand, the residue of Bangalores as his unit charged through the breach. Bernard blinked and the smell was gone. He decided then that he had had just about enough of these woods. The visions were getting worse, more real with every step.

He turned around to leave the clearing when he heard the voice. It was distant to be sure, well beyond the clearing, beyond the flowing river. It was just a muffled cry, but Bernard knew it belonged to a child. The voice called again and he could tell the little boy was calling out in German. Bernard looked over his shoulder and into the clearing. He saw no one.

"Nope. Screw that," he said to himself, his voice trembling.

He didn't dare continue on. He knew what he would find at the other end of those woods.

A flicker of movement caught his peripherals. He looked to his left; all was still. A twig crunched behind him. He spun around and whirled his M1 Garand with him, nothing. But there was something off about one of the trees, a distinctive looking maple. The tree in question was slightly closer than it had been when he stood at the edge of the clearing. He took a step back. The tree looked innocent enough, just a maple, its leaves beginning to change colour in the autumn breeze.

A rustling of leaves sounded behind him. The sweat was now pouring down his face. He shouldered the Garand and spun around. Nothing but forest all around. Just like before, some of the trees looked to be closer than they had been even a moment ago. He began to take another step backward, back toward the safety of the door. He turned to look at the maple once more.

Bernard had caught it by surprise. It was just a quick glimpse, a flash really. But he knew what he saw. A massive black insect that towered over him, multiple sets of eyes beaming down and legs covered in twitching feelers. He shook his head in disbelief.

None of that was present now, it was just a tree. Maybe he was losing his marbles after all. He took a deep breath and felt the forest's oxygen enter his lungs. He licked his lips. This air tasted off. It smelled rotten and sick.

He flinched and took a short, shallow breath to avoid tasting more of the air. Then, he realized the maple, the same one that appeared as a nightmarish creature a moment ago, was in fact closer. Bernard's pulse elevated, a bead of sweat stung at his eye. He had his rifle at a low ready position but raised it.

He fired a round from the hip toward the tree. The shot

cracked through the old woods with a deafening echo. The bullet flew past the maple. He had missed, badly. His shot slammed into another tree twenty meters farther than he had intended. The bark flaked off as the round dinged it, sending splinters flying in all directions.

Bernard was shaking and was never the best of shots, even in his prime. He raised his rifle to his shoulder and fired again, this time using the iron sight. This shot struck home. The bullet collided with the maple as the clap of the M1 Garand floated through the trees. Nothing moved. There was nothing wrong with these woods. He was just paranoid, just an old food. It was all in his—

A thin white film began to seep out of the bullet hole in the maple. It flowed like puss from a decaying wound. He was no botanist but he had never seen a tree leak something like that. The maple started to emit a hiss. At first it was barely audible to the human ear, but within seconds it filled the woods.

The maple started to shake violently. Branches began to thrash in the air despite there being no wind. Bernard took a step backwards and watched in horror as black spindly insectoid limbs appeared behind the trunk of the tree. They were covered in a tar like substance that began to shoot through the air as the legs whipped around. Bernard wasn't going to wait around and watch as this maple finished its transformation into a nightmare. He spun around and screamed when he saw that he was face to face with another maple. This one was even bigger than the other. Its branches were curved in a way that looked like they were about to converge on him in a twisted embrace, an embrace he wanted no part of.

Bernard jumped back and fired two shots into the truck of this enormous tree. He took off running and within seconds could hear a second set of hissing join the first. He sprinted toward the doorway. He could see it in the distance, but something was different. The door was closed. His basement gone.

All he could see was the oak panelling and that heavy door-knob. He began to panic. He could hear the rustling of leaves behind him, the snapping of twigs, the sound of legs scuttling across the forest floor, bearing down on him.

He reached the door and spun around. Twelve maples sat in a staggered semicircle around him, the closest being less than a meter away. Bernard steadied his rifle with his left hand and took his right from the trigger, keeping an eye on each tree as he did so. He groped blindly for the handle. He found it and turned the knob.

There was a shriek so loud that it could have broken all the glass in Manhattan. The shrieking lasted only a second and then all the trees started to shake. All of them, the maples, the oaks, the pines, every single one of them. Bernard returned his hand to the trigger and whipped his rifle around trying to keep an eye on all of them. He could see the clearing in the distance but the woods beyond it had gone black.

Dachau was coming, and hell followed with it.

A moment passed and the clearing went black as well, almost as if someone was frantically ripping the fuses out of the forest. Bernard pressed his elbow against the door and heard it creak behind him. The darkness was approaching. The forest was going dark. Seventy meters, sixty meters, fifty. It was coming, pitch black. He took a step through the doorway and felt the solid concrete under his right foot. He went to pull his left leg back as well, but it was too late. The darkness had swallowed him.

Bernard came to a moment later. He was standing upright. He wasn't sure if any time had passed at all or if he had even lost consciousness. All he knew was he was still alive, somehow.

The woods were gone. He was now in a desert. The sun

beating down on him mercilessly. The dunes that surrounded him in the distance looked calm and untouched by time. The desert was still, no wind, no movement. Then, Bernard saw it, fifty meters in the distance, the door, and it was still open. Just a sliver of light came through but he could see his basement. He'd recognize that old water heater anywhere.

He began to run and felt the weight of the M1 Grand still firmly in his hands. He wasn't sure if it had always been there or if it just appeared, but it didn't matter, he still had his weapon.

Bernard was forty meters from the door when he saw a dune begin to move in his peripherals. He looked to his right and saw bulges of sand slithering towards him, at least ten of them. He didn't dare look behind him; he knew there would be more.

He was eleven meters away and drenched in sweat when he heard them surface. Claws digging frantically into the sand, the same sand his brother had died in, fighting for Patton. He recognized it now. The sands of Morocco. He had never been to this desert before but knew it well. It felt like he had been here all his life, a life he had been able to live while his brother did not.

He reached the door and heard the drool seeping into the sand behind him with a wet crackling sound, God they were close. He dove through the opening and landed on his face. The cold concrete of his basement caught his fall. He tasted the blood in his mouth but there was no time for that. He flipped onto his back and fired the remaining four shots through the doorway. The M1 Garand pinged as the steel ammo strip hit the floor, empty. The shots hit the sand dunes that now stood motionless in the doorway.

They sat still for a moment, the sand crumbling slightly around the bullet holes. Bernard got to his knees and crawled along the floor. He grabbed the corner of the door and threw it closed just as the sand dunes started to shake, puss filling their wounds. The howls that filled his basement were gut-wrenching.

Bernard Steinman sat in his living room. A lit Marlboro hung from the corner of his mouth as he studied the daily paper. Two weeks had passed since he had wandered through the mysterious forest. To his surprise no one had come knocking on his door to investigate the gunshots. Bernard hadn't dwelled on this notion long, believing that the basement had either contained most of the noise, or that the neighbours had assumed teenagers were setting off firecrackers in the ravine again.

Only yesterday had he built up the courage to go back down into the basement and pick up the spent ammo casings and sweep up the sand and dried leaves. To his relief, the door was gone. Just the bare concrete wall remained, the way it always should have been.

For the first four nights after he had slammed that door closed, he had slept with every light in the house on and his Garand across his chest, loaded. Two clips under his pillow just in case. He didn't really sleep, and he could have sworn he heard thousands of footsteps scuttling up the stairs. They would run right up to his bedroom door and then stop. That's when he would wake up, every time.

Even with the nightmares, he didn't dare go see a doctor. They would send him to see a psychiatrist. He would lie on the black sofa and the doctor would ask him a lot of questions about his mother and he would smoke like a chimney. The doctor would chock up what Bernard had seen to shell shock or battle fatigue and would say the party line, "You know, sometimes it takes years for this sort of thing to manifest. Sometimes you get flash backs."

Bernard would be let off with a clean bill of health and

maybe a bottle of sleeping pills. He would be told to find a hobby like assembling model airplanes or fishing. But Bernard knew he hadn't hallucinated. Battle fatigue hadn't created that door out of thin air, nor had it conjured that forest or those shifting sands. Bernard didn't know what made that door appear or why it had chosen him. But it had, and he knew it was real, all of it. An alternate reality that sat just outside his own. He had the spent casings and muddy shoes to prove it.

Bernard knew that if he continued to spout off a tale about what he had seen in those woods, he would have a problem. They would lock him away in the loony bin, white walls and no laces. Bernard decided to cut out the middle man and avoid doctors all together. Besides, he had found the only doctor he needed. Dr. Jim Beam, and that guy was always writing a prescription.

Bernard leaned over to grab his third cup of coffee for the morning. His fingers reached around the brim of the mug when he saw his mantle was gone. He snapped his head forward.

The oak door loomed there, waiting.

He froze and the daily paper fluttered to the ground. "Why are you after me?" he called, "Why torture me like this?"

The door remained silent, watching.

His mind raced as he remembered he had left his M1 Garand upstairs, leaning against the nightstand. He felt vulnerable. A single bead of sweat brushed past his temple as he stared at the door, the words spinning through his mind, *why does it target me?*

He put his hands on the edges of the chair and began to raise himself up, slowly. The sound of a dead bolt being drawn back echoed through the house and the door knob began to turn.

SIDE TWO

ECHOES OF ETERNITY

I watched as the copious flashes of electricity danced around the tops of the portals. These gateways changed the weather around them, making the storms more erratic than they otherwise should be. The hovercraft jostled against the wind as we reached the climax of the bridge. The troopers in Alpha Company had been clever by calling the racing body of black water underneath us "The River Styx." That was three years ago and those boys were all dead.

I looked past my boots as they dangled over the side of the craft and watched the water slam into the rapids far below. If I could trade places and be down there, I would. Anywhere would be better than where I was headed. I looked up and glanced to the far side of the river ahead. From up here, a hundred meters above everything, one could really see the storms raging. Rain poured down, lightning scorched the sky; the explosions continued.

I could smell the gun powder already. My nostrils filled with the scents of burning steel and decomposing flesh. My body instantly stiffened. Three years of combat on this back world will do that to a man. I was like Pavlov's dog, except I wasn't getting a meal and there sure as hell was no bell.

The closest substitute would be the air-raid siren: a wretched death call like no alarm I had ever heard. A series of awful electronic beeps that sounded like a swarm of angry bees mixed with a power drill. I could hear it in the distance. Another wave was coming through one of the portals. The symphony of explosions continued, becoming more frequent, and were backed by a rhythm section of gunfire to add the bass to the cacophony. Supposedly the attacks had been more sporadic during the two weeks my unit was on leave, but the sights and sounds now suggested other-wise.

Two weeks' leave, that's all they gave us. They shipped us to some pleasure world to "relax." All the food, drinks, and whore-houses you could handle. Most of the guys couldn't even tell which brothels used real woman and which used the pleasure models. I could; the pleasure models laughed at more of my jokes.

"Relax," the officers always said, but of course didn't partake in these activities too much. The M.P.s were always watching. They didn't want us losing our edge. They wanted us to forget, but not enough that we would lose focus. I just wanted to go home, but I knew with the time dilation, home would be a very different place than when I had left it. Two weeks was not enough time to recover from this place.

The hovercraft stopped at the barricades on the far side of the bridge. I could feel the sweat begin to pour down my face. This power armour was heavy, and my body was already anticipating the closed visor.

A fellow team leader in Charlie Company preferred to keep his helmet open at all times. He repeated at nauseum that he liked to smell their fear as he "stomped the critters." It gave the new guys some hope, a thing growing increasingly harder to find around here.

Replacements were something of a frequent occurrence. Fresh meat for the grinder. There were twenty of them, squeezed into this hover transport with the other veterans and myself. I knew at least half of them wouldn't make it through the first week.

I looked down at my rifle. One round from this thing would tear a man in half, closed casket funeral. But the things we were fighting? Four, five rounds to the head. *Maybe* then it might go down. If you were hitting it in the ribs or guts? Good luck—at least twenty. Sergeant Rickman called 'em bugs. Corporal Polaski called the ugly suckers critters. I called them what they were: first contact.

Within three hours of the first portal opening, they were coming through. Just a few dozen at the beginning, that was still enough to completely wipe out the science team and surrounding mining crews. Those poor bastards didn't stand a chance.

A few hours after that, four hundred of the beasts came through. Colonel Janzen was there but he was just a lieutenant back then. He said that he could see everything from the gunship he was riding in and that the ground looked black as the hoard rushed from the portal. Humans had made contact with extra-terrestrials and they were hostile. That was five years ago.

The critters originally pushed the science teams and their security escorts all the way back to the mainland. That's when the navy flew in and destroyed the bridges. The things didn't like the black water of this world and refused to swim, at least at first. Once they got wise and started entering the river, the navy bombed them back to the portal. Took awhile, but they did it.

Thousands of bodies. Tens of thousands of bombs.

The army went in next, and was told to dig in. They started to construct a series of trench lines—some of which are still used today on the left flank. That kept the suckers pinned to the portal for a few months. It cost a lot of lives, though. The brass thought they were sending everything they had at us then. We found out later that those numbers were just a warm-up.

During that same time, the science team found four more artifacts scattered around the continent. These relics showed similar markings to those found on the stone orb that spawned Portal One. While prepping the discoveries for excavation the scientists accidently activated three of them causing more portals to open.

Portal Two was the largest by far, and a nightmare to be stationed at. Thousands of the things stormed through within minutes of it being opened. The captain of the U.F.S. Dreadnaught panicked and nuked the whole area. Hundreds of troops died in an instant because some officer, thousands of meters up got trigger happy and wanted a medal.

Portal Three was the most northern and I found it to be particularly fascinating. Despite its size, hardly any of the critters ever came through it. A couple dozen every other week or so. A lot of the troopers guarding it joked that these bugs were lost from the main packs that came tumbling through the other portals. They probably weren't far off. Everyone wanted to be stationed at Portal Three, but in all my time planet-side, I'd only served two rotations there. Barely a month, once it had all been added up.

Guard duty on Dig Site Five was also desirable, but I didn't want it. The air smelled off and the sky had a sort of pink hue eternally looming overhead. That was the only artifact that had yet to be activated, and I didn't want to be there when it did. Rules were to stay a solid two kilometers back from the relic. Since we still weren't sure how we opened the other four, they didn't want anyone to look at it, let alone touch it.

The Federation tried fighting the things off for a little over a year before deciding that their mining operations weren't worth the risk. Before that though, they tried everything, and I mean everything, to close those portals. They sent unmanned drones to explore inside. The moment the drones entered the swirling abyss of Portal One, their sensors and camera feeds went dead. Next, command tried blasting the portals from space. Left an impressive crater but the portals still sat there, unfazed by our weapons. Their ever-present hum still ongoing.

Some pencil pusher then thought of the genius idea to fire nukes directly into them. Six of the fat boys flew into Portal Two alone. That just made the critters more aggressive. They kept on a continuous charge for a week straight. No breaks, no gaps, just hundreds upon hundreds of thousands charging at our trench lines. That level of attack had never happened before, nor since. After that incident—and a causality rate of over ninety percent—command ruled that nukes should never be fired directly into a portal again.

Once the Federation decided to get off world, that was when things got really interesting. Headquarters figured they would cut their losses and let the bugs have the planet to themselves, as they had clearly earned it. Within six months of abandoning the world, satellite imaging started to pick up structures being built on the surface, major construction projects. Enhanced imaging came back clear as day. The bastards were building starports.

How could a quad pedal creature with no opposable thumbs, and as much military strategy as a group of lemmings build any structure, let alone intricate ones like that? The brass wondered the same thing. They sent in some fighters with surveillance equipment to do a low altitude fly by. All of them were shot down, but the images they sent back before hitting the dirt, were haunting.

The critters had a leadership of some sort, a caste system. The pictures were grainy, but depicted a different type of creature among their ranks: builders. Tall, lanky bipedal looking things. Other than the starports, they were also manufacturing surface to air missile systems, war ships, bunker complexes. They were even turning our abandoned bases into a make-shift command and control by the looks of it.

The navy had a fit over that and blew the whole continent into the stone age. They used a whole lot of nukes, but you'd be damn sure they managed to miss the portals by a wide margin. The fly boys weren't going to make the same mistake twice.

Next, they sent in the army to mop up. They pumped all those troopers full of antiradiation pills and fitted them in special power armour. Even with all that ordinance the navy dropped, it still took another three weeks to retake the planet and get back into position around the portals. Some guy at command told me once that they still didn't have a complete casualty list for that battle. The critters just kept pouring through. After being pushed back to wherever they came from, the bipedal leadership caste hadn't been seen since.

The navy then decided to change tactics and bomb the area around the portal sites into submission. It didn't work. Too many of the bugs made it through the carpet bombing, forcing the army commanders to step in and take control of the operation once again. I believe the line commonly used was, "If you want something done right, you send in the army. If you want to waste a lot of money, you send in the navy."

The army brass had a plan of their own. Build walls around the portals, solid reinforced concrete. Easier said than done. The constant storms and relentless attacks made it hard for the concrete to form. After more than a month of trying, they finally managed to get a wall to stick together around Portal One. It stood tall for two whole days before it came crumbling down, taking the entire garrison's morale with it. No one could explain it, but the sensors showed the portal's energy levels had spiked rapidly when it was encased. It knew it was boxed in.

So, status quo it was. We keep throwing troops at the problem until command comes up with something better. This was supposed to be a temporary solution, but you know what they say. "Nothing more permanent than temporary."

It'd been three years since their little walls collapsed. Three years I'd been doing this. I'd killed more of them than I could ever count and they'd returned the favor.

The new guys beside me were getting restless; they wanted some action and for their sins they would get it. I learned to appreciate these few minutes of downtime while we waited for the lieutenant of the command post to unlock our chair restraints. I looked down at my suit and ensured all my gear was in place. Four magazines for my rifle sat next to two pocket nukes that were held in place by webbing on my chest plate. I could feel my sidearm on my right thigh strapped firmly against my armour, with two mags for it on my belt.

They used to give each of us a med kit, but after losing so many troops, replacing those med kits began to get expensive. Besides, if you were close enough to be slashed by one of the beasts, you were already as good as dead. A med kit did nothing to help someone who's been disemboweled.

I watched as a lieutenant exited through the curtains of the command post. He looked like an old grizzled veteran, but he couldn't have been more than twenty-four. Being stationed in hell had that effect on people. He wandered up to the hovercraft and several of the old timers started to hound him for taking so long. Rickman was the loudest and McFadden was the most profane. She was some hard-looking convict, incarcerated for assault and drug trafficking. A perfect fit for Charlie Company. Her blonde crew-cut and scarred face made her look more masculine than most of these eighteen-year-old replacements that sat beside me.

The lieutenant walked to the back of the hovercraft and I could see his armour was still dripping with blood. This guy had probably been in the shit not even an hour ago. I think Baxter, the college dropout three seats down from me, noticed this as well. He stopped his hollering a moment after.

I swung my legs around anxiously as they hung free over the side of the craft. I knew the jolt was coming. The lieutenant typed in the code and my shoulder restraints came free. I dropped into the red mud, my boots sinking into the surface. The new guy beside me wasn't expecting the jolt and fell face-first into the muck.

Corporal Horvath picked him up and quipped, "Bout time you got that shiny armour dirty."

He always had a soft spot for the new guys, but then again, Horvath had only been here a year. Give it time, he'll be jaded like the rest of us lifers soon enough. You see, enough guys get chewed up by the grinder and you didn't care anymore.

I heard yelling and took my eyes off the fresh meat that was private Fredrickson—at least that's the name that was printed on his armour. I looked to my left and saw some bald beast of a man come lumbering toward us. He had the gunnery sergeant insignias painted on his shoulders. He held a classic KPH Storm Rifle in his fat mitts with another slung around his back. Why some guys preferred to carry two rifles around was beyond me. Then again, the obsolete piece of junk that was the KPH was prone to jamming with all the mud on this back-water. So, I guess there was a method to his madness.

I didn't recognize this sergeant; he wasn't the normal guy. Gunnery Sergeant Calazo had been "greeting" me for the better part of two years, but I guess his clock ran out. He finally bought the farm, or mud puddle if it was anywhere around here.

I could tell this new gunnery sergeant wanted to make a difference and felt like the louder he yelled the more motivated we would become. His armour had the name "Mannix" etched in black paint underneath a few white skulls. A mix of human and critter. I doubt he'd even seen a bug outside of a holotape, let alone fry one. I knew a hack when I saw one.

Gunnery Sergeant Mannix grabbed two recruits out of

the mud and slugged another in the jaw for daring to talk while he was calling out orders. He yelled something at me but kept on walking and continued to harass the new people. I rallied up my team and motioned for them to follow me.

We moved into the trench complex and headed to the assembly area. A single captain and his two bodyguards stood at the front of the open area. I approached the weathered officer and handed him the signed document that the pleasure world had given my unit. It signified that we were on approved leave and had returned at the required time.

He looked over the papers lazily with his one good eye and said, "Company?"

"Charlie Company, Seven-Hundredth Division. Sir." I nearly forgot to add the sir, but he didn't seem to notice.

"Right, Portal Two," he mumbled, as he crumpled the paper into a ball.

I nodded and gestured for my team to follow me through the trench line. I rolled my eyes the moment my back was turned. It was always Portal Two. I couldn't complain too much and, judging by the sounds coming over the trench walls, Portal One was in the thick of it right now.

The artillery thundered nearby and the rifle fire was picking up. The critters were closing the gap. I heard a private who was manning one of the rear machine gun emplacements yell something about a "third wave," before firing off a quick burst.

Portal One became a distant memory as we trudged along the trench line for a little over six kilometers.

Just before we reached the first bunker of Portal Two, Gunnery Sergeant Mannix started yelling something at a few of the slower members of our troop. "What? Are you guys tired? Half of you just got back from the whore houses and the other half are greener than piss." He shoved a few replacements around.

One of the females looked like she wanted to take his head

off, but resisted the urge. I already despised this man and I could tell he hadn't been planet-side long. Probably never even been in the shit. I guarantee by next month he will be begging to get some leave for himself.

As we approached Bunker Seven, I watched as a group of medics carried body bags from the front lines. I counted at least eighteen dead, but knew that had to be only a fraction of the losses that Portal Two would have suffered from the last attack. Some of the body bags looked lighter than others. A corpse missing its limbs weighed a lot less.

A second group of medics followed a few seconds later carrying a soldier who was still alive and screaming. Both legs were gone and his left arm looked to be barely attached. He'd live, and I'd probably see him with some mechanized prosthetics fighting beside me in eight to ten months. They'd just keep patching you up and sending you back. Got to keep that organ blender fed. Death was the only permanent escape from this hell.

I checked in with the lieutenant at Bunker Seven, and he said the same thing he always did. "I need you to man those machine gun emplacements and give the boys there some much needed relief."

I liked him. No bullshit, no power trips, just straight up orders. I heard he used to be an accountant before joining up and volunteering to come here. Can you believe this moron actually volunteered of his own accord?

"How long ago was the last wave?" I asked him as he studied a monitor on the wall that listed, *KILLED IN ACTION*. It continued to grow longer by the second.

"Nineteen minutes ago was when the last round was fired. They've been going pretty easy on us this past week. Daily average is a wave every sixty-seven minutes. You've got some time sergeant. Maybe they're running out of fodder."

A sergeant with a prosthetic arm positioned behind the lieutenant laughed and grumbled something to himself before returning to his disassembled rifle that lay on the table beside him. I'd seen this guy before. The psycho liked to collect trophies, mainly the critter's tongues. I had no idea where he stored them or how he kept track of his kills but that wasn't my problem.

I saluted and left the bunker, my team and Gunnery Sergeant Mannix stood waiting. Several of my boys already had their visors down. I don't think the smell of death agreed with them so much. I relayed the orders of the lieutenant and nodded at Mannix. He returned the nod, knowing he was now free to leave and return to the bridge. Someone had to welcome the next hovercraft full of unwilling participants to this conflict.

Mannix had successfully escorted us to our A.O. and could go to the relative safety of the rear. Despite the gruff exterior he put on, I knew he wanted nothing more than to be as far away from Portal Two as humanly possible.

I felt rain hit my forehead and looked up. The clouds were getting thicker by the second, which was good. If it was raining, the portal wouldn't be sending anything our way.

Sergeant Rickman took Team One to the far-left trench line. He loved it over there, with its nice clean line of sight. McFadden and Horvath went with Sergeant Yumi. She was a tough old broad. Hell of a soldier, but had a personality like wet sand. I split the remaining new guys and gals up between my squad and Sergeant Perez's who himself had less than a year out here. I remember when he started, I said he wouldn't last the week. I guess I was wrong.

I led my squad up to what they called "The Nest." It sat on the top of a berm and had a nice little rock slide under it. Those boulders slowed the critters down a lot. I motioned for my team to spread out and grabbed Private Fredrickson to follow me. I led him to Machine Gun Pit Six, my lucky spot. As I trudged up the berm, my eyes darted to a grotesque visage before me. Slouched over the gun was a headless trooper. I approached the guillotined mess and thought to myself, *I guess he won't be needing any relief.* I had known for a while that I had become desensitized to this place.

I looked around the pit for his wingman, but found no other body. The guy or gal must have turned tail and ran. I looked over the edge of the sand bags and saw about forty critter corpses laying in the jagged rocks below. All teeth and spikes, handsome bastards that they were. I heard the new guy gasp, either at the headless trooper or the mountain of corpses. It didn't matter, both unfazed me.

I moved over to the machine gun and pulled the corpse from it. The poor sod had already begun to stick to the barrel. The peeling sound of dried guts being lifted from cold steel, is something you never get used to. I flipped him over, expecting him to be some replacement fresh from the world, and looked at the black name printed on what was left of his armour. His name tag read *LEROY*.

"Shit," I said out loud.

"What?" Fredrickson asked as he looked up from the carnage that lay below.

"I knew this guy. Two and a half years he's been here. If there was anyone who would make it through this, I thought it would be him."

Fredrickson looked down at his boots and swallowed. I think he was starting to get an idea of where he was. This was nothing like the recruitment propaganda videos told you. I tossed Leroy's body down onto the rocks below, but not before grabbing the last magazine he had in the webbing of his armour. Fredrickson looked at me in shock. I knew he disproved of me discarding the body so nonchalantly like that, but I knew better. No one gets buried here, and the best you can hope for is incineration. At least this way, Leroy can lay with his kills and let the rain and mud preform an impromptu burial.

"Holy shit," Fredrickson whispered and I looked up.

He was staring at the portal. I don't know how he failed to notice it until now, but I guess Leroy's headless body slumped over the machine gun was bound to distract a person. I stared at Portal Two for a minute.

There it sat, towering over everything three kilometres away. Its black and purple mishmash of rings spinning inward but outward at the same time. An oval of nothingness that seemed to suck all hope into its massive belly and expel only horror. Its bright lights beamed down but cast no shadows. If humanity ever made it to the edge of the universe, I had a feeling it would look like that.

The rain was starting to simmer down, only a few drops hit my forehead now. I enjoyed the cool water on my face. Fredrickson had his visor down and I could see the water beading down the tinted glass.

"Do you hear that?" he asked as he pointed to his ears.

"What? The hum?" I replied. He nodded yes, so I continued. "Ya, that's the portal. Gets louder the closer you get and you notice it more when your visor's down. Guys who have stood beside it too long say they started to see stuff that ain't there. They usually get the shakes a little bit after that."

Fredrickson stiffened up and peered into the void of Portal Two for a while.

I broke the silence after a minute by pointing and saying, "See that blob of colour over there?" He turned and his eyes followed my gloved finger. I continued. "That's Portal Four. Judging by the smoke, looks like a big wave is coming at 'em." I paused for a moment and looked at the carnage as someone set off a pocket nuke. That wasn't good: that meant our forces were getting pushed back. "If these hills weren't in the way, behind us you would see Portal One. It's about the same size, just a whole lot closer to us."

Fredrickson was about to speak when I heard the clunking of power armour coming up the hill behind us. I turned around and saw a corporal. I didn't know his name but I'd seen him around. He was carrying two duffle bags in his gloved hands with his rifle slung across his back.

He came up beside us and dropped the duffels in the mud. "Ammo?" he asked, his voice was distant, that thousand-yard stare was a familiar sight.

I gestured for him to hand over some magazines. He reached into the bag on the right and tossed me two mags for my M78 Vulture.

The corporal looked at Fredrickson before saying, "And you?"

Fredrickson shook his head and replied, "No. I'm good. Thanks, though."

"No, you aren't," I said as I gestured for the corporal to hand me two more magazines.

The corporal acknowledged the request and said, "How's your machine gun looking?"

I walked over to the weapon and saw the ammo reader was flashing, *38/3000*. I looked down in the mud beside the machine gun and saw two more drums of ammo, fully loaded. Leroy didn't even get through his first drum before they got him. I swear these things were getting faster.

"Hand me a fresh one so I can reload this," I said.

The corporal complied by taking a fresh drum out of the duffle bag by his left boot. He handed the case to Fredrickson who immediately went to work on reloading the weapon. At least the kid was good for something.

The corporal nodded at me and picked up his duffle bags. He looked up at the cloud cover and muttered, "At least the rain has stopped." He was too new to know what that meant.

I grunted and the corporal headed down the line to the next machine gun post. I turned around and saw that Fredrickson had finished reloading our machine gun. I handed him two of the magazines the corporal had given me.

He replied, "Sergeant, why did you take the ammo? The

academy told us Federation policy is a thousand rounds max, per soldier."

"Screw the policy. The asshole who came up with that has clearly never fought here. You'll need those extra rounds, trust me. Tuck them into the webbing on your thigh, they should fit."

The roar of Warbirds flying over head caused Fredrickson to jump. Seven of them blazed across the sky, no doubt to assist Portal Four with their bug problem. Fredrickson watched as they dropped their ordinance on Portal Four's position a few seconds later. I didn't bother to look; it was always the same.

Instead I walked over to the machine gun and made sure the new guy had loaded it correctly. Not that I didn't trust him, just there was a trick to loading it right. The ammo reader glowed blue and displayed *3000/3000*. Good work kid.

"Why are we so far away, anyways?" Fredrickson asked.

"What, you want to be closer to that thing? Be my guest, nobody is stopping you. Just know that the entire stretch of no man's land has been pre-sighted for mortars and artillery. I wish we were even farther away but our weapons lose their effectiveness after two kilometers. They could still split a man in half, but just start to bounce off the critters," I responded as I checked my gear one last time.

"All these gun emplacements and artillery and they still get through?" Fredrickson asked as he looked around the red and muddy landscape.

"More often than not. When they start to break through, we fall back to the secondary line and if that fails, then tertiary positions are warranted. After that there's nowhere else to go. But they have never pushed us past our secondary lines. They usually run out of steam long before that."

The rumble of thunder caught my attention, causing me to look towards the portal. The lightning above it was getting fierce and the clouds began to billow rapidly. The black and purple mirror of the abyss rippled delicately.

I pushed Fredrickson's shoulder plate and said, "Get to your position."

"I don't hear the alarm," he said, as he knelt down on the wooden platform beside the machine gun and propped his rifle against the wall of the pit.

"I don't need no alarm to tell me they're coming," I retorted.

I grabbed onto the machine gun and cocked a round into the chamber. The thunder continued to grow louder and the ripple in the portal increased with an angry stir. I looked to the sky; no Warbirds or attack choppers yet. Not the first time they were late.

I looked down the right flank and saw our armoured core had begun to adjust their barrels as gunners manned their positions. I had met Captain Jackson before. Unlike most officers, he was on the ball and always ensured his boys were ready. The siren wailed a moment later. I could tell Frederickson wasn't used to it, as he looked to the sky nervously.

The roar of chopper blades boomed behind us as they came over the mountains. They flew directly over our position before hovering overhead, waiting patiently for a target. I scanned the no man's land; it was still, for now. I glanced up at the obelisk that sat between our pit and the next position over.

The tower loomed a little over forty meters in front of us. Some general somewhere thought it would be a good idea a few months back to place several sniper towers around. The first few were steel, the critters climbed up those no problem. The week after that they switched to concrete. The claws on those bugs go deep. They scaled those towers as well, like it was paper mâché. The brass couldn't believe it. Hell, it surprised me, too. We haven't built any since. I looked to the top of the tower and saw Ramirez's rotting corpse was still up there. No one had ever even bothered to bring him down, whatever was left of him.

The attack choppers fired a barrage of rockets causing me to snap my attention back to the no man's land. The bastards were starting to come through. The rockets slammed into the ground just in front of the portal and I could see the black masses of the creatures charging. The thunder of the artillery firing in the distance shook the ground beneath us.

"All gunners hold fire until they reach the two-kilometer warning line," an officer said over the radio, he sounded young.

The artillery and mortar rounds collided with the earth, sending dirt and guts into the air. Judging by the amount of movement at the portal site, this was going to be a big wave.

The attack choppers switched to their Gatling guns and thousands of spent ammo casings started to pour down on us. I lowered my visor to avoid one landing in my armour. You only make that mistake once. "Why aren't we shooting?" Fredrickson yelled, as the hot metal casings bounced off his visor.

"Still not close enough. The artillery will soften them up, it's just a waste of ammo at this point for us!" I called out over the thunder of ordinance that was slamming into the no man's land between us and the portal.

The chopper directly above us switched back to missiles. It fired off another barrage before it rose up and turned away. Two more choppers followed its lead, they wouldn't be back for twenty minutes. The tanks under Captain Jackson's command knew that was their cue and fired a mix of shells and rounds down range. The last chopper released its remaining missiles and pivoted. It tipped its fins towards the ground to wish us luck shortly before it whirled away.

"Here we go," I said and gripped the machine gun tighter.

Some of the boys on the left flank opened fire, but I knew the critters hadn't crossed the line yet. I watched as the black masses charged through the smoke, thousands of them, hundreds of thousands. The artillery continued to rain down, but it didn't matter. They just kept coming; they always did.

I pressed the trigger and my machine gun fired a short burst. Fredrickson followed my lead. From this far away, I couldn't tell if it was my bullets hitting the pack or someone else's. I opened fire again and continued to hold down the trigger until my machine gun clicked that it was dry.

By that time, Frederickson was already through his second magazine and the beasts were nearly on us. They had started to climb the rocks at the bottom of the berm. I knew if I wasted time reloading the steaming machine gun we would be overrun. I unslung the rifle from my back and looked over the side of the hill.

At least thirty of the uglies had made it through our cross-fire. I squeezed the trigger and watched as two of the critter's heads exploded. Black brain matter sprayed the bugs directly behind. The mob of beasts were unfazed by the gore of their dead comrades.

I fired another eighty shots and Frederickson reloaded again. The kid was too trigger happy; at this rate he would be out of ammo in a matter of minutes. The critters were almost up the hill and past the rock slide. Between Frederickson and I, we must have popped a good sixty or seventy of the things, but a hundred more just replaced the dead ones.

The screams on the radio caught me by surprise. You never get used to the blood curdling yells. The voices were a mix of familiar and unfamiliar, male and female. Most were dying troopers, but a few officers were still barking commands. I turned my head and looked down the left flank. Team Two had already been overrun. Their bunkers were crawling with hostiles and their rocket pits were already abandoned.

I looked over the berm again and saw their teeth, spikes, claws, and eyes. Ravenous, feral beasts. They were close, less than ten meters. It was just a matter of seconds until the first ugly bastard was up the hill and a few hundred of its friends would be right behind him. My weapon clicked as I fired a barrage that shredded the closest one's front legs. It fell face first into the mud and tumbled down the rockslide taking four of its brain-dead comrades with it. They were all tramped by the pack and their howls of pain were silenced. I reloaded in record time and popped three more of the beasts in the skull just as the pack began to close the last four meters.

I knew it was time to fall back, the left flank was completely gone. The troopers didn't last as long as they usually did, too many damn replacements. The radio filled with another set of screams as some corporal had his vocal cords ripped out. I grabbed Fredrickson by the shoulder and yelled at him to follow me. He fired a quick burst and complied. I heard a critter emit its glass shattering wail and I knew the bullets had hit their target.

We took off sprinting. I was faster than him, but not by much. I looked to the horizon and could see the familiar hills ahead of us, jutting into the sky. The ruby coloured mud looked ominous with the amount of smoke from the battle-field fluttering overhead. My eyes wandered to where the left flank had been. Everyone who was still alive had broken rank and were heading to the secondary rally point. Some of the slower privates weren't so lucky and the critters jumped them. I turned away as I saw a chest cavity open up.

I looked over my shoulder and saw the bugs had reached the top of the berm. They had made it to our machine gun nest. I turned and fired a burst, as I started to back peddle. My shots were clumsy and went high left. Fredrickson charged past me; he didn't dare look back.

I fired again and hit one ugly square in the jaw. Hundreds of rotting teeth fragments expelled from the wound. The dazed critter staggered to the right for a moment before shaking off the pain and continuing its charge. Half of its face was missing but it didn't care, it just wanted me. It lurched forward another three steps before it exploded along with the rest of the hill. The blast was powerful enough to send me flying backwards.

I landed on my back but kept my rifle pointed at the massive hole were the berm had stood, mere moments ago. I could see another series of flashes in my right peripheral. Captain Jackson's armoured core had turned their attention to our primary firing positions and were attempting to cover our retreat. The tank crews had never done this before, and it scared me. How big was this wave? I watched as the second volley collided with the hill, the explosions were deafening.

I got to my feet and raced up the hill. I could see the back of Frederickson's helmet a good clip ahead of me. Its grey hue quickly became indistinguishable as it mixed in with the rest of the retreating troopers. I made it half-way up the hill before I saw the familiar yellow and black paint scheme of eight Hornet walkers saunter over the hill. Their left arms were fitted with Gatling guns, while the other hand supported wrist mounted rocket launchers. Judging by how fast they were burning through their ammo, the bugs must be right behind me. It was just a matter of time until their Gatling guns would jam. There's a reason why command keeps these walkers in reserve.

I made it to the top of the hill and sprinted past a Hornet mech. Hot discharged shells slammed into my visor and chest, but I shook off the multiple pings. I spun around and my jaw nearly hit the bottom of my helmet. The entire no man's land between us and the portal was black and moving. Hundreds of thousands of blood thirsty critters charged our position, and more were still coming through the gateway by the second.

The armoured core had now fallen back, desperately firing shells at random as they headed down the dirt road. Two tanks had already been swarmed by the critters. Their turrets rotated frantically trying to swat off their attackers.

They reminded me of horses galloping away while wolves clutched onto their fatty stomachs. The crews in those tanks would be dead in a matter of seconds.

A voice called my name and I turned my attention behind me. A squad of troopers were hunkered down in the trench line. Sergeant Sarah Wilmer sat with a bunch of pimply faced privates, Fredrickson among them. She gestured for me to join them in the relative safety of the trench line. I complied and jumped into the muck. She had always taken care of me, even when we were both recruits at basic. Maybe that's why she was my main squeeze when I was there.

She slapped my shoulder and said, "Done taking in the scenery, hot shot?" Her visor was open and her long black hair had come undone from the ties holding it back. It hung down in front of her face, and was definitely not up to regulation standard. But no lieutenant in the galaxy had the balls to tell Wilmer to cut it.

When I didn't answer her little jab she spoke again. "That bad, huh?"

I nodded and checked the ammo reader on my rifle. Ninety-eight rounds were left in this magazine. The howls and thunder of paw prints in the mud reminded me of just how close the critters were getting.

"Heads down. Navy's going loud!" A captain screamed in all of our ear pieces.

Not even a second passed before my teeth rattled in my jaw and my armour shook. Hundreds of pounds of ordinance struck the no man's land. It would hurt them for sure, but it wouldn't be enough to stop them. Hundreds, if not thousands would still get through the barrage.

A Hornet to our right turned tail and ran after its arm cannon clicked dry. I stood up on the wooden platform and pressed my rifle against the trench wall. I was in an absolutely terrible firing position with an awfully big blind spot. The hill slanted in such a way that I wouldn't see anything until they were less than two meters away from me. Sarah rallied the men and woman of her squad and they jumped up on the wooden platforms a little bit farther down from me, much better firing positions. Fredrickson came up on my right and pointed his weapon to the sloped entrance of our trench line.

Sarah's squad began to open fire and I jumped. I still had no targets. All I could see was a few meters of red mud and the sounds of death fast approaching. The pebbles in front of my rifle skipped into the air as the blend of the navy and army ordinance continued to hammer the no man's land. I looked to my left and saw the critters had made it up the hill. The troopers there were fending them off well with the help of a Hornet that still had ammo.

The hulking mech fired its last rocket from its wrist and raised its arm cannon at a pack of the bastards that were moving into the western trenches. The Gatling gun spooled up, but no rounds exited the barrel. The operator of the mech raised his left arm and scanned the weapon with horror. We both knew it had jammed.

The pilot frantically brought the weapon to his mech's right hand in an attempt to reset the cannon but it was too late. A pack of eight critters jumped him simultaneously. They bit through the metal cockpit in seconds. The operator flung his walker's arms around helplessly as the entire mech became black and buried as more of the things piled on. He managed to get off two pistol rounds before his head was separated from his body.

Sarah's squad had adjusted fire to assist him but it was too little too late. The Hornet slumped over and tumbled to the ground with a thud. Even over the gunfire I could hear it make contact with the earth.

The artillery and mortar fire grew louder as the troopers manning those guns shifted their coordinates to start hitting the base of the hill, giving us a moment to reload. We were danger close, but I think everyone was willing to take the risk.

Fredrickson fired his weapon and I turned my attention to the entrance of the trench line. Two of the uglies sat in a pool of black blood at the private's feet. He got down on one knee into a firing position and took pot shots at a pack as they ran by the trench entrance. They didn't even stop to enter the ditch and come after us. It only took me a millisecond to realize what they were charging at, the last operational Hornet still in the game.

I jumped from my platform and raced to the opposite wall of the trench. I pulled myself out of the crevice and could see the Hornet had back peddled a good twelve paces from its original firing position. The critters were almost on it, but this operator's Gatling gun was still functioning. It glowed red hot, as hundreds of rounds sliced the merciless onslaught in half. I could see Fredrickson's shots were doing some damage to the advancing pack. Several of the beasts were limping as they pushed past the entrance of the trench. A few only made it a couple of bounds past Frederickson's position before falling dead in the cold mud.

I fired at the critters as they charged the Hornet. My rounds were hitting them in the back of the head and dorsal spikes. If these things were smart, they may have figured out they had been flanked and adjusted accordingly. They either didn't notice or didn't care. Every critter that fell dead was immediately trampled by the endless hoard.

My rifle clicked dry and I cursed its maker. I moved my hand to my chest plate, grabbed a fresh magazine and proceeded to reload the weapon. There was a noticeable lack of bullets erupting from the entrance of the trench meaning Fredrickson had paused his fire to conduct the same operation I had. I pointed my rifle at the endless wave of black unleashing a hail of bullets. The thump of gunfire to my left suggested that Fredrickson was back in the fight as well. A fresh set of two hundred bullets ready to be spent.

The Hornet had taken another five paces backwards and

the operator was getting desperate. He switched to his wrist rockets and fired a volley. The missiles decimated at least twenty of the critters, but that did not even put a dent in their ranks. Another volley, and another twenty uglies exploded in a heap of gore. The pilot went to let fly another salvo when an exceptionally agile bastard leaped up and bit onto his wrist mounted rocket launcher. The volley of rockets left the launcher and flew straight down the critter's throat. A flash of light erupted as both the black beast and the Hornet exploded simultaneously. Guts and steel rained down all along the trench line.

The pack, now realizing that their main target had expired, began to turn. They started to run parallel to our trench line, making us the ones being flanked. I jumped down from the ledge and back into the trench. I landed on the skull of a dead critter with a satisfying crunch. Its brain fluids covered my boots. Multiple bodies littered the ground around me. Fredrickson still had his back to me and was hosing the pack as they tried to enter. I looked to my left and saw Sarah icing a critter as it jumped down from the north side of the trench. It cried in pain and died after having eight bullets sever its spinal cord.

She turned, her brown eyes locked onto me and said, "You're welcome."

I nodded in thanks and watched as she fought her way back down the trench to rejoin her squad, whatever was left of it. The screams on the radio were getting worse. No commands were being issued, just cries for help and the occasional call for ammo or a medic.

I must have killed forty of the things and burned through two more mags before I realized the trench line was lost. Fredrickson had long run out of his own ammo and had resorted to taking mags off a dead private that lay limbless in the mud. I couldn't make out the name, as her armour was covered in blood, but I could see her red hair and freckled face. She had the looks of a prom queen. Hell, she probably was, six months earlier, on a planet far away from here. She didn't deserve to die like that. No one deserved to die like that. We were surrounded. Most of the unit had retreated to the tertiary positions about half a klick behind us. The few that remained in Trench Line 218 didn't have that luxury. Most of Sarah's squad was dead, or moments away from it. She and a few replacements had been pushed back so far that they were almost on top of me. Critters rained in from the top of the trench line. I knew this was it. I dropped my rifle in the mud and grabbed a pocket nuke from my chest. I set it down next to my rifle and popped open the command pad. The keys glowed white and the female robotic voice stated, "Select distance."

My hands were shaking and the gloves made my fingers the size of sausages. I attempted to type in a distance of five hundred and fifty meters but my adrenaline was pumping too high. I missed the zero and hit the *ENTER* key instead. "Error, invalid distance set. Minimum safe distance is *five hundred* meters."

"I know, I know. Shut up!" I screamed at the pad.

My friendly neighbourhood pocket nuke continued, completely oblivious to my screams. "However, if you wish to override the minimum safe distance protocol, then enter the code. Seven. Seven. Five. Zero. Then press the *Enter* key three times. Warning! Warning! You will not survive if you override minimum safe distance protocol."

I screamed at the nuke again and tried to steady my hands. *Goddam they make these numbers so small*, I thought.

Spent casings from Sarah's rifle bounced off my helmet with a loud ping. She and the remnants of her squad were less then a foot from me, as I knelt in the dirt arguing with the inanimate object. I closed my left eye and typed in a distance of five hundred and fifty meters. I didn't want this thing falling short.

The command pad blinked green and my future ex wife's robot voice said in a friendly tone, "Select direction. Press *One* for north. *Two* for—"

"Whatever you're doing, hurry the hell up," Sarah yelled as she slammed a new magazine into her smoking rifle.

I pressed the command console so hard I nearly broke my finger. The number "One" glowed green and I moved as far away from the nuke as I could. It shook for a second before its primary booster rocket blasted into the dirt of the trench. I was still too close and it scorched my armour. The nuke flew straight up for what felt like an eternity before changing course and heading north.

My vison of the rocket was suddenly blocked as a massive black object jumped into the trench line. A critter landed directly on top of me, knocking the wind out of my lungs and pressing my rifle into the mud. I should have been terrified, but in truth I was annoyed. I just wanted to live long enough to feel that nuke go off and take thousands of those things with me. That need for blood kept me in the fight.

I grabbed the critter by the nose—or whatever this thing with three nostrils was that was steaming up my visor—and used all my power-armour-assisted strength to pull it to my chest. While it wheezed in pain I reached to my right thigh and brought my side arm to its left temple. Six shots flew into one side of its skull and out the other. Its full dead weight was on me now and even with my visor closed and the air filtration unit on, the stink was unbearable. I saw the light of the nuke's engine cut out and watched as it lazily came tumbling back towards the ground.

"Incoming," A corporal from Delta Company yelled over the radio.

I watched the pocket nuke drop until it went low enough in the sky that I lost sight of it behind the trench wall. The creature's weight was crushing me, forcing me to take shallow, stabbing breaths. Despite the pain, I was willing to bear it.

This disgusting corpse would offer me some protection from the coming fallout, however slight the protection might be.

The explosion was enormous. Mud, sandbags, steel and guts flew into the air and landed in the trench. Fredrickson took a heap of barbed wire to the back of the helmet and flew forward. A corpse of a critter hit Sarah square in the chest but she remained unfazed. She shook it off and placed her boot on the skull of a bug that was still twitching and fired. An extra layer of black blood covered her lower body. The critters that survived the blast, charged into our trench. I wasn't sure if it was to attack us or to escape the explosion.

I watched as Fredrickson got to his feet and iced two critters before noticing I was pinned. He grabbed the beast's oily skin and tried to drag it off of me. I heard the roar of chopper blades and looked straight up. Gatling fire followed the scream of missiles that filled the air. Judging by the lack of new uglies entering our trench line, I would say the choppers were hitting their targets.

It took Frederickson and another private from Sarah's squad to finally push the heavy monstrosity off of me. I got to my feet and could just see the remnants of the mushroom cloud over the trench wall. I knew we were all hopelessly irradiated at this point, even with all our armour. If we didn't get to the aid station within two hours, we'd be in serious trouble.

The military used to supply us with antiradiation meds that would give us more time in the event we ever had to resort to the use of nukes. Those key items were located in the med kits, the same med kits they stopped handing out to cut costs. Despite being only a pocket nuke, it still packed a hell of a punch. I knew we wouldn't be able to use our primary fire lines for at least three weeks, or whatever was left of them after all that that shelling. A set back to be sure, but that was not the first time we had to rebuild those positions.

I grabbed my rifle from the watery ground and dug the caked-in mud out of the muzzle with my finger. I knew it would still work, unlike those KPH Storm Rifles they used to supply us with. I looked up and saw Sarah and her remaining squad mates were beginning to climb out of the trench. Frederickson and I followed their lead and sprinted to the tertiary defensive line.

The roar of Gatling gun fire echoed behind me, but I didn't dare look back. I followed Sarah to a sandbag parapet on the left flank. I jumped over the wall and pointed my gun towards the secondary trench line where we had been just minutes ago. The choppers were starting to run dry on ammo and some had turned back already. I could see critters had made it to the top of the hill and were charging over the secondary trenches.

All that firepower, the pocket nuke, the artillery, the navy's barrage, only slowed them down by a few minutes. Clearly this wave was much larger than any other I had seen. They should have run out of steam by now, yet more continued to come through that swirling gateway. Their numbers seemed impervious to the amount of ordinance we sent down range.

The last chopper fired its remaining three missiles and banked left, its thundering blades trailing off behind the mountain that loomed behind us. The right flank opened fire with their machine gun emplacements and rocket launchers. I steadied my rifle and opened fire on the advancing bugs. Within seconds they were almost on us. God they were fast.

I looked to my right as a group of troopers shifted their fire and saw that the most forward bunker was in trouble. The two machine gunners had been pulled out and were long dead, leaving just a handful of replacements with only their rifles to hold back the coming tides of death. I watched as the muzzle flashes from the bunker's slotted firing ports became less frequent and eventually stopped entirely. A pack of the things crawled through the front facing opening of the bunker. I knew they wouldn't get far. No doubt the guys in the control center had already shut the blast doors leading to the rest of the complex. Those doors were thick, too thick for even the critters to get through.

I opened fire again and saw three troopers to my left had lobbed off a pocket nuke each. The rockets drifted across the sky before plummeting down and detonating at their programmed distances. We were in trouble, no doubt about it.

The thunder of cannons rang overhead as the defenses that were burrowed in the mountain hammered away at the onslaught. It would only be a matter of time until the critters scaled the rocks and entered the base that way. Another pocket nuke was launched by someone on the right flank. Sarah handed her last mag to one of her troopers and I reloaded my rifle as well. The right flank was falling fast. Then I heard it. The roar of engines overhead.

The Warbirds came in fast and low. They carpet bombed the entire secondary trench line and when they got past the hill, they switched to pocket nukes of their own. The number of explosions was nearly blinding as thousands of bombs erupted. I hosed down the last few stragglers and watched as the smoke drifted out of my weapon's barrel, hugging the rifle in a cloud of grey.

I turned my head and saw that to my far-left, a few snipers had set up a position overlooking the portal. I needed to see if there were still more coming, if any had survived the fury that had just been unleashed on them. I didn't know what I would do if there were more, but I needed to know. I moved down the line and reached the snipers. The hill they were positioned on slanted in such a way that despite the smoke, you could see the entire no man's land unhindered.

"Whaddaya got?" I asked the nearest sniper.

He was looking down the scope of his rifle scanning Portal Two in the distance. "Nada," he said and lowered the scope from his helmet. "We pushed 'em back. 'Bout goddamn time, too. Did you see the size of that wave?"

I nodded and watched as he lifted his visor and grabbed a

package of cigarettes from the webbing on his chest plate. I gritted my teeth and thought, *Of course I'd seen the size of it. I was in the shit every step of the way while you were up here safe and—* I quickly stopped myself from getting worked up by his comment. He was just vocalizing the thought that we all had. Those numbers were unbelievable, I still couldn't wrap my mind around it. If it wasn't for those Warbirds, well, that would have been it for us. I shuttered just thinking about how close we had come to being wiped out.

A few rifle shots echoed from the right flank but I knew they were picking off stragglers.

The sniper stood up from his firing position and said, "After a hit like that we probably got six plus hours to regroup. They gotta replenish their lemming stockpile after all." The cigarette bobbed around his mouth as he spoke.

I was only half listening to what he was saying. The clouds around the portal were still swirling violently and multiple bolts of lightning flashed overhead. The smoke started to settle and the no man's land was becoming more visible. The black and purple abyss of the portal rippled ominously.

They were sending more through.

"Movement!" a sniper shouted over the radio. I heard clicking as troopers reloaded their weapons and got to their feet, attempting to get ready for a second wave.

I typed a command in my wrist computer and my visor entered into its zoom mode. I hated this function; it gave me crippling motion sickness which made me nearly combat-ineffective. I looked at the base of the portal and saw something I never thought I would see.

The humanoid creatures. Their leadership caste—they were back. More than a hundred of them.

They looked to be wearing their own version of power armour and had blue rectangular beams of light coming from their left forearms. A cannon of some sort was mounted to their right shoulder.

A sniper fired, a standard three-round burst. The bullets collided with the lead humanoid's blue rectangular light and bounced off. These bastards had shielding. I watched as a few of the humanoids pointed to the hill tops and directly at our sniper position. Several shoulder-mounted cannons adjusted and aimed right at us.

"Run!" I yelled. "They have us zeroed!"

A few snipers listened but most stayed behind and continued to fire. I un-zoomed my visor and took off towards the center of the tertiary defensive positions. I looked back and saw no less than twenty beams of light shoot straight up from the base of the portal. The beams hovered a few hundred meters in the air and then raced towards the sniper positions. The light seemed to lock onto their targets. As the troopers tried to scatter, the beams adjusted to their movements, following them. The explosions were smaller than I expected, but then again, I didn't know what it would look like. The resulting burst of light incinerated anything that was caught in the blast radius.

"All units. All units," a lieutenant yelled over the radio. He was probably the last officer alive within four klicks. "Move up to the secondary defensive line."

We all complied. I knew what he was thinking. He must have seen what I had. We were sitting ducks here. At least if we moved up, we could engage them across a wider plane. The artillery had adjusted their fire and was set to begin bombing the area around the base of the portal again.

By the time we made it to the secondary line, the artillery began to rain down again. The explosions looked different though, something was off about them. I just couldn't quite put my finger on what it was. I zoomed in again and observed that most of the humanoids had their shields raised. The clever bastards had set up a phalanx defense similar to the warriors of old. These troops were clearly much craftier than their frontal assault subordinates. The artillery shells collided with their raised shields and detonated. The humanoids stood firm under the onslaught and began lumbering forward, keeping their phalanx steady.

I raised my rifle and fired, instantly regretting it. My visor shook and I became dizzy, I forgot the zoom mode was still active. I grabbed my helmet and tried to steady myself. I watched as my rounds fell short, really short. I fired again, this time ready for the shaking of my vision. The rounds slammed into the mud a solid meter in front of the pack of advancing bipeds. A few other troopers began to open fire as well. I could see white ripples forming on the leading humanoid's shields. The rounds deflected into the dirt in front of them. I raised my aim slightly and fired a few bursts. I fought the disorientation from my zoomed in vision, and saw my rounds hit the shields as well.

A few of the humanoids in the front of the brigade were becoming exhausted by the amount of ordinance coming their way. They let their shields drop slightly, just enough that the top of their heads were visible. A few snipers on the right flank took advantage of this. I watched as a lead humanoid's armoured skull exploded in a pink mist. The creature's lifeless corpse fell into the mud and left a sizable hole in the phalanx. Its alien brothers attempted to seal the hole but the snipers were too quick for them. Four more fell dead beside their comrade.

I fired a single shot at one that had turned its shield to reflect the incoming sniper rounds. My bullet flew past the right most edge of the shield and caught it in the neck. The armour must be softer there. It clenched its wound with its free hand and disappeared into the center of the phalanx, pink liquid dripping down its arm. For a moment, just before it vanished, I thought I saw fear in its yellow eyes.

Their right flank was much less coordinated than the rest of them. They had broken rank when the front of the phalanx collapsed, and the artillery finished them off. Their left flank began to return fire. Hundreds of beams of light flew into the sky and hovered. The light stared down our positions and seemed to be picking targets.

A moment passed before the arching light raced towards our hilltop. The trench line next to mine ceased to exist as the beams eviscerated the area. I dropped my third humanoid from the center of their phalanx and was starting to feel the effects of motion sickness. I un-zoomed my visor and could now see that six choppers were flying in from Portal Four's location. They must have pushed those critters back, about damn time.

The choppers swooped in and unleashed an unholy amount of ordinance on the left flank of their phalanx. The helicopters were sure to strafe the side of the no man's land to avoid being taken out by our own artillery rounds that continued to rain down. The choppers lasted roughly seventeen seconds before our humanoid counterparts took notice of our air superiority. They locked on and fired before the choppers had a chance to react. Heaps of flaming scrap crashed down into the no man's land, tilting the playing field marginally in their favor.

Our position continued to be hit hard. I could tell by the gun fire that the bulk of our forces were either dead or out of ammo. Both were equally as likely and terrifying. I slammed the last magazine to my name into the rifle and zoomed back in. I fired a burst and watched as my bullets entered a humanoid's right eye. Its head flew back and it fell lifeless to the ground, only to be trampled underfoot by its brothers. I almost felt bad for it. If it had held its shield just a few centimeters higher my shots would have ricocheted off. I guess that's the price you pay for displaying weakness on the battlefield.

Another volley of white light hit the trench line behind me. Someone had yelled to get down but wasn't able to finish the thought. That trooper had turned to nothing along with anyone who had the unfortunate luck of standing next to them. Yet the alien phalanx was crumbling fast. Thirty of them had managed to regroup and make a circle. They were moving backwards towards the portal. The other twenty or so that remained outside the group weren't so lucky. They were executed by our artillery in seconds.

The circle of humanoids deflected hundreds of rounds and I could tell they were exhausted. Despite the incoming fire they managed to reach the portal. The back portion of their ring instantly disappeared into the portal, but the front stayed and continued to take fire.

In unison the remaining fifteen alien troopers fired their cannons once more in a parting gift. A humanoid on their left flank lowered it's shield out of pure exhaustion. Its body failed to keep up with what its mind asked of it. One of our snipers took the liberty and insured the top third of its head was no longer attached to its body.

The remaining humanoids didn't wait to see if their shots hit home and stepped backwards into the portal. Most of the beams of light went wild and struck the hill in front of us. Two of the beams hit someone on our right flank. I had followed the streak of light with my head and watched as the trooper exploded into nothing.

The artillery stopped a second later and the battlefield was silent.

"Shit we got lucky," Fredrickson said. "They must not have gone for a lock-on with the last set."

"Oh ya, real lucky," I retorted and checked my ammo counter, sixty-eight rounds remained.

Fredrickson was completely out, as was most of the troopers around me. Combined, everyone in my trench had less than four hundred rounds and I could tell our position was in better shape than most. I looked down the line and saw that our right flank had no more than ten troopers left. Our left flank wasn't looking much better.

I moved down our trench and could see Sarah was collecting magazines from dead troopers that had become buried in the mud. Despite her thin frame, she was able to roll men twice her size with relative ease. I knew from experience that she didn't need the power armour to be able to do that. I moved up behind her and tapped her shoulder.

She looked at me with the corner of her eye and, after realizing it was me, she stood straight up. She handed me a magazine that she had just recovered, the trooper's blood still on it. I could see the top six rounds were caked in the stuff. I accepted it and hugged her. I could tell by how she stiffened up that she was surprised, but she relaxed soon enough.

"What'd I do?" she asked into my helmet where my ear would be.

Sarah's voice was muffled, but I made out what she said. I released her and looked into her weary face. Those brown eyes stared back at me.

"I'm just glad you made it," I said.

"I'm glad I made it too," she chuckled to herself.

Sarah grabbed my chest piece and pulled me close, so our helmets touched. She moved her head and kissed the inside of her visor so quick that if you blinked you would have missed it. She winked at me and pushed me away. In an instant she pivoted and began to yell at a couple of replacements to stock-pile ammo. God she was smooth.

The flash of lightning caught my eye, the thunder only a second behind it. The portal was rippling again and the cloud cover was increasing.

"Oh, come on," a corporal standing beside me muttered.

I zoomed in with my helmet. Sure enough the portal was shimmering. It was sending something through. The lightning picked up and the clouds swirled rapidly. Whatever was coming through was big.

"Firing positions," Sarah yelled over the radio.

The few of us left alive didn't need to be told twice. We

jumped up on what remained of our wooden platforms and aimed at the portal. A minute passed and I suddenly became acutely aware of just how dry my mouth was. I would have traded my helmet for just one drink of water at that moment. I knew we were running out of time to counteract the radiation poisoning.

"Where's the back up?" a replacement, and the sole surviving member of Echo Company, asked. His voice trembled and was definitely not old enough to be here.

"What back up? It's just us!" another replacement yelled back.

Sarah was on the radio next and told them to stow it. We were all thinking the same thing though. Where was everybody? There had to be troopers still alive at base camp or even the reservists on the far side of The River Styx. They were coming, right? They had to be.

Another strike of lightning and rumble of thunder. The portal shimmered and then I saw it.

Two massive claws gripped the side of the gateway. I don't know how something could hold onto light, but it managed to. It pulled itself forward and its head came through next. It was the ugliest of all. Black and warped with multiple sets of different sized eyes that looked like streaks of white along its forehead. A gaping mouth dripped with drool. Each drop was the size of a waterfall.

It stepped through the portal; an armoured inverted leg came though. I realized at that moment that the creature was crouching to fit through the portal. Crouching. The twelve-story opening was just too small for it.

No one fired. We were all in shock. Then I saw movement at the base of the portal. Thousands of critters darted between the beast's gigantic legs, charging through the no man's land. The creature finished exiting the portal and stood straight up. It was taller than I could even describe. I just kept staring at the spikes, the teeth, the claws. It raised its right arm and I could see it had cannons attached to its forearms. They looked similar to the humanoid's shoulder mounted weapons, but were bigger. Much bigger.

The lumbering beast took a step forward and aimed its entire compliment of armaments at us. Blue dots began to move along its legs. Squads of humanoids were scaling the beast, attempting to reach the firing positions that were built into its enormous belt. More and more critters raced through the portal. Hundreds of them were mixed in with fireteams of humanoids forming organized lines of troops. The waves prior had been probing our defenses, whittling us down. This was the main force.

The Titan raised its head and let out a horrifying howl. My visor split from the deafening sound and I fell onto my back. If the visor had been up, I'm sure my ear drums would have burst. I went to stand but hesitated as I saw multiple exhaust trails shoot straight into the cloud covered sky. They raced upward and then headed north towards the portal. Some of the survivors on the left flank had launched their pocket nukes. Eight of them, and I knew they wouldn't do a thing.

The Titan shook its head with delight as its cannons spooled up. I looked down the trench line and met Sarah's eyes. Reflected in the remnants of her visor, I could see white streaks of light racing towards us. In an instant Sarah became a washed-out blur as a light, brighter than a shattered star, descended upon us with no remorse.

KOREAN STEEL

The crowd cheers like they always do. Nashville loves to scream our names when we come to town. Maybe tonight we are in St. Louis? I'm not sure, they all begin to blur together after a while. The crowd's roar echo through the tunnel backstage.

Jarrett, our drummer, runs out first, as is his ritual. The stadium's lights are off so the audience won't see him. The hungry people continue to cheer as the opening song plays from a tape over the sound system. Its purpose is two-fold: to hype up the masses, and to tell them to get their asses to their seats. Buy that beer, you've run out of time. The show's about to begin.

Our taped song is an old William Henry And The Troopers tune, one of my favourites when I was a kid. That said, I was getting tired of hearing it. Sixty stops on this tour so far. Hearing the same song every night gets to you.

"Clashes By Moonlight" finishes playing and Jarrett begins his open salvo to a little number called "Ace In The Hole." The crowd goes ballistic. I love this track. Some fresh blood from our new album. Admittedly, it makes me a little depressed. This was the only hit single off our newest LP, *With Overwhelming Force.*

I remember some snot nosed "music critic" named Eric Prince—a pretentious name if I'd ever heard one—jabbed us good in his one-star review of the album. He had called it "With Underwhelming Force." Real clever, you hack. Eric Prince was from Alabama, what did he know about metal?

Lance, our bassist, runs out next, followed by Hooper, our rhythm guitarist. They start to play and I can see the lasers are already flying. I know it is my turn to let the crowd have it.

The rhythm section stops for a moment and I begin my lead break. I enter from stage left and the moment I start playing the stadium lights shoot on. The crowd goes insane. My custom-built ESP guitar glistens in the spotlights. It shows off the 70s Korean Special Forces camouflage paint job perfectly. I love the design. It borrows elements from both the old North and South patterns, back when they were separated.

My time to shine is limited, however, as Nix belts out the opening lyrics. The cheers for him are the loudest, the people always love the lead vocalist. I roll my eyes and keep playing.

It's no secret that we are breaking up. I think the fans could see the writing on the wall when the album dropped and Nix only had one song-writing credit on the whole damned thing. Some saccharine ballad by the name of "Hold Me Close." The song blows, but the chicks dig it.

I think the bulk of fans agree with me, though. It's our second single from the LP and it didn't perform well on the charts in the slightest. As such, it might be the last single our record company drops for the album. Unfortunately, it's on our setlist tonight. Much to Nix's insistence, of course. Whatever, I don't play on it. Hooper preforms all the guitar parts, a trend with most of our ballads. Fine by me.

We haven't been getting along for a few years now. All the things you would expect: drugs, drama, infinite travel, the endless cycle of an album, then a tour, followed by another album, broads getting in our way, all that crap. Nix stopped being hungry and blew enough coke up his nose to kill a rhinoceros. The guy did so much blow, he made me look like Saint Francis by comparison. I'm not proud of it, but that's saying something.

We started the "Domination and Damnation Tour" in late March, beginning in South America. Only two short months after our latest record was released. I wanted to call it "The Overwhelmed Tour," but management thought that was too on the nose and would hurt sales. Regardless of the name, movement of tickets in that continent were abysmal. That's what happens when you release a subpar album by a tired band.

Our audience in Latin America had never been huge, but the sheer lack of interest was embarrassing. Young upstarts like Ripley's Riot and the German band The Warriors had outsold us by massive margins on their respective tours of the area a few months prior. I remember when Ripley's Riot were opening for us in '83 and we were on top. Those were the days.

After the first shows, our manager got some up and coming band from Miami called Lock Heart, to come out and support us. All of their members had Latin backgrounds and had a slew of songs in Spanish. They pulled our asses out of the fire, but it was clear they were playing us off the stage for the last eight shows of the tour. At least ticket sales went up, slightly.

After the South American leg, we had two weeks off. A band meeting was called and that's when Nix announced he was going solo—actually, sorry. That isn't true. He tried to vote me out first. Me! The lead guitarist. The founder of the band. The Korean in Korean Steel. Mr. Creative Seoul himself.

After a few smashed bottles and my fist nearly meeting his

face, the rest of the band stepped up and said it wouldn't be right to replace me. Lance was the most vocal in my defence and agreed that I wrote most of the songs anyway. It was my band, not Nix's.

Nix was furious and then dropped the bomb shell that he was leaving. He said World Hell Records had signed him to a four-album deal and were promising him more money per album than what we were currently getting. He said he signed it during the making of *With Overwhelming Force*. This surprised no one, least of all me.

Our manager announced the news the next day. Korean Steel would be breaking up once this tour was finished. You should have seen ticket sales skyrocket in North America and Japan. Korean Steel's last tour wasn't something they wanted to miss. Our sales were never huge in Japan but those dates were the most money we'd ever made there. I could never tell if me being half Korean hurt profits on that island or not, but enough of them showed up on this tour to see us play.

The band rips into our third song of the night: a banger called "Leave 'Em For Dead." I wrote it along with Nix and Lance. A fantastic track off our second album, *Break and Enter*. That's the album that put us on the map. The song starts off with an amazing rolling bass sound, excellent tone from Lance. Then Jarrett is supposed to come in with his drum fill, but nothing happens. A moment passes before the thunder of percussion fills the stadium. He is a full two seconds off.

I play my lead break flawlessly and shake my head. Jarrett had been saying for years how the booze wasn't affecting him. Right. You think on the tours to support *Night Danger* or *Indictable Offence* he was this slow? Not a goddamn chance. He would have been out on the streets if he had been. That new wife of his isn't helping, either. So what, she's an ex Miss July and Playboy bunny? If you get lazy and it affects your playing, you got to get rid of the girl.

You don't think I've had blondes of my own? Too many to

count. But if I lost focus on my playing, on my technique, I would drop them as fast as possible. I've given my soul to this band and I can't believe the others aren't willing to do the same.

"Leave 'Em For Dead" ends—faster than it should have I might add. Jarrett had sped up his tempo trying to mask that he was late on the intro. The spotlights shoot on and illuminate the stage. Nix introduces the band. Lance is first and plays a few seconds of a bass line to one of the deep cuts from our *Night Danger* album, our third LP. He does that as a tease, knowing some of our more devout fans would want nothing more than to hear it. It's a song he wrote a while back and is quite proud of. His original name for the track was "Tiger's Bane," but I reworked some of it and changed the title to "The Fox."

A few members of the crowd cheer when they hear that distinctive bass line. I wish everyone knew all our songs but I have to be realistic. Most of the audience is only here for the hits. I would love to play "The Fox" live, but Nix refuses to sing it. He just wants more room on the setlist for his sappy ballads. Hooper and Jarrett always agree with Nix on everything, so I guess we don't play that one anymore.

Nix introduces Jarrett next. He stands up from behind his kit, his long black hair sitting in front of his eyes, sweat dripping everywhere. He is shirtless, as per usual. I can really tell his muscle definition is lacking and he is putting on the pounds in the mid section. Those countless beers catching up to you?

Hooper is next. He takes two steps forward and waves to the crowd. They cheer louder for him than they did for Lance and Jarrett combined. He was always the pretty boy of the group. That blond hair, white unbuttoned dress shirt, black leather pants, a smoke permanently lodged in the corner of his mouth. He looks the part, and, at one point, he had sounded the part.

Sure, if you ask the rock magazines, they still love him. He had been ranked as one of the top five rhythm guitarists two years in a row, by three different magazines. In *Excitable*, they put him top three behind the guy in Dragon's Sorrow and Matt Brando, the legendary '70s guitarist who formed Panzershriek. A definite influence for me and my playing style.

Full Metal Magazine ranks Hooper fourth. Behind Brando and my friend Willi Snide from War Hammer in first. In third is the late Jamie "Animal" Jamison. Those three albums he did with Outlaw Vengeance were some of the best metal I've ever heard. "Animal" died way too young for the world to see what he really was capable of.

I'm not going to lie, I'm jealous of Hooper. You know where I fall in the rankings for lead guitarists? *Full Metal Magazine* put me fifteenth. *Excitable* didn't even mention me at all. Thirty players and five honourable mentions and I don't even get a footnote. *American Steel Foundry* put me in the top eight. That's great right? Except they put that no talent hack Max Vinnie in seventh. Max, ahead of me? How many platinum albums does Rapier have? The answer is easy, zero, only golds. I have three albums that have gone platinum, two of which even went double platinum. Hell, even our live album from 1985, titled *Liv, Live* has gone platinum. 1986's *Love Her Deadly* went to number eighteen on the charts. Beat by Max Vinnie? Get the hell out of here!

The spotlight pierces down on me and Nix belts out my name. I wave and instantly go into a five second solo. Something I just came up with last week; it slays. The crowd whistles, causing me to smile before pointing out to the audience at stage left. I see a few of them are wearing official Korean Steel fan club shirts and studded bracelets. Those things are old. These guys must have been with us since our first album, our die-hard fans. They cheer as I point at them and I'm pretty sure I've seen three or four of these kids at our last two shows as well. I throw them a few guitar picks from the mic stand

and watch them leap into the air to grab them. One kid hands a pick to his girlfriend. She is ecstatic.

I turn back to the mic and take a deep breath. I roll my eyes under my lids and say as coolly as I can, "And on lead vocals, the man himself, Nix McCruger." The cheers are deafening.

He bows, I don't think he or the fans can hear the hatred in my voice, but he would be an idiot not to know that it's there.

Nix then grabs his mic and waits for Hooper to start playing "32-32." Hooper has lead guitar duties on this one. I actually wrote it, but Hooper's tone and style sounds better playing the riffs. He bursts in with the solo that starts off the track and I come in with the chugging riffage. This song brings back memories.

It's the first song on the second side of our debut album. The LP in question was called, *Taste The Steel*, and it didn't sell well in the slightest. We didn't care. That was back when we all got along, back when we were just five young kids from the LA strip. We got our start along with all the other big names like Haunted Cathedral, Rapsheet, and Human Vulture playing the club scene together. What a time to be alive, the LA strip: 1980-1982. Pure magic.

I remember the guys from False Alarm would routinely hold never-ending parties at their apartment. The amount of times I woke up on the floor beside their couch after a show, insanity. Charles Whitney, their drummer, and I go way back. He always supplied me with booze, and other stuff. Usually fresh off the boat from Bogota.

He was a few years older than me and both our old mans had fought in Korea. Marines, same unit. When Whitney's old man found out his son was hanging out with Sergeant Campbell's kid, he told him to take good care of me. I guess Charles took that to mean always have a fridge stocked and a few hotties laying around, blondes, brunettes, red heads, Latinas, Asians, anything I wanted. A different assortment every night.

I zone back in and sing the backing vocal to the title track of our fifth album. 1984's, "Bombs Over Brooklyn." I penned this song after watching a documentary about the 1975 terror attack. The record gained a little bit of controversy when the song was released as the lead off single. There was outrage at first, but once people realized the message behind the song, they calmed down. I had to explain the fact that I was condemning the attacks and not supporting them at all. Still, the controversy helped push a lot of albums. Our back catalogue rose in sales too, *Indictable Offence* receiving the biggest boost.

I think that LP is my favorite that the five of us have done. So many top tier songs off that beast of a record. Nix was on a tear then. He wrote two of the best songs we ever laid to tape, "Blades In The Night," and "Dodging Bullets." Amazing tunes. That album also contains my mother's favorite Korean Steel track, "You Are Mine, After All," the second ballad I ever wrote. She liked that one because it wasn't just about drinking or sleaze or battle like most of our tunes up to that point. She'd said she liked it because it was a love song, but I think she knew who it was about. Kathy, the one who got away.

While my mother had been supportive of my passions, the same couldn't be said about my old man. He had been less than thrilled when I told him I was switching to playing guitar full time after I graduated high school. He couldn't understand why I would just, "throw away a perfectly good factory job." A quote he repeated ad nauseam.

He did eventually come around to the idea of me being a guitarist, no doubt my mother helped with that. He had always listened to her. They always told me that it was "love at first sight that one rainy night," when he was on leave in Seoul during the war. Everyone says crap like that, but with them I believe it. Sure, he could be a hard ass sometimes, but he loved my mother, no doubt about that.

Hooper finishes his guitar flourish on the seventh song of our set and I keep the rhythm going. It's one of our longer songs and has some progressive elements to it. I love the track, it's completely different from anything else we've done. I look over at stage right and roll my eyes. I've been playing flawlessly the whole night and sound excellent, but Hooper? He sounds sloppy. The guy has been slamming too much heroin into his arms as of late. It's affecting his speed. Me? I never touched the stuff. I saw how it destroyed Eastern Justice. Another set of souls crushed by the lights and glitz of the LA strip.

Hooper plays the final notes and begins smiling to the crowd. He has no idea how bad he's playing. Top five rhythm guitarist my ass.

Nix struts around the stage and says his trademark lines, "Everyone having a good time?" "Do you want some more?" crap like that, but the crowd eats it up.

He stops in the centre of the stage and says his standard intro to our next song. "Is everyone feeling hot? Anyone feeling red after driving down that main drag." He points to me and says, "Give it to 'em, Campbell."

I launch into the riff for "Tail Light Fever" and Hooper joins in to give it more weight. God he must be missing a third of the notes in this intro. He's really sliding. I shake my head and zone out again. This song holds a special place in my heart. It came off *Break and Enter* and was the second single.

After the fallout from our first LP and its underperformance, we begged our recording label, Birthstone Records, to give us another chance to prove ourselves. Between Nix, Lance and myself we had written enough material in the two years prior to fill another album, maybe even two. The label was hesitant of course—the suits always are—but I remember our manager rationalized with them that our first record suffered from too much interference from the producer. The label eventually agreed and gave us the green light to continue.

We booked studio time and within a few weeks began recording what would become, *Break and Enter*. I remember the all-female band Jagwire was completing their debut release in the studio beside us so we hung out with them frequently. There's quite a famous picture of our two bands posing together in the studio. I hooked up with their bombshell of a drummer a few times but I was always secretly after their guitarist, Tammy Vance. I couldn't get near her as Nix and her started to date on and off that summer. Last I heard she was married to the guitarist in Human Vulture. Now there's a raging alcoholic if I've ever seen one. I would treat her better than that.

I look away from the crowd and see Lance chugging away on his bass. He is still giving it all he has. He is the only person in the band I still genuinely like to be around. Every night on the tour bus is the same. Hooper goes to the back and shoots up. Jarrett and Nix drink at the front and once Jarrett begins to slow down, Nix brings out the coke. Recently, he's been handing out the white stuff earlier and earlier each night. That leaves me and Lance to party on our own in the center of the bus.

Lance was the only member I had invited to join me in my next band after this tour ends. The guy really is one of the best bass players I've ever seen. He's got the look: bullet belts, white sneakers, band shirt with a leather jacket overtop. But more importantly, he's got the sound. I've already talked with Richard "Turbo" Schaff from the German metal band Fire-flys to come play with us and we agreed to split the lead guitar duties and have a twin lead attack. I also sent a letter to Frankie Tilley, the former front man of the Birmingham band Her Majesty's Destroyers. He called immediately and said that he was eager to get started. He even offered to let us use his studio.

Talk about a super group. Two of the greatest guitar players in the business, a phenomenal bassist and a singer who played on the golden age albums of one the New Wave of British Heavy Metal top acts. All that we needed now was a drummer. Lance said he knew a few guys, so that shouldn't be a problem.

The stage goes dark once again and I gesture to the roadie to throw me a bottle of water. I catch it before making my third guitar change of the evening. This one has a simple artic camouflage pattern painted on it. A stellar looking beast of an axe. Nix sneers at me as he runs by to grab a towel from backstage. He disappears just as the intro to our next track starts to play. It's a snippet from JFK's farewell address to the nation in 1968, after a tremendous second term. Now there was a leader who lived like a rock star. He didn't take guff from anyone, least of all his own generals and his farewell address proved that in spades.

The intro ends and Hooper starts playing the main riff to the track. The crowd particularly loves this one. I come in with some guitar flourishes and Nix brushes past me and starts to sing. I watch him pace the stage and I have to admit he sounds good, phenomenal even. It's a shame we can't get along; he has one of the best voices in rock. I still remember when we found him in that dive bar singing some old sixties stuff. After just a few notes, I knew he was our new front man. If only his ego and the drugs hadn't gotten in the way. I rip right into my solo after the second verse. Not a single note missed, Max Vinnie eat your heart out.

Nix hits the high notes flawlessly after my solo. Despite my hatred, I recognize why the boys from Martian Outpost asked to play with him on his up coming solo albums. Between those three guys and Nix, they are going to write some kick ass tunes. Hell, Nix has already started writing for his new solo album. He thought I hadn't noticed but you would have to be blind not to see it. That bothers me. The guy contributed one song on our last record, but now he's writing like a mad man.

"Foreign Policy" ends with the pre-recorded gun shot sound effects. I remember Lance, Jarrett and I went out to the gun range that summer to capture those. A few M16s, AK47s and an M60 on a hot July afternoon. Those were the days.

The stage goes dark and I exit stage left. It's time for "Love Me" off of *Love Her Deadly*. The only ballad of the album. Hooper knows all the guitar parts and I like to use this part in the setlist as a chance to take a break. I have a feeling a lot of people in the audience take off to buy more beer during this song as well.

I get backstage and Rodney, the same roadie who threw me the water, is waiting with my drink. Gin and tonic, double shot. A throw back to my days when I was obsessed with all things British. Everything from the guitar players to the singers. What they drank, what they smoked, I copied it all. I downed the drink and Rodney handed me another one.

"I think you've had enough," someone says.

The voice is coming from somewhere farther backstage and I recognized it immediately: Michael Calhoun, our Manager. I turn and stare at him, a look like no other. He had been riding my ass all year, but gives Nix a pass when he goes on one of his coke-fuelled benders. I hammer back the second drink and stare at him through the bottom of the glass. He crosses his arms and shakes his head. What else can he do? Fire me? The band is finished anyway and I'm the core of it.

"You're playing like absolute shit tonight, same with last night," he says, the vein in his forehead about to burst from rage.

"I'm playing like shit? *Me*? *I'm* playing like shit?" I point to my chest and my voice gets louder echoing off the tunnel at the side of the stage. I look to my left hoping for Rodney to back me up but he has discovered that his shoes are the most interesting things on the planet. "Me?" I yell again as I wipe the gin from my mouth and continue, "Have you heard Hooper? He's been slacking the whole tour."

"I don't need to hear Hooper. I know you sound terrible. Like trash. Missing notes, a delay on 'Foreign Policy' just now. Frankly, the rest of the band is covering for you. Good thing Jarrett and Lance are keeping good pace or you would have no timing at all."

Rodney grabs the glass from my hand before I can launch it at Michael's balding head.

I throw my hands up and yell out, "How much can you play again? Oh, I forgot, nothing! What the hell do you know about timing?"

Michael turned and walked away, kicking a storage case out of his way. "Get me my Storm Trooper Gibson," I say to Rodney and see that he's already grabbing for it.

I snatch it from his hands and sling it around me just as I hear the ballad finishing up. I ponder on having another gin and tonic but think better of it. I wish they had warned me as a child just how easy it was to become an alcoholic. No one ever tells you such things, just another life lesson that slips through the cracks.

I take a drink of water instead and run back onstage just as Nix hits the final note of that god-awful song. I had liked it when we wrote it, but I think it's the weakest song on an otherwise stellar album. Of course, compared to "Hold Me Close" this thing comes out looking like a Mozart composition. The crowd cheers, but I can tell it's a lot weaker than it was for stuff like "32-32" or the second song we played tonight, "Fashionable Ecstasy."

I nod to Hooper and he starts to play the riff to "Red Lightning." I demanded this one be on the setlist for this tour. Something to wake up the crowd after the snooze fest that was "Love Me." It's one of our deep cuts off *Bombs Over Brooklyn*. On an album full of singles, I wanted to play something different. Every tour since 1984, we've been playing the hits off that record. While we still had a few on the pecking order tonight I wanted a lesser-known track as well. A song with one of the best riffs I'd ever written.

Jarrett comes in like a roar of thunder. I know he loves to play this one live; he gets to show off his drumming chops. The group of guys and gals from the fan club light up the moment they hear the opening notes. Before this tour, it had never been played live. Everyone was in for a wild time.

Nix trots out to the elongated part of the stage and belts out the opening lyrics. I see a flash come from the third row of the pit. Nix falls backwards. I stop playing and hear the screaming. A second and third flash erupt and then I can hear it.

Gun shots.

The crowd attempts to scatter but are packed in too tight. The shots slam into Nix's side causing his body to convulse. I turn and start to run to the wings of stage left. I make it a single step and that's when I see another flash in the peripherals of my right eye.

Johnathan Edmond Gracey, who preferred to be addressed as Mr. Gracey, sat down on a bench in Central Park. He was eight minutes behind his normal schedule. It was a Monday morning and he had already been to the bakery for his bagel. The Irish girl behind the counter had taken her sweet time making it, which caused him to fall behind. She had put too much cream cheese on it as well which made the first bite too soggy. *Minimum wage broad,* he thought to himself.

Mr. Gracey was already in a bad mood; he would have to spend the better part of the day going over case files that his junior associates at the firm had screwed up last week. Liebowitz

Gracey & Weiss had prided itself on its work ethic, perfectionism and more importantly, its ability to win high profile cases. But these young hot-headed lawyers that Weiss had been bringing in were rapidly soiling their good name. Losing the Abbotsford Technologies case had been a major blow to revenue. It would take Mr. Gracey and Mr. Liebowitz a great deal of glad-handing and backroom politics to attract those lost clients back to the fold.

Just last week, during one of his frequent Scotch rampages, Mr. Gracey had thought of pulling the trigger and banishing Weiss from the firm for good. The thought of allowing their bumbling associate to fend for himself in the cutthroat trenches that was the New York law industry pleased him greatly.

Mr. Gracey shook his head after a moment and leaned back on the bench. *Being senior partner isn't all it's cracked up to be*, he thought. *I never knew I would have to deal with such stupidity on a daily basis. God, I miss the Sixties.* He rubbed his temples as his migraine flared up. The doctor had informed him that these bouts of headaches were from lack of sleep and dehydration. Jonathan Edmond Gracey knew his body better than anyone and ignored this unwanted opinion. He only needed five hours a night and had trained himself to not require a minute more.

He grabbed his daily paper from beside him and unfolded it. It had been bought from the news stand beside the bakery. Today there had been a line. *No doubt someone trying to pay in Mexican pesos. Typical immigrants,* he had thought while he tapping his expensive shoes on the dirty sidewalk.

He skimmed the headlines on the front page, something about an oil pipeline and then a Chinese-American trade agreement being settled. He flipped to page two and something caught his eye. He read the small headline and smiled, rereading it to make sure his eyes weren't playing tricks on him:

KOREAN STEEL'S 'NIX' MCCRUGER AND DARIN 'JETT' CAMPBELL IN CRITICAL CONDITION.

The sub headline then continued:

SHOTS RANG OUT AFTER A DISGRUNTLED FAN OPENED FIRE AT A SHOW IN CINCINNATI ON SATURDAY. MORE ON PAGE ELEVEN.

"Good riddance. Bunch of loud-mouth burn outs," Mr. Gracey said to no one in particular.

The pigeons in front of him poked their heads up at the sudden noise and then went back to eating the bits of bread someone had left behind for them. Mr. Gracey licked the tips of his fingers and turned to the stock information on page eight. Gold was up.

DAWN PATROL

Technician Stanley Higgins tapped on the gauge that sat directly to the right of the black egg-shaped mass. The number "98678" was painted proudly on the front of the uniform steel. Higgins, like nearly all of the air crews, was new to this war. Today would be their first taste of combat. Only six months in the Northern Alliance Military and seven months after his twenty-first birthday, here he was. 35,000 feet flying over the Atlantic Ocean, headed to the Republic of Free States.

For seventeen years the war had raged on, but the Oligarchy assured the populous that the end was finally in sight. Not that the promise mattered to the billions that had perished.

Nuclear weapons of any kind were outlawed at the New Delhi Convention of 2109, or maybe it was 2118 the records were fuzzy. Most of the data had been lost or corrupted when the first bombs fell sixty years later. Those politicians all smiled and waved to the cameras at the convention and said, "Never would a nuclear weapon be used against mankind ever again."

Humanity couldn't keep its word. How could they be

expected to turn their back on a weapon so powerful? Mars and Aries would have been proud of their children.

The war had started out with three major factions, but quickly dropped to two when the nuclear holocaust knocked out The Eastern Conglomerate. It's ironic, they had been the last to sign the pact at New Delhi but were the first to be utterly decimated by the same bombs they wanted to preserve. A splinter cell of a few hundred thousand still operated in a remote region, but they were not recognized as a government entity by the other two surviving factions.

Higgins was still confused as to why these black egg-shaped objects had temperature gauges at all. What sort of bomb needs to be checked for temperature? He was smart enough to know they weren't nuclear, at least not by any design he was familiar with. Higgins wasn't even sure they were bombs, but the officers had said that they were and to argue with one resulted in correction by taser. He had enough scars from basic training that he didn't wish to add any more to his collection. 98678's temperature was on the low end of the spectrum, so he pressed a few buttons to raise the heat by seven degrees.

Higgins felt the bomber's direction change before making a smooth descent. He knew from his two training missions that they were getting close to the target. He couldn't understand why they needed to descend to drop their ordnance, but again, he didn't ask questions.

The wave of nukes fired off during the opening hours of the war had been much less effective than one would have expected. Fighter response teams and anti-aircraft intercept missiles took out about sixty percent of the onslaught. Still, with that forty percent, millions died, and it was enough to take out the Eastern Conglomerate. After that, there were almost no nukes left to fire.

The war then took a four-year break while both sides rearmed and regrouped. The Northern Alliance built more nukes, bomber crafts, and tanks. The Oligarchy, in their infinite wisdom, were going by a more traditional manifesto of war. The Republic of Free States went in a different direction and revived their old shield technology prototypes, a remnant idea that existed long before the war.

After the rearming stage, both governments sent in the infantry. Battles were fought constantly, but no clear winner could ever be decided. The R.F.S. would take land in South America while the N.A. would claim pockets in Europe. This went on for nearly four more years until the Northern Alliance finally managed to push the R.F.S. back to their final strongholds.

The war then reached a true stalemate. The Free States' investments in shield technology paid off. They were able to construct defensive barriers around entire cities. Their last twelve metropolises became completely impenetrable by bombs, bullets, or shelling. The only way to enter the barrier was to march in by land.

The R.F.S. attempted to sue for peace, but the N.A. refused. They wanted to wipe the Free States from the globe. The Northern Alliance and their warmongering Oligarchy answered the request with the only way they knew how: a bombing raid. Hundreds of nukes were dropped on the Free States' most northern shielded city.

Despite the show of force, no damage was done to the barrier. The Oligarchy was outraged and sent in their Grand Army. Still a significant threat, even after so many years of bloodshed. The army marched in with everything they had and were told to show no mercy.

After receiving half a million casualties in only a matter of days, the Grand Army retreated to the Alliance safe zone. All those people blown apart and for what? The Northern Alliance forces didn't get any farther than six blocks past the shield wall.

After the massacre of the Grand Army at Havalon, the

N.A. switched from bombing to lasers. The idea was that if light could pass though the domes, then a laser with enough output should cripple the city beneath it. The science team could never get the power high enough to pierce the domes.

Republic of Free States cities were more or less self-sustaining. They grew their own food, and mined their own ore where they could. The resources the R.F.S. couldn't extract, they recycled from tech they no longer had a need for. Anything they couldn't make themselves was scavenged from the surrounding area or bartered for by working with smaller bands of survivors. They had set up a complete trade network between their few surviving cities. Alliance hunting parties that went out after these convoys suffered heavy losses.

Higgins took his attention from the explosive device in front of him and looked down the bomb bay of the ship. A corridor of steel, copper, rivets, and the menacing black egg-shaped bombs. One hundred of them on each side, fifty a row, double stacked. This particular bomber was one of hundreds in the current formation, and this was just one of the blitzes planned for the day. Three separate offensives were occurring within a ten-hour period. Nearly every bomber in the Northern Alliance arsenal was airborne and heading to the assigned drop sites. The fleets were flying with no fighter escorts, the N.A. had held air superiority for over four years.

Higgins and his fellow crew members were en route to New Johannesburg, a city that had once been home to a great deal of history. New age paintings, museums filled with Second Renaissance sculptures, stunning architecture, and the Northern Alliance was going to bomb it into rubble. What a waste. Higgins still couldn't understand how this next generation of bombs would penetrate the city's shields, but again, he didn't ask.

The bomber started to rattle as it evened out and then Higgins heard the explosions. Long range anti-aircraft batteries had opened fire. He was trained to expect this, but the sounds were unnerving. The Republic of Free States had set up a network of defensive bunkers outside their shield domes. The Northern Alliance had bombed these sites in the days before, but it seemed the missile attacks weren't very effective.

The anti-aircraft fire increased and the aircraft swayed left and right. Higgins walked over to the view screen and activated the bomber's nose camera. A lowly technician such as himself was not permitted on the flight deck and was confined to the bomb bay hold. These cameras were the best view of the battle he would get.

The screen came to life and Higgins could see that the air was filled with black, pluming smoke that swirled in front of the bomber. The amount of flack that ripped across the sky was enormous, but through the debris Higgins could see the green dome over New Johannesburg. It flickered in the distance in benevolent majesty. His view was momentarily obstructed as multiple rockets soared past the bomber. The missiles flew off course and headed up toward the heavens, only narrowly missing their targets due to the bomber fleet's new scrambler technology.

The bomb bay doors opened and Higgins felt the rush of the cold air hit the uncovered portion of his face. He adjusted his oxygen mask to ensure it was snug and pulled his fur flight jacket closer to his neck. He looked over the guardrail and could see the surface below. They couldn't be more than six thousand meters above the ground. *Why the hell are we flying so low, and why did the doors open so far away from the city?* Higgins thought, as the barren earth passed by below him.

The surface was chock full of craters and upturned dirt from previous bombardments. Several grey dots littered the ground and Higgins knew these must be the flack towers. No doubt they were connected to the city via underground tunnels. The roar of the exploding shells blocked most of his view.

Higgins' aircraft was toward the back of the formation and he could see through the view screen that the bombers in front of them had already started to drop their ordnance. Thousands of the black objects raced to the surface. *Why are they dropping them outside the shields? Are the other bomber's guidance systems that off?* Higgins thought.

His mind raced as he imagined this whole operation failing as a result of a faulty system. The corrections the pilots and bombardiers would receive when they returned to base would be excruciating.

The bombs hit the ground but to Higgins' surprise there were no explosions. More and more of the black objects collided with the earth outside the shield wall, but nothing happened. He turned as he heard a click, and watched as the egg-shaped devices behind him were released. The first row exited the craft and plummeted in free fall to join their dud counterparts below. The second row immediately followed, leaving the bomb bay completely empty. The fleet had dropped all their ordinance. Tens of thousands of bombs, and not a single one had detonated. Their designers would be lined up against the wall the moment this was reported.

Higgins zoomed in the view screen and surveyed the bombing site. He jerked his head back as he saw movement at the drop zone. Something was slithering out of each bomb that had collided with the earth. Massive yellow blobs scuttled toward the Free States' defensive positions. The fleet hadn't been dropping bombs.

They were dropping living beings.

The defenders turned their attention from the skies to the surface as thousands of the feral beasts charged their positions. Higgins' eyes widened as the wave of death swallowed up the grey bunker complexes below. He stood up and moved away from the screen, haunted by what he was seeing. He sauntered over to the guardrail and felt the wind blow past his breathing mask. The view of the battle below was lost, as the bomber flew over the green shield of New Johannesburg.

The skyscrapers contained below gleamed in the sun, their windows reflecting the light like emeralds. It looked peaceful and serene, like a relic from a long-lost age. A community park came into view. Its green grass and children's playgrounds had been removed and replaced with countless white tents, no doubt holding thousands of refugees.

From up here, with the wind in his face and the smell of jet fuel in his nostrils, Higgins could almost forget there was a war. But he knew this artifact of a city would be destroyed, along with everything else. The wave of creatures would be charging through that shield wall in a matter of minutes. What exactly were these beasts? In what dark crevice had the N.A. found them? Were they alien? Born in a lab? The result of the massive amount of fallout on the ecosystem? Higgins could only guess, as he stared at the endless green shield that passed below.

The door leading to the front of the aircraft opened and the ship's bombardier, Jordan Thomas, entered. He walked with his shoulders and chin held high. Despite the oxygen mask, Higgins could tell he was smiling, the standard expression for a citizen in the Northern Alliance. Jordan approached and Higgins forced his mouth to smile under his mask. Failing to do so would no doubt be reported.

The bombardier spoke. "Mr. Higgins. I see you ensured all our little bombs were dropped on the enemy. Excellent work."

Higgins nodded and replied in the standard polite tone of the Northern Alliance. "Mr. Thomas, great work today on completing your mission. I will serve as a witness if you wish to use this as an example of a field competency met."

Standard conversation etiquette was to always give someone a compliment and to be positive. To not do so was considered a slight and rude. To ensure that one did not stray from these social expectancies, the Northern Alliance had each of their citizens on a daily routine of medications.

Higgins took the issued pills every day, as instructed. They were meant to guarantee you never became depressed, always staying happy and cheerful. All of the time. Every waking minute. God forbid you actually showed some real human emotion.

Higgins had known for years that these medications were not nearly as effective on his psyche as they should be. His comrades were able to always maintain a smile and say the right thing, something he struggled with on a daily basis. The doctors stressed that if the tablets weren't working, then it must be reported immediately so they could up the dosage.

Call Higgins a conspiracy theorist, but he didn't think there was a higher dosage.

He had proof of this theory.

The few people that the medication didn't work on, always seemed to disappear. Mr. Clarke, Higgins seventh standard year teacher was a prime example. Mr. Clarke had recognised that the medications didn't work for Higgins only a few weeks into the year. He then advised him that he shouldn't seek out more pills nor tell the doctors about this fact. Mr. Clarke's responsibility and duty as an instructor was to report Higgins to management, without hesitation. But he didn't, something Higgins was entirely grateful for.

Halfway though the curriculum Mr. Clarke suddenly vanished. Some N.A. government jockey from *The Department of Health And Wellbeing*, came in and said Mr. Clarke was severely ill and would be back when he was feeling up to it. Mr. Clarke never returned. Higgins remembered sitting at his desk the following week thinking, *they found out the pills didn't work on him. They took him away and he's never coming back. I have to pretend the medications work or I'll disappear too.* In all the tests that followed, Higgins was always sure to state answers that were overwhelmingly positive and conformed to the N.A. policies perfectly. He knew his life depended on it.

Higgins was brought back to the present when he heard Jordan clear his throat. Higgins looked down and saw that Jordan had his hand extended out to shake. A thin, brown leather glove covered it. This was standard practice of someone who was about to leave.

Higgins shook the hand and said, "Mr. Thomas, an additional moment of your time before you go, if you please."

Jordan released Higgin's hand and replied, "Excellent."

Higgins tried to pick the most positive sounding words he could as he said, "Mr. Thomas, I am curious. I noticed that today we were not dropping bombs on our enemies but some sort of living entity. Did you notice this as well?"

"But of course," the smile still plastered on his face as he spoke.

"Did you know of this ahead of time?" Higgins asked.

The corner of Thomas' eye flickered slightly as his smile thinned.

"Of course," Jordan replied simply.

Higgins could tell Jordan wished to speak more but it would be considered rude to say so much to such a simple question.

"Please tell me how that makes you feel?" Higgins asked, his smile now completely divorced from his lips.

Jordan's eyes squinted even more, the smile was massive under that air mask, "It made me feel excellent. The pilots went low enough so that we were under the enemy's missile defense nets and to ensure the pods did not fall off course. The wind was so slight that it did not carry them outside of the drop zone. To have the pods fall elsewhere would be considered—pardon my curse—a waste."

"Oh, your curse has been forgiven. Excellent choice of words my friend," Higgins said, even though he was not particularly fond of Jordan Thomas.

Higgins continued. "But you don't find it odd we are dropping living things on our enemies? Flesh and blood?"

The smile melted away from the corner of Jordan's eyes, "That sounds like negative speech. Possible insubordination."

"No, of course not. Forgive me, Mr. Thomas. Perhaps I am being unclear or have misspoke as a result of the adrenaline. I'm asking purely as a matter of philosophy," Higgins replied quickly, the sweat under his fur lined flight hood was starting to form.

Jordan's smile slowly crept back onto his face. "Then as a matter of philosophy I must ask, how is this any worse then dropping bombs on an enemy?"

"I don't know. It just seems—" There was silence as Jordan stared at Higgins, waiting for him to conclude his sentence. To finish someone else's sentence would be unwelcomed by most. "It just seems, odd, to me," Higgins continued after a moment.

"I must respectfully disagree, but I appreciate your opinion and this talk on military strategy. Unfortunately, I cannot continue this enlightening conversation at this time. I have other duties to attend to. Good day," Jordan said.

Despite the smile, Higgins could tell the man was furious, or as furious as someone could be when they were stuffed full of pills.

The two men shook hands again and Jordan headed back through the door that lead to the front of the bomber. No doubt he was off to congratulate the pilots about being able to maintain the correct height despite coming under heavy fire.

Higgins looked at his watch; it would be less than an hour until he needed to take his second set of tablets for the day. In case of an emergency the military had issued everyone a two week's supply inside each member's personal med kit. *I wish the pills worked on me the same as they do on everyone else,* he thought, listening to the howl of the wind through the bowels of the bomber. *Then I wouldn't feel ashamed about being a part of this geno-*

cide. He sighed and turned around before leaning forward against the guard rail. *Jordan does have a point,* he thought as he looked down the empty bomb bay. *How are bombs any better? How would sending an additional half a million N.A. troops to their deaths on the streets of Free State cities be preferable?*

His mind left him as it travelled far below into the streets of New Johannesburg. He imaged what would happen when the massive beasts tore thought the city, block by block, until they reached the refugee camps, sparing noone.

Seven days later, Higgins found himself in the back of the same bomber, returning to the scene of the crime. Seven days was all it took for the creatures to move through the entire city and eradicate nearly three million people. The drone fly-by had confirmed no movement from enemy personnel in a little over fifteen hours.

Command guessed that there might be some survivors hiding in the subway tunnels or fallout shelters, places the creatures couldn't claw their way into. The Oligarchy ordered for ground troops to be ready to move in and gas the tunnels. How the military planned to get boots on the ground with all those mindless beasts running around was beyond Higgins' imagination. It was unlikely that the Northern Alliance had domesticated them enough to be able to distinguish friend from foe.

Higgins' bomber was one of three that were heading to New Johannesburg once again. He had not flown since the initial wave seven days prior, which he considered a blessing. Rumours fluttered about that command had sent in a second wave the day after their initial attack. Another fifty bombers swooped in and dropped reinforcements. An additional ten thousand blood thirsty abominations entered the fray. There had supposedly been a plan to send a third wave the next day, but there was no need. The bio-weapons had done their job and pushed to the city center. They sustained heavy casualties, but the beasts were clearly expendable.

All three bombing operations that were carried out that day had been equally successful. The city of Mazran hadn't even needed a second wave to be sent in as the initial three hundred bombers and their payloads had been enough to eliminate the entire populace.

Higgins could think only of the civilians, the people who would have grabbed their rifles and fired entire clips into the massive monstrosities praying for them to fall. That would have been their last thoughts before the tide consumed them.

Higgins looked around the nearly empty bay and his eyes locked onto the only thing loaded in the bomber's clutches. It had been a surprising revelation when the aircraft took to the skies without a single bomb or pod being loaded. The object in question looked like an oversized sewing needle, double a man's height and about as thick as Higgins himself.

It swung delicately in the breeze as it looked down, past the open bomb bay doors. Four more of these objects were secured to Higgins' immediate right. The ordinance officer had given him strict instructions not to load them unless the first one failed to complete its task. Since Higgins had no idea what this needle was supposed to do, the idea of it functioning properly or not was moot.

The three bombers didn't have the clear blue sky all to themselves. This time, they were accompanied by nine Grand Army dropships. Three escorts per bomber. The dropships were instructed to take out any anti-aircraft guns should there be some still active. The creatures had all moved to the city center at this point and were too far away to hear the gunfire on the outskirts of the metropolis. The dropped soldiers should be safe to work without worry of "friendly" hindrance. So far not a single shot had been fired at the bombers. The Grand Army troops must be growing restless.

Higgins looked to the monitor; New Johannesburg was fast approaching. He cocked his head in curiosity as he noticed the surprising lack of green that should have encased the city. The shields had been shut down, their generators long dormant in the damp bowels of the metropolis. Whether it had been the creatures themselves who had somehow managed to deactivate the shields, or perhaps an N.A. special forces team sent in to complete this mission, the correct answer was anyone's guess.

If it had been a spec-ops team, Higgins felt terribly for them. He couldn't imagine anything more terrifying than having to go into that city. The same city into which their supposed "leaders" had just dropped thousands of scurrying death machines. Claws, teeth, tails thick as steel. All snarling their way. Little-chance they made it out after blowing the generator.

Higgins' viewscreen displayed the suburbs of the city as the bomber drifted overhead. No movement or weapons fire. Just a desolate wasteland. Higgins could have zoomed the viewscreen in for a closer look, but he couldn't bear to look at the bodies in the streets. Despite not being able to see them at this height, he knew they were there.

The slight click originating from the back of the bomb bay forced him to take his eyes from the city below. The rod had been released from the bomber. Higgins turned back to the view screen and watched as the mysterious object fell through the air before eventually crashing onto the streets below.

The bomber banked left and Higgins attempted to keep an eye on the massive needle. He realigned the camera and spotted it sitting at the intersection in front of what used to be a shopping mall. A wide-open parking lot sat behind the needle, the remains of what appeared to be aid stations and food distribution centers looming within it.

A few moments passed before a light on top of the steel spike began to flash red. The bomber circled the block again and Higgins could now see hundreds of the creatures beginning to flock toward the flashing light. It was summoning them, calling them from the blood-stained streets. They charged to it from their nesting pools: emerging from basements, apartment complexes, parking garages, any dark corner they had constructed their hovels. Higgins knew that the other two bombers would soon be dropping rods of their own, if they hadn't done so already.

The bomber continued to circle as hundreds more of the beasts sprinted to the ominous light source that was no doubt emitting a frequency audible only to them. This continued on for a long while as more of the monstrosities appeared. Thousands crowded the needle, jumping and nipping at it. The device was oblivious to their ferocity as it continued to flash in the sunlight.

The grainy footage of the viewscreen picked up the fur and the claws. A terrifying image, even thousands of feet in the air. Higgins couldn't imagine being down in the streets with them. He felt sorry for his so-called enemies and the weapons used against them.

The beacons must be attracting the beasts to a few central locations so they will be easier to round up. Higgins thought as he continued to study the viewscreen. *To be used again as a weapon of mass destruction by The Oligarchy. Dropped in another raid against an enemy that is already against the ropes.* He tugged at his breathing mask, finding it increasingly claustrophobic. *How the Northern Alliance plans to sedate the thousands of—*

There was a burst of light as the beacon detonated, decimating the entire block.

Higgins heard the explosion, followed by two more claps of thunder shorty after. He stood there, numb, his knees trembling as the weight of the world came crashing down. His soul ached.

Just like that, all those beasts had been extinguished. Their purpose fulfilled, no longer useful to the Northern Alliance.

Easier to destroy than to reuse. The N.A. would just create more, by growing or mutating or whatever the hell they did.

The bomber completed another pass. A new layer of smoke billowed up from the city, no movement on any streets. Higgins was focused on the suburbs but he assumed the other two needles had been just as devastating.

The door leading to the flight deck opened and Jordon Thomas strolled through. His fur lined coat flapped in the breeze as he spoke, "Mr. Higgins. Excellent job once again—"

"How can they just blow them up like that? Living things? They made them and used them, and then just executed them like—like they were nothing!" Higgins yelled cutting off Thomas mid-sentence, a major slight indeed.

Thomas' smile melted from his eyes and he replied, "How is this any different from a traditional bomb. It is made for a purpose and then ceases to exist once that purpose is completed. Bombs are much prettier though, and easier to control." His voice had an edge to it, a tone Jordan Thomas had never used before.

"But bombs aren't alive. Those—those things were," Higgins stammered.

"This is the second time you have talked with an agenda of insubordination. I must report this immediately, Mr. Higgins. I'm sure you understand, but to be frank, I do not enjoy your negative tone."

"Report me. I can't function like this anymore. To be associated with mass exterminations. Two in one week."

"This is a war, Mr. Higgins. The R.F.S. are trying to kill us, we must win to ensure peace can be restored and the world can be rebuilt."

"Do you actually believe that? How are people in the Free States any more despicable than us? They've have never dropped ravenous monsters on their enemies and then summarily annihilated them when the job was done."

"Who's to say they wouldn't do the same if they had found

the technology first?" Jordan sighed and then continued. "But Mr. Higgins, I am going to be honest. I am becoming annoyed with this conversation. I'm sorry to be rude, but I am leaving now. Goodbye."

Jordan turned and left. The door closed behind him and Higgins knew where he was headed. Straight for the captain to tell him of the insubordination that had just occurred in the bomb bay. Higgins knew he had crossed a line but at least he wouldn't be contributing to this unjust war machine any longer. He just hoped the execution was quick.

A typed letter, its wax seal still warm. Hand-delivered by a sergeant with biceps the size of Higgins' head. That's how the Northern Alliance notified him of his immediate transfer to frontline infantry in the Grand Army. Jordon Thomas had reported the insubordination all right, and then the pilot followed procedure and conveyed it to Bomber Command.

Less then twelve hours later, Higgins was sitting in front of the base psychiatrist. He answered all the questions correctly. After all, he had been passing tests like this his entire life. Still, he was surprised that the psychiatrist didn't ask about the incident or his opinions on the bombing missions. The doctor reviewed the grades and signed off that Higgins' mental heath was adequate. He was still fit for combat.

A nurse ensured that he'd been taking his pills and that was it, no further questions. Less than a week after his comments of disobedience, he found himself where he was now, in the troop bay of a dropship headed to the R.F.S. capital. The three cities that had been decimated in the previous attacks had ensured a clear path for the Northern Alliance to fly straight to the Free States' seat of government unhindered.

Higgins had heard in the news reports the day prior that the Republic had again requested a surrender. This was followed by the Minister of *The Free Press* addressing the unions. He shouted that it was The Oligarchy's wish to continue the war. Only after full decimation of all Free State cities would they then be satisfied. He said it was revenge for the R.F.S. firing the first nuclear missiles of the war in an unprovoked attack. Higgins had bit his tongue during the broadcast as it ran throughout the base. Insubordination towards a member of The Oligarchy's cabinet was punishable by death. A slow and painful one to be sure.

Higgins knew that the accounts of who actually started the war were long gone. The notion that the R.F.S. struck first was nothing more than Alliance propaganda. And did the Minister say unprovoked? Nothing could be farther from the truth. All three sides had succumbed to the military industrial complex. Adding fuel to the fire by taxing and blockading each other constantly. A war had clearly been in the making, it was just a matter of time.

The dropship shuttered as the flack started again like clockwork. The two window gunners at either side of the troop carrier fired at unknown targets below. Their small explosive shells would do nothing against the well-crafted bunkers, but it made them feel like they were contributing to the battle.

The Grand Army was flying behind the bomber formation. Thousands of troops had been tasked with probing the outskirts of the metropolis to pick off any resistance that attempted to slip out of the city and escape. Each solider had been briefed and shown pictures of the R.F.S. leaders in the event they attempted to flee like rats from a sinking ship. They were Priority One and would be dealt with accordingly.

The N.A. had pulled out all the stops for this one. Six hundred bombers, all loaded with their steel drums of death. The population was estimated to be a tad over six million. Military intelligence was confident it should take no more than two weeks for the city to be devoid of life. To ensure their estimates stayed true, they planned to send another two hundred bombers before dawn tomorrow in a second wave.

Radio chatter over the dropship's loud speaker indicated the flack fire was much more accurate this time around and the R.F.S. missile defence net had increased. The bomber crews were taking causalities and a few had already been shot down. Higgins hoped command wasn't surprised by the fierce resistance, as they had given the Republic citizens no other choice. This would be their final stand. Higgins knew he should feel terribly for those dead men and woman on the crashed bombers, but he felt nothing.

The soldiers in the troop bay were all strapped into their seats just like he was, with one exception. Their belts could be unlocked manually. The harness Higgins had been thrown into could only be unlocked by his squad leader. His unit was aware of his transfer and his rebellious comments. As such, no one talked to him or even acknowledged his existence. He wouldn't be surprised if a round found its way to the back of his head the moment they exited the craft, fired by a loyalist fanatic of the Northern Alliance. Higgins liked to think he would welcome the bullet, but there was no guarantee how one would act so close to death.

The dropship banked a sudden left as the radio chatter indicated another bomber had been shot down. Their craft was the closest to the crash site and Bomber Command had requested that they survey the wreckage, providing extraction to any survivors.

The dropship dipped under the cacophony of flack and circled over the crashed bomber. Higgins could see the damage through the windows across from him. A scorched ball of twisted steel and white flames. No one could have possibly survived—

A flash erupted from the cockpit of the wreck, followed by another. Someone had opened fire.

The dropship circled the crash again, movement in the

windows on the bomber's flight deck. Another flash from a sidearm, and then nothing. A hundred of the monstrosities jumped from the debris and scattered in several directions like cockroaches in the light. Several headed to the nearest Republic bunkers while some ran toward a far-off canyon. The bomber crew had been killed by their own ordinance.

The pilot of the dropship confirmed with command that there were no survivors before raising the craft up and away from the crash. The radio chatter on the comms was becoming more frantic by the second. There were several reports of a new anti-aircraft weapon of some sort. The calls for assistance were hard to follow. Talk of possible boarding parties? No, that was impossible. The Northern Alliance still had complete air superiority. None of it made any sense.

The pilot turned off the comms before Higgins could get any additional details. The captain didn't want the soldiers to get spooked before their big drop. The troopers sitting across from Higgins had lost their smiles and appeared fearful. The N.A. wouldn't be happy about that, years of mind conditioning wasted.

The dropship jerked as the pilot dropped once more to avoid the flack. They were almost upon the edge of the city. The craft shuddered as a round burst beside the ship. Higgins could hear the rivets connecting the metal tremble under the pressure as steel smacked against the hull. The troopers gripped their harnesses tighter. This mission was not going as smoothly as they had been led to expect.

Another burst of flack, this one to the starboard side of the craft. The window gunner a few places down from Higgins had his jaw removed as a piece of shrapnel ripped through the troop bay. The body fell to the steel floor and a spray of blood covered the smoking weapon. The troopers near the body swore at the sight, but the window gunner on the opposite side faced outward and took no notice. He continued to fire at the various defenses below, completely unaware of the corpse that lay behind him.

The pilot activated the comms again and Higgins could hear the desperation in his voice as he informed them that most of the bombers had been shot down. The captain went on to say that the R.F.S were firing something bigger at them and he was trying to fly around these new projectiles.

Higgins didn't hear anything else the pilot said after that. Something had slammed into the side of the dropship. A steel rod pierced the port-side hull of the vessel and impaled the poor sod who had been sitting there. The rod emerged from the soldier's ribcage and extended into the troop bay by two meters. The device was far too large and uniform to be a piece of flack. Too clean, too perfect in its design. It had clearly been manufactured to pierce through steel.

The troopers who sat beside the mysterious object unbuckled their harnesses and moved away from it as quickly as humanly possible. Their dead comrade's lifeless eyes watching as they pushed away. A sergeant yelled out orders and a corporal took a step closer to the tip of the projectile to get a better look. No doubt he was counting his blessings that this object, whatever it was, had been a dud.

A second passed before the tip of the projectile began to turn. Unscrewing itself, accompanied by the sound of grinding metal. The soldiers gasped and several moved to the back of the troop bay in an attempt to distance themselves from the object. No one remained seated, no one except Higgins.

The lid from the capsule fell to the floor and a curious green mist poured out of the end. The few troopers who were near the object yelled in pain before falling to the ground a moment later. They clutched their chests, blood pouring from their noses. The troop bay was filled with yells as the mist continued to spread. Higgins was sitting far enough away that all he could do was look on in horror as the green hue grabbed another set of troopers in its grasp. They attempted to cover their mouths but were not nearly quick enough to escape its reach.

Higgins was trapped, unable to unbuckle his harness no matter how much he fumbled with the latch across his chest. He looked up to see how far the mist had progressed and saw something entirely unspeakable. The impaled trooper, the man with the projectile sticking through his abdomen, had begun to move his arms. His legs twitching only a moment later.

The dead man sat up as much as he could in the chair. His face was already a horrifying sight to behold as it decomposed rapidly from the mist. A low growl emitted from the deceased trooper's vocal cords. Its eyes were now red as rubies, the soul that once inhabited them, long gone. Pushed onward to the next life by the mist, leaving behind only an undead husk.

The troopers that lay lifeless on the cold steel floor started to stand, skin falling from them as they lurched forward. Their hands disintegrating into claw like abominations. Screams of terror filled the dropship as rifles were fired at the approaching mob of decaying soldiers. The bullets pierced the shambling crowd but to ill effect. No cries of pain, no guttural roars, just a constant lurching forward.

Higgins' rifle was stowed beside his left boot but he couldn't reach it. He pulled nearly every muscle in his neck attempting to squeeze out of that infernal harness and grab his weapon. All he could do was grope around blindly and feel the muzzle of the barrel taunting him.

Higgins screamed in rage as his pulse pounded in his ears. He couldn't retrieve his rifle; the harness was too tight. He straightened up and moved his right hand to his hip, pulling out his side arm. He pointed the weapon and fired eight rounds into the chest of the closest shambling corpse. Just like all the other bullets, these shots did nothing.

Twelve of them were almost on him. The troopers

continued to fire and some dropped empty magazines to the ground as they fumbled to reload. One solider struggled with a control panel, attempting to open the dropship boarding ramp. A jump from this height would surely be fatal, but that death somehow felt preferable to the alternative. Anything was better than being ripped apart.

There was another sound of ripping steel as a second rod pierced the dropship. This time towards the back of the craft, near the pack of surviving soldiers. The tip started to unscrew just like the first, and Higgins could see the mist beginning to escape its prison. There was a wet tearing sound and Higgins looked to his right. He was face to face with two red eyes that sat in a decaying skull. The rotting face was missing its jaw.

"SNIPES"

There I sat, looking out at the woods through the cracked windshield of Henry's Mustang. The trees swayed lazily in the warm summer breeze. I was seated in the passenger seat and peered over at him. He could tell I was nervous.

"We're here man, now or never," he said, looking annoyed by my obvious hesitation. Then again, when didn't he look like that.

Originally, the plan was for me to stay in the Lastikuta State Park for the night. Just as all the other members of our motley crew had done, at one point or another. But when Henry and the rest of us pulled up in the Mustang, we saw that the cops had the place locked down. A search party was being put together. Apparently, some hikers had gone missing two days prior. Their car was still in the lot; they were in the park somewhere.

Vince, the blonde kid with a pocketknife obsession who sat in the backseat directly behind me, had suggested we drive up to the nearby Catholic bible camp and I spend the night there instead. Henry hadn't put up much of a fuss, he wanted to stay as far away from the cops as possible. He was driving underage, and after his older brother had been sent to prison, he loathed any man with a badge. The Mustang had belonged to his brother, and he had given it to Henry to look after just before he became a resident of the state. The jailbird must have known that if he didn't lend it to his kid brother their old man would end up selling it for beer money.

So, there we were, at the Holy Rosary Bible Camp. While I couldn't see any buildings from the parking lot, I knew it was out there. Waiting patiently for me to wander in like a lost baby deer.

"How far is it?" I asked, my voice cracking as I spoke.

"'Bout a klick, maybe a shade under," Henry said, as he pulled a carton of smokes out of his rolled-up sleeve.

"How long did you guys say it was abandoned for again?" I clutched my rolled up red sleeping bag tighter as I spoke.

"I heard it hasn't been used since eighty-eight I think," Henry responded as he placed a cigarette between his lips and struggled with the lighter to get a flame going.

"Good year for metal," Malcom said from the backseat directly behind Henry.

Malcolm was obsessed with guitar players and found every opportunity to bring it up. It was obnoxious. He always talked about the seventies and eighties like he was there, and somehow survived despite his rock star lifestyle. This kid was little more than a thought in eighty-eight, but here he was talking about it, as per usual.

The tape deck clicked as some Metallica album ceased playing. This Mustang was old but was in surprisingly good shape. You could call Henry's brother a lot of things, but untidy wasn't one of them. He loved his car, and so far Henry seemed to be taking good care of it for him. The cracked windshield was its only sign of wear. Henry had said on numerous occasions that he wouldn't get it fixed because he thought it looked tough. I knew the truth; he didn't have the money to fix it. Malcom said it looked "metal," so I guess that helped Henry justify putting the repair off.

"Well?" Henry said breaking the silence. "Do you want to join our crew or not?" He stared at me, his green eyes locked on my pale face.

"Ya, of course I—"

"Don't be a pussy, man," Vince said, cutting me off. I could hear the clicking from his pocketknife as he spoke.

"Ya, don't be a pussy," Malcom chimed in. "Last guy we wanted to join, chickened out big time. Like, wouldn't even get out of the car."

"Last guy *you* wanted to let join," Henry corrected him.

"I ain't no pussy, I'll do it," I said, as I unbuckled my seat belt and threw it aside.

I opened the door and exited the car. I could feel the sweat running down my back as a mix of nerves and that hot July sun began to work its magic. I placed my sleeping bag on the ground and pulled my backpack out from underneath the passenger seat.

I shut the door and peered into the car through the open window. Henry took a drag of his now lit cigarette and nodded at me with approval. I think he was happy that I didn't back out. After all, it was he who suggested I join.

Henry grabbed another smoke, immediately handing over the fresh Camel cigarette to me. I accepted it with such a cool confidence, you'd swear I'd been partaking for years. The truth was I had never smoked a day in my life.

Henry closed the package and tucked it back into his sleeve. He took another long drag and said, "See you in thirteen hours."

"Ya, thirteen hours, and don't let the wolves getcha," Malcom wheezed from the backseat.

I looked to Vince as he said, "Nine o'clock sharp, you meet us here. If you ain't here we's gonna make you stay till the end of the weekend," he laughed like a seal.

I glanced back at Henry and he shook his head to imply that Vince was full of it.

"Lucky thirteen," Malcom added as Vince continued to laugh.

I pushed off from the car and watched as Malcom handed Henry another cassette to play. Henry popped the old one out and slammed in the new tape. The tires spun in the dirt and the Mustang peeled out of the parking lot to the sounds of Megadeth's *Peace Sells* album, one of Malcom's favourites. I stood there for a minute and watched as the Mustang turned left onto the country interstate, toward the town of State Grass.

Within seconds, Dave Mustaine's blaring guitar riffs were gone and only the sounds of the mosquitos remained. I turned around and peered towards the entrance of the forest. The lonesome trail that led to the campsite was oddly still. Now I was really beginning to have second thoughts. I wanted to join their crew and make friends, but I was nervous.

I was the new kid in town and had the disadvantage of moving in at the start of June just as the school year was winding down. If I didn't make friends now, I would have to go the whole summer alone.

I looked at the bible camp sign. The wood was weathered, and the paint had nearly all flaked off. A tangle of spider webs sat between the wooden planks and swayed in the breeze. I hated spiders; their presence made me uncomfortable. My mind wandered as I thought of my first few weeks in town.

I had met Henry and the others in school, and for a few weeks I thought they didn't like me. Always seeming to ignore me whenever I approached them. That all changed just six days before the summer break started. Henry had approached me in the school yard and introduced himself. I hung out at his house the first day of summer and that's when Vince and Malcom seemed to warm up to me as well.

I remember Henry had handed me a Budweiser, my first beer ever and asked me if I wanted to join their club. I'd said yes, but that was when Henry dropped the news on me: I would have to pass a test. I'd thought it would be something embarrassing like asking the fat girl in class out on a date. But when Henry told me that all I had to do was stay in the woods for a night, I'd thought it would be a piece of cake. Every member of the club had completed it as a rite of passage, even wheezy Malcom. If that dweeb could do it, so could I. Of course, the major difference between their test and my own was that they had all stayed at the state park, not the abandoned bible camp like I was about to.

I knelt down and opened my backpack. It was relatively empty. I had only packed the essentials: a flashlight, an extra pair of batteries, two bottles of water, a can of bug spray, a granola bar and a small zip lock bag of trail mix. I felt around in my right pocket to ensure my swiss army knife was there. A birthday gift from my dad two years ago, back when mom was still alive.

Satisfied that all was in place, I swung my backpack onto my shoulder and picked up my sleeping bag. I passed the decrepit sign and entered the trail that led to the camp. A transport truck whizzed down the highway behind, startling me. I put my heart back in my chest and took several deep breaths to lower my pulse once more. I gave my head a shake and continued to walk down the path.

Multiple sets of tire tracks were imprinted in the dirt. They looked to be much newer than 1988, I was sure of that. I reached into my pocket and retrieved the cigarette Henry had given me along with a book of matches I brought along in case I wanted to start a fire. I struck the match against the box and lit the cigarette. I took a drag and coughed for a solid minute.

8:37 PM

The walk to the camp was quicker than I anticipated. I had followed the tire tracks up and around a bend in the road and before I knew it, there it was. Standing before me, more ominous than I had expected. The main building was a massive log cabin that sat in a clearing. It overlooked the road like a sentry, its windows dark but ever vigilant. A white flagpole sat in front, its banner long removed and its paint peeling away to reveal the rusted steel underneath.

I looked to the right of the cabin and noticed that a second parking lot was present, tucked neatly into the clearing. No doubt this lot was used for the pickup trucks that could make the journey on the trail. As I approached the building, I became aware of the items in my backpack jostled with every step that I took.

Despite the obvious exposure to the elements, the cabin was remarkably well preserved. No broken windows, no graffiti, no logs missing. I guess teenagers in this town had more respect than the ones where I was from.

I walked up the wooden steps. Each one creaked under my weight as I ascended. I came to the main door and peered inside through the glass. I couldn't make out any details as only a intense black could be seen. I reached down and turned the handle. To my surprise, it opened. I guess no one had bothered to lock it the last time they were here. I pushed the door open and could see several turned over chairs and a few rusted out cooling fans sitting in a corner.

I placed my backpack down onto the old deck and reached into my bag to retrieve my flashlight. I raised my head and looked up at the wooden banister hovering beside me. I gritted my teeth as my eyes locked on what sat an inch from me.

I was face to face with the biggest, meanest spider you'd ever had the displeasure of seeing. Its red and yellow body was sitting comfortably in a web made of silk and dried out flies. Its colourful legs flicked gently on its web. It knew I was watching it.

My imagination ran wild, as I pictured this thing jumping onto my face and going down my throat. As I conjured up this image, the spider spun around in its web and went to the far side. I tumbled back in sheer panic waving the unlit flashlight in the air frantically as a make-shift weapon. I must have looked completely ridiculous if someone had been watching, and I felt like someone was.

I pulled my backpack up and lifted the sleeping bag with my free hand, never taking my eyes off the spider. I turned on the flashlight and entered the building. An empty assembly space greeted me. I'm sure this hall was originally used to hold presentations and games, but with the lights off, it looked more like a crime scene.

There was a stage sitting off to the left, and a fireplace to the immediate right. Multiple benches and fold up tables littered the floor. A clothing rack stood at the center of the stage. Children had once worn these items for the countless plays, talent shows, and skits they were required to preform. The grimy clothes hung ominously as their headless collars watched me intently. I knew ghosts weren't real, but if they were, I'm sure these would be the clothes they'd wear. The entire interior was covered in dust and cob webs had encased the unholy number of crucifixes that hung from the walls in a thick silk. I placed both my backpack and sleeping bag down on a nearby bench and decided to explore.

9:07 PM

The sun was starting to set and the sky was turning orange over the tops of the trees. I had finished exploring the main building and had concluded it was too dirty to act as my base of operations for the night. That, and the number of crosses and spiders had freaked me out. The rest of building was pretty boring, a small kitchen, a set of bathrooms and a few more materials for crafts, long left behind.

I had less than half an hour until the sun went down, so I picked up my pace. I left my sleeping bag and backpack in the main building until I could find a more suitable sleeping spot. I covered myself in half a can of bug spray and exited the cabin, flashlight in hand. The sweet smell of repellent wrapped around me in a cloak of fumes.

I walked down the wooden stairs and turned to the right. A short distance away was a trail going up a steep overgrown hill. I climbed the path and entered a clearing with six cabins, three perched on either side. They were made from logs, just as the main building had been but looked more run down.

I approached the first cabin on the left and twisted the door handle after reaching the top of the stairs. The knob turned with a satisfying click; it wasn't locked either. I had to slam my shoulder and use some elbow grease to get the weathered door to budge, but it gave away quickly enough.

After walking inside, I noticed that a bunk bed sat on either side of me. A closet was positioned on the left side of the room and a few metal coat hangers jangled as the breeze from outside stirred about the room. The air smelled of dead leaves and old wood.

I moved farther into the cabin and into the next room. This second area was larger and had two sets of bunk beds on either side. A few sky-blue sheets littered the ground and a stained plaid jacket hung on a hook beside the back door of the cabin. The amount of beds meant there would have been twelve children per cabin, assuming each structure was constructed with the same design. In its prime, this camp could house a lot of children.

I headed outside and searched the next cabin over. It was exactly the same, six sets of bunk beds and some left-over items, including a dusty Mets hat. I was already becoming bored and wondered why I had ever been scared of this camp in the first place. It was just a bunch of run down and weathered lodges.

I exited the cabin and walked to the end of the row of buildings. An outhouse complex was to my left and I knew there was no way in hell I would be exploring that. I could just imagine the smell, decades old feces rotting in the dirt. Spiders, rats, snakes and a million other horrors burrowed in its midst.

Directly beside the outhouses was a building made of brick. A sign hung over top of the entrance stating that it was the showers. I made a mental note to examine the inside of that later once I had found a spot to set up my home base for the evening. The shower shed would be my first excursion, my first patrol of the evening. I looked to the row of cabins once more before turning to the right and heading down a short trail.

A large log cabin sat at the end of the path. Like everything else in this camp, it too was unlocked. The door opened with a distinctive creak and I entered. This cottage was the nicest by far. The walls were decorated with cheap art and the floors were covered in a shag carpet. A bookshelf sat off to the far side of the room containing multiple copies of the New Testament and other books about the good news of Christ.

The building had a distinct scent of old papers with a slight hint of mold floating above it all. A leather sofa sat peacefully against the wall and a set of chairs were stacked over in a corner. In front of them was a cheaply stained table. Heavily used board games rested on top of it. The standard fair, Monopoly, Game of Life, Clue, nothing that would be perceived as violent by the holy sisters or priests of the camp. Of course, Monopoly could always turn into a brawl if one wasn't careful.

I walked over to the window and realized I was on something of a high ground. The main building of the camp that overlooked the entrance sat below me. I turned to my left and looked down the hall. Another window sat at the far end. Through the dirty glass I see a set of eight rotting benches resting before a heavily weathered altar. They were waiting for a congregation that would never come. A cross loomed at the front the scene, a haunted looking thing. I swallowed hard at the sight. This was clearly the spot where the camp once held mass, but it looked so sinister and old. A path went from the right of the altar area and down the hill towards the assembly hall building. I turned my attention back to the leather couch and decided that this cabin would be my main base for the night.

9:55 PM

The sun had set by the time I finished exploring my new command and control. I had reasoned that this cabin was where the priests and councillors slept. There were multiple bedrooms, each containing two double beds. The mattresses were long gone, leaving behind steel frames. The steel skeletons still looked to be more comfortable than those bunk beds ever hoped to be. This cabin had indoor plumbing and housed its own bathrooms, complete with showers and sinks. The last area of the lodge I stepped foot in was the basement.

After some cautious exploration, I had realized it was just a cold cellar. It contained a kitchen, a small eating area, a rusted-out water heater and a few fuse boxes. A mildew-laden door sat at the far side. Curiosity had told me to open it and I saw that it led back outside and faced the mass area. That horrifying decaying cross watched me as I stood in the doorway listening to the sounds of the sleeping forest all around. After snooping around a bit more, I walked back to the main building of the camp and retrieved my backpack and sleeping bag.

I had just reached the front door of my headquarters and was about to open the door when I felt the need to look behind me. I saw lights, multiple set of them, darting through the trees as they moved down the dirt road. Their beams cutting through the woods, making disfigured shadows in the moon light. As they made their way into camp, I realized they were headlights.

I stood on the stairs of my base and listened. The sound of truck engines growing louder and louder. Rocks, mud and dried leaves being crushed under rubber. I knew the sound of Henry's Mustang, and this wasn't it. I panicked and swung open the door to my cabin, closing it behind me the moment I was inside.

At first, I thought about dropping my gear on the leather sofa and watching these newcomers from the window, but I thought better of it. I knew these visitors might decide to explore the buildings just like I had. If they did, they would see my items and know I was here. I had to remain undetected.

I ran down to the basement and looked around for a spot to hide in the likely event these intruders decided to have a peak around. I moved to the kitchen and remembered the cabinets, perfect. I flung open the doors and turned on my flashlight for a split second to see if anything had been left inside them or if any spiders were present. The coast was clear, thank god.

I turned off my light and shoved my backpack and sleeping bag inside. Now it was time to watch these hostiles and scout their movements. The unprepared warrior is the dead warrior.

I closed the cabinet doors and ran to the basement window. I could see the side of the main building as well as the second parking lot sitting to the right of the camp. I watched as three pickup trucks rumbled past the treeline and rolled through the grounds. They circled about before parking in front of the main cabin. They were loud, black and rusted out hulks of machinery.

I could see that men sat in the beds of the trucks but their attire was odd. From this distance it was hard to make out, but it appeared as though they were each wearing black hoods of some sort, coverings that shrouded their faces. A glint of steel, some of the men had guns. My eyes widened.

The enemies exited their trucks, twelve men in total. The figures in the beds of the pickups jumped out first, pulling something behind them attached to a rope. I could hear squealing and watched as a pig was dragged from the back of each truck. Judging by how poorly these animals were being handled, there was no love for them.

The men trudged up the hill behind the cabin, hauling the three pigs behind them. I noticed they had left their trucks running, which I found strange. Dad was always talking about gas prices being on the rise and joking about money not growing on trees. I wished he was with me now, but he was likely deep into a double shift.

The figures walked in silence as they moved up the hill and headed towards the altar. I lost sight of them as they moved out of my view upon reaching the top of the hill. I hurried along the wall of the basement to a new window. I could see now that a few men were holding kerosene cans. They began to gather twigs and dry leaves, piling them hastily behind the cross.

Three men stood guard, two at the sides of the group and one at the rear. This brooding menace of a man was the closest to me, but his back was turned. He was facing the altar, watching as everyone moved into place. He seemed calm compared to the rest. The double barrel shotgun he wielded was broken over his forearm but was loaded, ready for use at any moment. A lit cigarette sat between his third and forth finger and he dragged on it every few seconds.

His two comrades that flanked him were not nearly as relaxed. Their rifles shook in their hands and they jumped at every sound the woods made around them, every hoot of an owl or snap of a twig. Now that these figures were closer, I could see that every man was wearing a black cloak over dark pants and a robe as dark as the woods around it. Some of the men wore masks with eye holes cut out, while others simply had their hoods pulled over their heads. I couldn't be sure which version of their uniform I found to be more frightening.

I saw the gleam of a revolver tucked into the belt of the man who stood before me. Its cold steel reflected the moon light brightly. He lit another cigarette and watched as a few men with gas cans poured their contents onto the tepee of wood. They threw matches at it until it caught ablaze.

The light from the flame was intense and completely illuminated the altar. I saw that eight of the men had now moved over to the benches while another emerged at the front of the congregation. He stood with his back to the cross and looked to the three pigs that stood beside him, their ropes fastened to the altar.

My bowels turned to water the moment the flock of onlookers started to chant. The language sounded old and backwards. Their incantation went on for several minutes, lead by the man at the front who waved his hand around and chanted louder than the rest.

I could see the guards on either side of the group were getting more nervous with every second that passed. They gripped their rifles tightly and kept pointing them at the tree line. The man on the left was overweight and I could tell he was sweating thick beads under his heavy hood. He rubbed at his forehead and adjusted his cloak incessantly. The beast of a man to the rear watched him with a keen eye.

The cult's chant continued to grow louder and louder, more and more disturbing. Once the chanting reached its climax, the leader fumbled with his robe. A second passed and I could see he was brandishing a knife. Its blade appeared to be a piercing blue in the moonlight. He grabbed one of the pigs and held the blade over its head. Its squealing was deafening.

Just as he began to bring the knife down towards the pig, the guard nearest to me turned and looked towards my cabin. I hit the floor as fast as I could and waited in silence. I was too terrified to move. I stared at the door in front of me, expecting it to swing open as a mob of hooded figures stormed in. The door did not budge. I heard the pigs squealing in pain and then a moment later, silence. The sounds of the night had stopped, the chanting, the pigs, all of it.

I slowly got to my feet and looked out the window. The congregation was gone, only the fire and three bloody pig carcasses remained. I looked around to ensure I wasn't missing anything, someone lingering behind, but the coast was clear. I shifted over to the original window and watched as the men returned to their trucks. They walked briskly and slammed the doors shut the moment they were inside. They were in a hurry.

The vehicles took off and headed back towards the interstate. Their tires spun in the mud and gravel as they departed. One stalky man was almost left behind and had to jump into the bed of the last truck. Once he was secured, the other men in the back frantically hit the roof of the vehicle, telling the driver to speed up. The red taillights disappeared through the trees and before long, I couldn't hear the engines any longer.

11:54 PM

I jerked myself awake. Somehow, I had fallen asleep at my post. The stress and the dump of adrenaline had no doubt taken their toll. I stood up and brushed off the dust from my jeans. A bug scurried across my arm and I swatted it away. I returned to the window and saw that the second parking lot was empty. An icy wind fluttered through the woods which caused the branches to blow around angrily.

I still couldn't understand what the hell I had witnessed. I'd heard of Satanists before but I never thought they actually existed. Definitely not in a small town like this. I moved to the other window that overlooked the altar. The fire was nearly extinguished with only a small dot of light remaining. The cross still hung over the altar and the pigs—

The carcasses were gone.

I rubbed my eyes to ensure they weren't playing tricks on me. I looked again and saw that only the altar and aging benches remained. I turned around to face the dark basement, hoping to see Henry or Vince standing there laughing about how this was the greatest joke they had ever played. Hell, I would have even taken Malcom at that point. The basement was silent and still.

I decided I would go out and have a look around the altar to see if I could find any evidence of where the pigs may have gone. Most likely an animal had come by and had dragged them off somewhere. I had heard black bears were a common sight in this area so they were the probable culprit. I felt the weight of my swiss army knife in my pocket as I went over to the kitchen cabinets to get my bag. I was dying for a drink.

I opened the cupboard and rustled through the backpack to retrieve one of my water bottles. My hands froze as I heard a sound that sent shivers down my spine. A squeaking sound coming from upstairs, the same distinctive creak the door had made when I originally entered. I sat there and listened but heard nothing other than the sound of wind fluttering down the stairs and into the basement. I relaxed and exhaled sharply; the breeze must have opened the door. Then I heard the footsteps.

The floorboards creaked above me. Heavy shambling feet lurched around the main floor of the cabin. My pulse went into a frenzy and the little amount of hair on my arms stood up. I immediately turned off my flashlight and dove into the cupboard shutting the door quietly behind me. My mind was racing. Did that cultist see me? Did he stay behind? Did they all come back? My brain scrambled to come up with the most likely scenario, until I heard the stairs to the basement groan under the weight of something. My mind went blank and the blood flushed from my face. I stopped breathing, remaining perfectly still.

Three separate creaks filled the basement as something moved down the stairs. I waited in horror for the fourth and fifth thump but there was no more movement. Whoever it was had stopped on the third step. The basement was as silent as a tomb, not a single sound. Then a distinctive clicking noise started from the third step. It sounded like a grandfather clock ticking, except with less rhythm and more grinding of teeth.

12:57 AM

I sat in that cupboard for nearly and hour. That was the amount of time it took to build up just enough courage to turn on my flashlight and look down at my watch. That clicking had continued for an eternity before the footsteps trekked back up the stairs and trudged around the main floor for a little while longer. I heard the creaking floorboards shift towards the main door and then silence. I figured at this point I had waited long enough, whoever it was must be gone by now. I prayed I was right.

I took a long gulp of water and opened the cabinet, shining the light around the dark basement. I was careful not to point the beam at the windows in case the cultists were still lurking around outside. If they saw my light, I would end up like those pigs, sacrificed to whatever pagan god those nut jobs worshipped. I exited out of the cupboard and felt my Swiss Army knife press against my thigh, realizing it was still in my pocket. I hoped I wouldn't need it.

I crept over to the stairway and switched my light off as I approached. I stood at the base of the stairs for a long minute, listening to the wind funnel through the cabin and down the stairs. Leaves rustled outside. Judging by how much noise they made, the front door must still be open.

I turned my light on for only a moment and fully expected someone to be at the top of the landing, peering down at me. Their black hood shrouding the evil that their eyes would have surely shown. But all was still, my imagination had run off without me again.

I switched off my light and moved up the steps, a creak after each one. I attempted to evenly distribute my weight on every stair but the result was the same. No matter how much I watched my footing, the stairs continued to grumble under me. My right hand gripped the flashlight and my left clutched my pocketknife as I removed it from my jeans.

I reached the top of the stairs and peered into the hallway. All was calm. Even the leaves stood still and lay lifeless on the carpet. I exhaled and turned left, entering the main room as I did so. The leather sofa and board games were all in the exact same place. This minor detail, this small dose of familiarity in the otherwise unfamiliar predicament I found myself in, calmed me.

The wind picked up and I felt a breeze against my face. I turned my head to the right and looked down the hallway. The front door swung in the wind, completely open. I listened for a moment but only heard the howl of the night. It was a cold and bitter draft. I let my shoulders drop and felt my pulse even out.

I turned back and approached the window taking deep breaths as I did so. The moon was huge tonight, nearly full. I noticed now how much it illuminated the campground. I looked down at the main building, then to the parking lot where the trucks had been.

And that's when I saw it.

A figure stood in the center of the grassy parking lot. While the moon was indeed bright, I couldn't make out its finer details, only basic characteristics.

He stood on two legs and was tall, unnaturally so. His arms were thick mounds of muscle and much longer than they should have been. Each hung down by his sides and dug into the dirt. It stared straight up at the moon and watched as the clouds moved across the sky with a breakneck speed. I had never seen anyone stand quite that way before. It was so... inhuman.

A twig snapped outside the front door and my heart leapt from my chest. The blood in my face turned to a hot ice and I bit down on my teeth. I turned my head towards the entrance but kept my flashlight off. I didn't dare press the button. I looked down the hall and saw that the doorway remained empty. I took four cautious steps towards the empty entrance way, before I heard another branch break off. They sounded close, only a few feet from the cabin. I stopped walking and listened, the grip of my knife burrowing into my hand.

Footsteps sounded off again, but this time they were getting quieter. They were running off into the woods. Twigs cracked in the dark and leaves crunched under the weight of whatever it was that darted through the trees. At first, I thought that maybe it was a deer, but these footfalls sounded heavy and less graceful. Whatever it was, it didn't gallop, it ran. I moved back to the window and looked out into to the parking lot.

The figure was gone.

My eyes darted back and forth. The only light on the grounds was from the all-seeing moon, watching me and whatever else patrolled these woods.

I stiffened up and felt a chill like no other rise through me as I heard the moldy old basement door's handle jiggle before releasing. It creaked open a moment later. Something had found its way in. I panicked. There was nowhere to hide up here. The sofa, bibles, and boardgames would offer little solace from the woodsman that was coming for me, trudging along the stiff concrete of the cellar, towards those creaky stairs.

I turned toward the front door and ran, sprinting as fast and as silently as I could, working to control my breathing as I did so. I didn't want my deep raspy exhales to give me away. I exited the house of horrors I had found myself in, and headed back towards the smaller cabins. I stopped beside the cottage closest to the trail and listened. Only the hoot of an owl echoed through the woods. Whatever was in the counselor's lodge with me had not heard me leave, or if it had, it didn't think it was worthwhile to follow me.

I took a deep breath to try and collect my thoughts and come up with some assemblance of a plan, but my peripherals stole my focus once more. Something was standing by the brick shower building. A figure taller than any man alive. Out of pure fear I raised my right hand and turned on my light, pointing it towards the shape. The moment the beam of light pierced the darkness, the figure moved behind the brick building and out of sight. I couldn't tell if my eyes were playing tricks on me or if something had really been there. My heart raced, and my shirt was drenched.

My hands were shaking and the light from my flashlight danced on the trees and outhouses. I turned to my left and pointed the light down the rows of cabins. As I did so, I glimpsed a second figure, green as camouflage, its elongated limbs reflecting the moon light. I could now see that its "arms" were actually scythes, dragging in the dirt behind it. The creature lurched behind the farthest cabin before I could study it any further. It didn't seem to take notice of my flashlight, or maybe it had. Maybe they were toying with me, playing with their food, a lamb to the slaughter.

I switched off my light and fumbled to unfold my swiss army knife. This three-inch dagger of mine would do nothing compared to the blades that these horrible figures dragged along behind them. I heard a series of clicks originate from deep in the woods behind me. The same grandfather clock ticking and scratching of bone sounds. The clicks became louder, faster. Leaves rustled, twigs snapped, and the owl stopped hooting. It was moving fast. The beasts were done playing, it was time for a hunt.

I bolted to the nearest cabin and thought about racing up the stairs, locking the door and hiding under one of the bunk beds, but I quickly tossed away the idea. I knew I would make too much noise and would no doubt be found within seconds. Those guillotines would come plunging down immediately after.

Instead, I pivoted and dove under the wooden stairwell of the nearest cabin. I was careful not to impale myself on my open knife. I felt cobwebs hit my face and a group of startled spiders scurry across my nose and down my arm hair. I was too frightened to care. I flipped onto my back and tucked my legs as close to my chest as I possibly could. I pointed my knife at the side of the stairs where I had just entered. My hands were shaking so badly, I could hardly grip the damn thing.

I listened as the booming footsteps continued to get louder and raced towards the wooden stairs of the cabin. Several branches trembled in the moon light. One snapped violently and thudded to the ground. I stayed as still as I could, I knew the darkness under these stairs would protect me from these unseen predators. That is unless it could see in the dark. I hadn't thought of that. I swallowed hard and held my breath, hoping that night vision wasn't an ability this hell spawn possessed.

A figure, the same as the others, emerged from the woods.

Its scythes raised in front of it as it bounded past my hiding spot. The clicking and footfalls moved farther away from the cabins, farther from me. I continued to lay in that place trying to calm myself, but none of the usual tricks were working. All I could see in my mind's eye was that misshapen, bony body, and those scythes. They were hungry for a kill. The blades had tasted the pigs but now they wanted something bigger, something alive, with blood still flowing, the taste of adrenaline still pumping through its veins.

My terrified brain immediately retreated to memories from the time I was a cub scout. The older boys had told me and all the other newbies about these wild creatures that patrolled the woods, scouted the quarries, hunted the campgrounds. Anywhere that little cub scouts might be. The story changed from troop to troop, storyteller to storyteller. Only one thing was constant: their name, "Snipes."

I don't know what I had seen in the woods tonight, but my mental image of what I thought a Snipe would look like as a child was pretty damn close to what was stalking me. I knew I needed to get out of here. I had to make it to the road, then I could run back to town. I had no idea how long it would take, but I would rather be running down a cold stretch of highway with the moon at my back than here in this godforsaken bible camp.

I crawled out from underneath the stairs and looked around. The breeze was getting heavier and on any other night I might have been freezing, but not tonight. My back was drenched in sweat, I hoped they couldn't smell it. I jogged to the end of the cabins and carefully looked to the left, where I had seen one of them. Nothing was there, just some tall grass and a pile of lumber.

I heard a few hoots from the same owl and decided it was now or never. I moved down the hill and tried to stay as quiet as I could. My breaths were short and stabbed at my lungs. I stumbled multiple times as it was now almost pitch black, the moon had become blocked out by the dense trees. I reached the gravel road and sprinting towards the interstate. *Almost there,* I thought, *almost free.*

I continued through the trail and nearly tripped in the tire treads that the trucks had left behind. I decided to fold up my knife and store it in my pocket so I didn't accidently disembowel myself if I fell to the ground. What a way to go, escaping from ten-foot-tall creatures with scythes for arms only to be gutted by my own knife as I tumbled over a root.

I could see the clearing ahead, the parking lot where Henry and the others had dropped me off all those hours ago. The air here was fresher than it had been in those musty woods. The smell of death was behind me now, far behind. I sprinted into the parking lot. The moon light shone on my face, giving me life. I took a few controlled breaths and listened to the woods that lay behind me. They were silent.

I breathed a sigh of relief and heard the wind move through the trees. I looked at the highway and hoped a car would drive by soon so I could hitch a ride back to town. I wouldn't breathe a word of this to the driver. They would either think I was insane, or even more likely, part of the satanic cult itself. A sentinel patrolling the highway in the event someone had witnessed their beasts.

No, I would go back to town and find a way to get proof. I would tell Henry first, then dad. Dad wouldn't believe me but I had to tell him. He needed to know. I was about to take a step forward when I heard the clicking. The sound of pincers salivating. It was right behind me.

THE LAST COSMONAUT

Carl Doyle stood in his apartment drinking his first cup of morning coffee. Snow blew against his plexiglass windows and the wind howled outside. What else was new? He hated mornings, waking up at the ungodly hour of 4:30 AM for a 6 o'clock start time. It was still dark out and would continue to be for a few more hours.

Carl watched as the snow billowed atop the steel and concrete buildings of the compound. The streetlamps hummed, making the whole area look serene, almost peaceful. Then he remembered he would be working in this weather all day. He grumbled.

Carl walked over to his couch, grabbed his blanket, and wrapped it around himself, cloaking his body. He reached for the viewing monitor controller and sat down as he selected a sports game that had ended nine months prior. He'd seen it three times before and knew how it ended, but this was one of the few things he had saved to the monitor's hard drive.

It was also the newest sporting event he had. It was old even when he'd recorded it two months ago. The battleship that sat in orbit at the time had been constantly behind on their entertainment broadcasts. Most of their frequencies were tied up with military jargon and they didn't want to waste bandwidth on the newest sport matchups. Plus, by the time they received the broadcasts from the Capital Ring they had already aged like a fine wine. That's the problem with colonization: you aren't near anything until you build it, and the moment you do, they ship you off to the next planet to repeat the process.

Ever since the Ulysses battleship had left orbit, the colony was effectively cut off from anyone else. Even the colony on the next planet over couldn't communicate. The only time the installations could chat was when the resupply ships landed and the installation piggy-backed off their transmitters. The neighbouring planet was some desert world. Hot sun, even hotter sand. Carl could go for some warm weather right about now. He chuckled to himself as he thought back to his time there. He had hated it when he was assigned to that posting, but anything was better than the project he was on now.

The Ulysses had gone tearing off after the Tatalilian Scourge, an alien race favoring barbarism over any real form of centralized government. The Ulysses, being the most forward ship to their territory, headed to meet the rest of the Colony Defence Fleet and organize an attack plan. The Scourge wasn't much of a threat, all things considered. They had poor strategies and slow ballistic weaponry. The navy never had any problems knocking them back, and yet the cycle continued none-the-less.

Every few years, the Scourge would make an unwelcome appearance and go after some poor spacer colony. The three hundred pounds of green stink that was the average Tatalilian thought of human meat—specifically biceps—as a delicacy. They didn't bother to use humans as slave labourers or anything similar. If someone was unlucky enough to get captured, they were dead. In recent years, now that the colonies were getting increasingly closer to Scourge territory, the attacks had become much more frequent.

Ever since the attack on Perseus Minor, the navy had made it a policy to put at least one ship in orbit around each colony until a satellite defence network could be established. The rock Carl found himself on was still under construction and had relied solely on the Ulysses for defence. The navy was confident that this world was far enough away from the Tatalilian hunting fleet's flight path and should be relatively safe from attack. The corporations instructed everyone to continue building the colony. Carl had rolled his eyes when he had heard the news and thought, *Of course. Don't let man-eating aliens stand in the way of progress.*

The first quarter of the recorded game ended. The Hunberg Rebels were down by two but they would come back in the next quarter. Carl looked at his watch and the red display showed the time: *5:04 AM.* He was going to be late. He scarfed down a protein meal bar and a peanut butter flavored sandwich. It tasted like drywall, but was supposedly healthy. He'd never gotten used to the taste.

Carl went to his quarters and put on the multiple layers of clothing required to prevent freezing to death on this ice ball: thermal underwear, multiple sweaters, lined pants, coveralls. He grabbing his lunch, put on his boots as well as his two coats and was out the door by 5:19 AM.

Carl felt the cold air sting his face the moment he stepped outside. His hands began to ache and his exposed face was already burning by the time he reached his truck. The starter on his battered vehicle turned over multiple times, sputtering after every press of the button. Even with the overnight heaters, it still had a difficult time waking up in the sub-zero temperatures. After the third turn over, Carl was able to get the engine running. A jet of cold air blasting from his vents filled the cab of the truck. He didn't wait for the engine to warm up before shifting the vehicle into drive and heading toward the compound's main gate.

II.

Carl pulled up to his office building after a white-knuckled slide down the ice-covered roads. The I.N.J. Telecommunications sign was half-submerged in snow drifts and the two-story structure sat in complete darkness. Being the only employee from his company still planet-side, he didn't need to worry about leaving a light on for the night crews.

When work on the colony had begun to slow down, the entire telecom crew had spent most days standing around, not accomplishing much of anything—other than drinking coffee and flicking cigarette butts into snow drifts, of course. After all, if the construction guys didn't dig the trench or build the junction boxes, then the I.N.J. crew couldn't run the cables or build the site. They had tried to keep themselves busy, but one can only clean the shop and reorganize the trucks so many times.

I.N.J. took note of the little amount of work being completed and decided to pull everyone—save for a skeleton crew of five—off-world. Despite the company's best efforts to buy the construction crews time, the short-staffed team was still able to keep a steady pace and catch up with the builders. I.N.J. then dismantled the skeleton crew and left only two employees and a worker drone to complete the project. A punishment for working too effectively, Carl assumed.

It was determined Carl would be one of the two workers to stay put and was promoted to field foreman. A made-up position that meant he didn't receive any extra pay, only the blame if the wrong choices were made. Carl's "crew" consisted of Adrian Wilcox, and a Hypercom Industries Mark IV Construction Bot. The I.N.J. team had thought that designation was too long and convoluted and instead named the drone "Old Reliable" for short.

Things went awry for Carl the moment he received his "promotion." Only a week into their two-man crew dynamic,

Adrian started to feel "ill." He told Carl that he had to leave the colony and return home. The company, of course, approved the request. If Adrian left the colony and breached his contract, I.N.J. wouldn't have to pay him any disability or severance.

Adrian had hopped on the transport ship a month prior, leaving the inhospitable ice world far behind. Only Carl and Old Reliable remained, expected by their employers to build a whole telecom network by themselves. Progress had been slow but I.N.J. couldn't care less, they had diverted Carl's old crew to a brand-new project. This colony was quickly becoming a side show.

Carl stepped out of his truck; his boots completely submerged in snow as he did so. As the only I.N.J. employee still on this rock, he was instructed to check on the office building every day to look for damage. The structure appeared secure from where he was standing. Besides, they weren't paying Carl enough to go wading around the backside of the building in unplowed snow drifts that would be up to his chest. If anything had been damaged from a storm, Carl would know. He had the alarm system and motion sensors synced to his tablet. Nothing of relevance had ever been reported.

The only reason he had gotten out of his truck and braced the elements was to scan his pass on the front door of the I.N.J. building. This was how he punched in for work and started getting paid. The company disabled the online time sheets when they forced the team down to a skeleton crew. Management had been worried the team wouldn't show up to work and would lie about their start times. As a preventative measure to this likely scenario, they made it a requirement to arrive at the office and scan in before going to the job site.

Carl swiped his pass and heard the acceptance beep as he did so. The black screen glowed and Carl cleared the frost that covered it. The familiar blue writing stated: GOOD MORNING EMPLOYEE, DOYLE, C . . . CURRENT TIME IS: 5:58 AM

He sauntered back to his truck and climbed inside. The heat in the old truck had taken its time to climb to an acceptable temperature, but now warmth flowed into the cab. He took a few moments and felt the hot air blow on his face, it was glorious. Carl wouldn't be getting paid until 6:00 AM and he wasn't going to leave this parking lot a moment earlier.

III.

The glow of the atmospheric processor lit up the horizon to the west, filling the sky with an array of curious purples and blues. Its black towers and massive body could be seen peering over the jagged hills. The processor, along with its four brothers, had been humming away for a shade over ten years now. One processor for each major continent of the planet.

The timeline for colony construction was standardized and had become routine. A planet would be probed and determined if it was to be a suitable home for humanity's expansion efforts. If the world was deemed profitable then the processor construction crews would be sent in and get down to business. Factors such as planet size and how much atmospheric transformation was needed to make the air breathable, would determine the number of processors built. Once construction was finished, the crews would vacate and let the processors do their job. All anyone could do was wait for the facilities to work their magic.

In the case of Carl's current planet, the colony of Tokyo-Miami, it had taken nine years to get all the readings to a steady level. The Colonial Expansion Initiative had run out of interesting or scientific names for colonies decades ago and began naming them after two cities. One that still existed and the other, a city from history.

Once the atmosphere was in an acceptable range, a second set of crews were sent in. Their tasks were to raise up living compounds and company offices. Once the primary buildings were complete, then came the secondary techs, which included the telecom crews. Carl's job was to construct a network, complete with radio communication towers, and eventually link satellites that the Ulysses was expected to drop into orbit. These satellites would then give the colony enough range that it wouldn't need to piggyback off the navy's frequencies any longer and could communicate on its own.

Progress was slow and the construction crews were even slower. Their equipment continuously froze, and the incessant plowing of snow drifts was dragging their operation down to a crawl. This was not the first ice-world humanity had colonized, but turn over on these construction crews were high. The companies needed to continuously hire and train new people, something that took time.

The radio station playing through Carl's truck speakers went to static as he descended a steep hill. His tires slipped on the ice and the traction warning light lit up on his dashboard. He had faith in his old truck. He hadn't gotten in an accident yet on this ice cube, and he wasn't planning on breaking his streak.

The radio reception came back clear as day once Carl's truck reached the bottom of the incline and entered the plains of the job site. There was only one radio station on Tokyo-Miami and it was run by an engineer that worked in Processor Four. Some old cowpoke who liked to play ancient country and western songs about horses and girls and heartbreaks and saddles. Real gritty, ye-haw type stuff. Carl hated this type of music, but it was nice to hear something different every now and then.

The disc jockey's track selection had been limited ever since The Ulysses left orbit. The guy had to rely on the few albums that he had saved as backups on a hard drive. Due to this technical limitation, Carl heard the same hundred songs or so repeatably for the last few months. Despite his annoyance with the repeats, he was becoming a fan of some guy named Nathan Winslet.

When Carl finally managed to get the tower dish operational, he might have to download some of Winslet's body of work. According to the old disc jockey, it was quite a substantial catalogue. The Ulysses leaving orbit had taught everyone a valuable lesson: always backup files. Even when streaming entertainment is so convenient all it takes is a loss of connection and all the data is gone.

The worksite was a massive clearing containing the unfinished satellite uplink tower in the middle. Snow-covered hills filled the horizon as far as the eye could see. This area was the flattest plain for hundreds of miles. Everything else was hills on top of hills. Short, tall, wide, narrow, but all hills by definition. This clearing was one of the few areas the tower could be constructed without having to worry about interference from the surroundings.

At the base of the tower was a concrete hut where all the communication wires and terminals led to. This was Carl's work location, a concrete bunker with no heat except for a portable heater unit he had bought from a plumber who had departed the colony two months prior. The guy had gouged him for the beat-up device. *Typical union guys*, Carl had thought as he handed over the money.

As Carl approached the tower, he could see the construction crews were already hard at work, which was an odd sight. He had grown accustomed to their routine by now. The crew would warm up in their trucks and sip coffee for almost thirty minutes before they started up their equipment for the day. Carl wasn't judging them of course. Their work consisting of grueling back-breaking labour, especially in this weather. They were becoming less and less enthusiastic about exposing themselves to the elements with each passing day.

The construction crew was out in force, gas-powered augers, back hoes, tractors, the whole eighteen-man team was not only working, but also on time. Something had these crews motivated to work. Perhaps they had been promised a bonus if they finally finished the telecommunication trench lines that were a month overdue.

Carl turned off the main road and entered the trail that led toward the job site. The truck fishtailed as it made the turn, kicking snow and ice behind in a plume of white. As he approached the scene, he noticed that a marshal's vehicle was parked beside one of the larger tractors. Something was up. The marshals always stayed near the living compounds or the atmospheric processors. Rarely venturing this far out, unless there was an accident. Carl hoped this wasn't an emergency of some sort, but what else could it be?

Carl parked his truck in the usual spot beside the bunker and watched the marshal as he stood to the side of the massive hole the crew was excavating. Whatever was down there had his undivided attention. Carl had no idea why the crew was digging such an enormous hole. They were supposed to be adding a second and third line of trenches. *No wonder these teams are so far behind,* Carl thought as he shook his head. *They can't even read a blueprint.*

He shrugged his shoulders. His job was telecom and he wasn't overly concerned about what the construction crew was doing. No doubt Old Reliable and himself would be out there in the muck tomorrow or the day after, running those accursed cables once the lines were finally dug. At least their excavation project had bought him another day inside the concrete bunker and out of the searing wind.

Carl exited his truck and walked over to the building. As he hiked through the snow, he looked to his right and watched several machines as they moved dirt and ice from the hole to a pile near by. The foreman was in the process of guiding a dump truck over to the mound of frozen dirt. No one had seemed to notice or even care that Carl had arrived. It didn't bother him. Due to the high turn over, he didn't even know most of their names.

Carl entered the punch code on the bunker and the door opened. The cold air flew out and bit him in the face; he flinched. It didn't get any easier doing this every morning. He turned on the light switch and the bulbs flickered on one by one.

In the left corner was a brown slab of metal, Old Reliable. Carl activated the aging drone and waited for the smaller cube to slip out of the top of its body. Two blue lights illuminated on the display and served as Old Reliable's eyes.

"Good morning, Carl. Please select personality type," the worker bot said in its monotone voice.

"Something quiet," Carl replied as he sat down on a tool box.

"I have vaguely surly, or calm and collected."

"Calm and collected please, Old Reliable," Carl said as he closed his eyes and leaned his head against the wall.

"Carl, would you like me to begin work on Program Six? Same program as the last . . . twenty-seven . . . days?" Old Reliable asked, switching its tone of voice to match its new personality setting.

"Sure, you do that," Carl replied hoping the robot would be quiet.

Carl knew it was just programing and the drone's creators had tried to make the drone as helpful as possible, but sometimes silence was the most help. The droid was equipped with sixteen different personality settings.

Mickey, the company's tower climber and rigger for this colony was a talker. He always liked to set the droid to the "Chatty Cathy" mode. The guy even made that personality Old Reliable's default setting. Once Mickey left, it took Carl and the rest of the skeleton crew a week to figure out how to turn off the defaults and get the droid to stop babbling. It would talk for hours about all sorts of useless trivia, the weather, old sports scores, and the proper way to grow corn on some colony called Vancouver-Rome.

As for Program Six, that was some make-work setting Carl had compiled his first day alone with Old Reliable. Simply put, it entailed going around the bunker ensuring the satellite dish didn't have any burnouts and to put away any objects left laying around. Once those simple tasks were complete, the drone would go outside and melt snow around the tower.

The old robot unpacked itself. Its "limbs" moving away from its brown body and its engines warming up. The droid hovered in place for a moment before puttering around the bunker, checking on various terminals and gauges.

Carl pushed his head from the wall and stood up with a deep sigh. He was growing bored of his profession. *When I was young, I never imagined I would be working in the less-than-riveting world of telecom,* he thought as he looked around the concrete room. He wasn't sure what he would rather be doing, but this wasn't it. He didn't hate his job, just disinterested. His creative mind wasn't sure what was worse.

Carl wasn't sure how he would spend his workday. There were several fiber optic cable endings that needed to be fusion spliced, but that would only take a couple hours. What would he do with the other ten in his shift? He could only check the azimuth and calibrations for the antenna so many times.

"Excuse me, Carl. Where would you like this to go?" Old Reliable said, as it held a piece of conduit in its pincers.

"I don't know. Um, over there, I guess." Carl gestured to the far westward wall next to two radio packs that still needed to be mounted.

Old Reliable knew where tools needed to go but when it came to building materials, he always felt the need to ask. Carl could deactivate this feature if he wanted, but even though he would snap at the drone, he appreciated its company.

Carl moved to his overstuffed tool bag and grabbed an

adjustable wrench and a screwdriver. He may as well attach the RF cable ends to the Alpha and Bravo radio packs that were mounted on the eastern side of the bunker. He looked up from his bag as he heard a thud on the bulkhead of the bunker.

Old Reliable stopped its puttering and looked to Carl.

"Keep working. I'll get it," Carl mumbled.

The worker drone beeped indicating it understood, before pivoting. Its little hover jets whirled behind him as he returned to gathering items. Carl opened the door and exposed the bunker to the harsh winds that thrashed outside.

Before him stood a construction worker in full winter gear, complete with a face mask and goggles. Carl couldn't disseminate who was under all that clothing. Foxford? Or maybe Silverman? No, this guy was too tall to be him. The masked man was out of breath and appeared to be sweating under to all his layers.

"You have a degree in history, right?" the young labourer asked, his voice indicating that he was in fact Foxford.

"Ya, I guess. Who's askin'?" Carl replied as he pulled his toque down over his ears. The wind continued to pick up outside.

"All of us. Come outside, quick."

Before Carl could answer, the young man was already jogging away toward the plains. Carl put on his gloves once again and wandered outside. He could see that all the construction equipment had ceased operations and were still. All eighteen labourers, as well as the marshal, were huddled around the massive hole they had created.

Carl pushed past a few workers and looked down into the hole for himself. At the bottom lay a gigantic object made of steel. A hatch of some sort sat at the far-left side of the hole, just barely excavated by the digging crew. Whatever this entity was, it looked like the workers had only unearthed a small portion of the object.

SONGS OF THE ABYSS

Then Carl saw it. Right above the door, a red star with a yellow hammer and sickle inside it. The letters *C.C.C.P.* etched in black paint below it.

"Well, Doyle, do you recognize that symbol?" Dwayne, the construction crew's foreman asked as he looked to Carl.

"Ya, it's Soviet," Carl replied as he zipped up his jacket.

"Is that like an alien?" Foxford asked from behind Carl.

The kid was twenty and not the most educated of individuals. He had been hearing about the Tatalilian Scourge his whole life, not the long dissolved Soviet Union.

Before Carl could answer, another member of the construction crew spoke up. "No, idiot. I told you it was manmade. I knew I'd seen it somewhere before."

Carl was as excited as he was nervous. This ship, or satellite or whatever it was, was old. It had been over four hundred years since the U.S.S.R. fell and even then, it had limped its way to the finish line. This craft was most likely even older. *What the hell is it doing way out here?* Carl's mind raced with the possibilities.

Carl had focused his studies primarily on the first two great wars, and while he knew about the rise of communism and the fall of the Tsar dynasty, he was hardly an expert on their inner workings.

His knowledge of their space program was even more limited. It was one thing to know of the feats of Yuri Gagarin, the hero that he was, and of course there was Sputnik, but the rest was a red blur. Alexei Leonov rang a bell, but Carl couldn't remember for the life of him what the man had done specifically.

Carl's brain was working in overdrive, trying to figure out how this craft had traveled to the other side of the galaxy in such a relatively short amount of time. *It would have taken hundreds of thousands of years or more to get here using the archaic engines of that era,* Carl thought as he felt the chill of the air bite at his neck. *Did the Soviets have Hyperdrives? Did they know about worm holes or—something else we don't know about?*

He shook his head, realizing the idea was absurd. If the Soviet Union had that type of technology back then, no doubt it would have been discussed openly. Such advancements would have propelled the U.S.S.R. to new heights. They would have been at the forefront of a brand-new age of space exploration. His thoughts continued, *surely they didn't have tech like that way back then. But then again, this ship being here should not be possible. Yet here it is, right in front of me, trillions of kilometers away from its home.*

He wished at that moment that he had payed more attention in Astronomy class in school instead of chatting to the girl next to him. Then a moment of clarity took Carl by storm. The Russians had sent an animal into orbit before they had ever sent a man. *What was it? A monkey? No that was the Americans . . . A cat? No . . . A Dog!* Carl thought and straightened up.

He hoped this wasn't the remains of the ship that had launched the canine into space. The last thing Carl wanted to see today was a dead dog, especially one that had been deceased for over four hundred years. He couldn't remember if that craft had ever left Earth's atmosphere or if it had burned up upon re-entry.

But what else could it be? The Russians never launched anything this far out. Still, the size of the craft had him curious. It was much too large to only hold one dog. The ship looked like it could hold an entire assortment of crew, if need be.

"Well, are we opening it or what?" Marshal Wyatt asked. His voice was shaking but he still had the raspy tone of someone who had been smoking the better part of thirty years.

"Shouldn't we call someone?" Foxford asked, his question aimed at no one in particular.

"Like who?" Dwayne retorted. He adjusted his ski goggles

as he spoke. "We have no range. The resupply ship is still weeks away. Not a chance our transmitter will reach them. It's just us out here."

"I say we open it," Marshal Wyatt said, his voice full of excitement. "Once we see what's inside, we tape it off and wait for the resupply ship to come into range. Then we report it."

"You're the cop," Dwayne replied as he looked off into the horizon at the rising sun.

"So, these Soviets," Wyatt said as he turned to Carl and fumbled with the turtleneck under his uniform. "They spoke Russian, right? Or was it Polish?"

"Russian. It was Russian," Carl answered as he continued to study the hull of the ship.

He was still attempting to figure out how this ship got here. Playing hundreds of scenarios about in his head.

Objects in motion stay in motion unless acted upon by an outside—

"Can you read it?" Wyatt asked as he squinted, attempting to decipher the various labels.

"No, and I've never met anyone who could. Then again, I've never asked anyone either."

"Well you recognized the symbol. You should go first. Maybe you'll remember something else from your university days?"

"Ya, I guess, but I didn't specialize in world history, more the great wars and colonization of the 'Second New World,' stuff like that," Carl answered with reluctance.

Despite his rapid heartbeat, the prospect of being the first person to open something so ancient was an intriguing notion full of wonder and mystery.

"Well still. That's more than me," Wyatt said. He looked to the jagged edge of the hole, no doubt deciding the best way to scale down the slope. He plotted his path and continued, "Let's make history, gentlemen." As he spoke, he gestured for Carl to lead the way.

Carl went first and slid down the wall of dirt and ice until he was at the bottom of the hole. A distinct metallic ringing was heard as his composite-toed boots hit the ship's aging steel. A conversation was already brewing up top.

"Wyatt? Why do you have your gun out?" Dwyane asked, his booming baritone voice echoing off the craft's hull.

"I don't know. There could be anything in there. Alien pathogen, something like that. Better safe than—"

"Doyle said it's Russian. Aliens weren't even around when that space race stuff was going down. Besides, what are you gonna do if it is a virus or gas or something? Shoot it? Bullets against bacteria? Solid plan there, no flies on you. Use your head, man."

Carl tuned out the rest of the conversation. The fact that he was standing at the bottom of the hole alone had him slightly worried, but the fear quickly dissipated. He was too intrigued by this ship. A snapshot of history, a piece of science, possibly the last soviet object still in existence that wasn't behind the dusty glass of some museum. The harsh environment of ice did serve as its own gallery glass of sorts, forever preserving the craft.

Carl found the entrance hatch's handle and felt around for a release. There were multiple red warning signs written in Russian around the hatch. At least, he assumed it was Russian. Having never actually seen the language written down before made it look like hieroglyphs to his eyes.

He found two black handles and knocked off the leftover ice with the back of the wrench he had stored in his coat pocket. He tried to pull the handles open but gave up after a few seconds—they were frozen solid.

"Need some help down there?" a voice called out from up top.

It could have been Marshal Wyatt who spoke, but Carl wasn't paying enough attention to know for sure.

"Ya." Carl turned around and looked up to the group

gathered around the top of the hole as he called back. "Get my worker drone for me. He can cut this door open."

Foxford nodded and turned to leave when Carl added, "It wont respond to your voice. It isn't calibrated for it. You gotta say, 'Old Reliable, override code, seventeen zero nine.' Then it will follow you."

"Seventeen . . ." Foxford said as he hesitated trying to remember the rest of the code.

"Zero nine," Carl repeated himself.

Foxford nodded again and ran from the edge of the hole. The wind was picking up again as flecks of white buzzed around the surface.

IV.

The snow had already begun to build up on the hull of the craft when Foxford returned a minute later, Old Reliable hovering close behind. Carl could hear the robot happily beeping away as it wished everyone at the site a good morning.

Foxford stopped at the edge of the excavation and said, "Robot, he's down there."

"Oh. Pardon me," Old Reliable said as he gently pushed past a few construction workers.

The droid arrived at the top of the hole and looked down into it. His metal claws moved in the air with joy once he saw Carl. His programmers had added this in as a detail to help build familiarity. Similar to how a dog acts when it sees its master returning home after a long day. It was supposed to help build a bond between the robot and the crews that used it. In Carl's case, it worked.

"Carl, it is good to see you again. Do you require assistance with your current endeavor?" Old Reliable said. His voice sounding cheerful, as cheerful as a robot could sound anyway.

"Ya, please. I need you to use the cutting laser. Steel setting four should do it," Carl answered.

The droid hummed and clicked before bobbing up and down to simulate a nod. It hovered down to the base of the hole and turned to looked at Carl.

Its gears clicked before the drone said, "Please point to where you would like the cuts to occur."

"Sure," Carl said as he drew a rectangle around the edges of the hatch with his index finger.

"Ready to cut the designated spot. Please stand back," the droid said cheerfully.

His programmers had set it so that he liked to work and assist when needed. Not that he had a choice of course, but the old bot seemed to genuinely enjoy helping. Carl wished he could just flip a switch in his brain to love work as well, but such is life.

Old Reliable was through the steel in a matter of seconds. It stuck its claws into the freshly carved cuts and lifted the hatch into the air. Carl could see that the crowd was still looming above, more interested than ever, eagerly waiting for him to enter.

Several of the labourers had removed their goggles; they wanted to see with perfect vision, not through some cheap plastic. Carl pointed to the ground beside the craft and Old Reliable dropped the hatch onto the ice.

Carl searched his pockets for a flashlight but came up empty. "Light please," he said to his old companion.

The droid beeped in delight and activated a beam that popped out of the front of its rectangular body. "Oh hell, I'm coming too," Marshall Wyatt said as he slid down the side of the hole.

"Count me in. I gotta see this," Dwayne mumbled as he threw his lit cigarette onto the freshly laid snow.

Carl could hear a few other voices volunteer to join them down at the entrance of the craft. Just as Dwayne arrived at the bottom of the hole, Carl called up, "No one else, it will be too cramped. We might damage it. Just the three of us and the robot for now."

The crowd sighed and a few of them whispered to each other, no doubt thinking it was unfair they were being left out. Carl waited for Dwayne to stand up and get a solid footing. He was not nearly as graceful as Marshal Wyatt had been in the decent. The foreman stood up and brushed off his insulated pants.

He coughed and shook his head saying, "I'm too old to be doing stuff like this these days, this weather is murder on the knees."

Marshal Wyatt nodded, but Carl wasn't really listening, he was too focused on the portal of blackness that lay before him. A gateway that led into history, into the forgotten vessel. He took a long breath then stepped forward, entering the craft. Old Reliable and his hover jets puttered forward into the opening. Marshal Wyatt entered next, his hand still placed firmly on his holster. Dwayne brought up the rear, coughing a few times as he did so.

The first thing Carl noticed was the lack of smell. He had expected the inside to be musty and stale, like an old basement or factory that needed a thorough cleaning. He soon realized that due to the sealed air and freezing temperatures, this was not the case. Still, the lack of any aroma was curious and alien to him.

There was no doubt the craft was a manned ship. Multiple consoles and screens, littered the walls. The equipment was more than antique; it was ancient. The various screens had a thin layer of frost on them and the walls were shiny from the cool air. Carl looked to his right and saw a sealed hatch, its locks no doubt frozen in place, sealed for hundreds of years. If need-be, Old Reliable could cut his way through, but still the idea of a door being closed for generations was an intriguing notion to Carl.

To the left of the group was a corridor that continued far beyond the limits of Old Reliable's battered flashlight. Carl could just make out several strange looking steel drum-like objects that lined the hallway. In all his years aboard starships, he had never seen anything quite like them.

These curious devices were positioned sideways and sat on metallic risers. Copious amounts of tubing and cables ran out of all sides of the objects. Carl counted six of these drums but could see that more of them were sitting out of range of the flashlight. Their silhouettes beckoning him to explore, leading him further into the ship.

Carl walked forward and could hear Old Reliable's hover engines whirling behind him. Judging by the lack of footsteps, Wyatt and Dwayne were hesitating at the entrance, still taken aback by the sheer scope of this craft. Carl returned his thoughts back to the ship as he passed one of the massive steel drums. Each of the barrels had a curved monitor with a keyboard attached to it. The screens were completely blacked out, barren of any information.

All except one.

Carl looked at the third drum closest to him, a single green light flickering on top of its keyboard. The frost that covered it made the green node faint, almost invisible. The monitor that hung above it displayed two words in white blocky lettering, the same alphabet that littered the rest of the ship.

Carl approached the drum and ran a gloved hand over the cylinder. This container had more cables and tubes running out of it than the others. Carl touched the screen and wiped away the layers of frost with the back of his glove. *How could this thing still have power?* He thought.

Carl moved his hand to touch the lone green key when Wyatt said, "Watch it. We don't know what's inside, could be dangerous." The marshal's voice echoed down into the bowels of the ship.

"I have to know," Carl answered as his fingers slid delicately across the series of keys.

"Let's just report what we've found and wait for the supply ship. They can take care of it," Wyatt's voice cracked.

"We talked about this. That ship is at least a week away, and that's assuming it's not late," Dwayne retorted. "Can you really wait that long to find out what's inside these containers? Besides, the supply ship will just call someone else in, a science team or some other experts. We will have to wait even longer for them to arrive. I say we open it."

Carl couldn't wait any longer. A desire to know, so many questions he needed answers to. He pressed the glowing button on the control panel and waited, hoping it wasn't a purge switch that would destroy all of the container's contents. There was a series of clicks and the words on the screen changed to form a complete sentence. Carl backed away as the drum emitted a low hum.

It was warming up, waking from its slumber. A moment passed before the top of the container lifted up with a slight hiss. Ancient air rushed to escape the confines of its prison. Carl pushed the metal hatch aside and looked in. His mouth dropped in amazement at what he saw.

A man encased in a green slush was completely submerged in the drum. Electrodes covered his entire body and his thermal suit had several monitors and wires connected to it. A breathing mask extended from his face to a tube that was connected to the bottom of the tank. The man's chest rose and Carl gasped.

The man was alive.

Dwayne pushed past Carl and swore as he witnessed the man for himself. The familiar hammer and sickle symbol dead center on the mesh head covering. Carl watched as the slush moved around the man's right hand. Not only was he still alive, he was already waking up.

"What the hell do we do now?" Dwayne said as he looked around the dark ship, trying to think of a plan.

"We say hello," Carl answered simply.

Despite his calm demeanor, his mind was racing. Not only would he be talking to the oldest man alive, but he also knew there was very little chance this Russian would be able to understand a word they spoke. Carl was aware of the history of his language, commonly called "Western Standard." It was a combination of English, French, Spanish and some Portuguese. Even if this cosmonaut could speak any of those four languages, he would only be able to pick up certain key words or phrases, not enough to hold a full conversation. Language had evolved quite a bit in the four hundred years since this explorer had blasted off from the motherland.

"You're taking this really well," Marshal Wyatt said as he peered over Carl's and Dwayne's shoulders.

"What? He's just a man. An old guy, but still a person. I'm just curious how he got way out here."

The cosmonaut stirred and turned in the green slush. His hands raised to his head and removed several sets of probes that were attached to his face. His eyelids flickered for a moment before finally opening. It took the Russian a second to register what he was seeing, but when he did, his eyes turned from a sleep induced daze to a full-blown panic.

Upon seeing the group of three hovering over him, he shot up and pushed his back against the side of the tank. He started to speak in his native tongue. Carl was amazed by the sounds of the language. He had never heard anything like it before.

"What's he saying?" Wyatt asked as he took a step back.

"How the hell should I know?" Dwyane called out over his shoulder.

The cosmonaut cocked his head and said in the best

English he could muster, "English, Yes? America? England?" His voice trembled.

"America's long gone my friend," Dwayne replied.

Carl removed one of his coats and held it out for the cosmonaut to take. The Russian looked at it for a moment, confused. His eyes darted between the three stranger's faces. Not wanting to spook the man, Carl placed the jacket on the side of the tank for the Russian to take when he was good and ready.

Carl held out his hands with his palms open to show he had no weapons and wished to cause no harm. While the cosmonaut's adrenaline was running rampant at this moment and protected him from the sting of the cold, he would need to take the coat soon. He would feel the chill of the freezing air momentarily, no matter how afraid he was.

The cosmonaut gingerly took the coat and placed it over his chest. He was about to stand up when his focus shifted from Carl to the hovering brown rectangle with blue eyes and claws behind the group.

As he looked at the robot, Old Reliable beeped and said, "Good morning." His usual monotone voice echoed off the dormant steel.

The cosmonaut pushed his back farther against the side of the tank and his face flooded with panic once more. He pointed at Old Reliable and began to yell in Russian. No doubt asking what the robot was, and why it was able to talk. It only occurred to Carl at that moment that droids—something he took for granted everyday—hadn't existed when this cosmonaut had gone out into the final frontier.

Carl kept his hands out and said in as calm a voice as he could muster, "It's okay."

Realizing his words meant nothing, he then shushed the confused cosmonaut attempting to settle him down.

"You know he can't understand you," Wyatt said.

"I think it's working, though," Carl responded, trying to keep the Cosmonaut from lashing out.

The Russian seemed to relax slightly, and Carl could see his frosty breath was becoming steadier with every exhale. The cosmonaut grabbed the coat tighter as he tried to stand up. The moment his chest rose from the green liquid he lost his balance and nearly fell over. Carl and Dwyane grabbed onto his arms and attempted to steady him.

Carl realized that this man hadn't walked in hundreds of years. His limbs would need to time to relearn some of their lost memories.

"This poor bastard is going to freeze to death," Dwyane said as he continued to hold onto the Russian.

"I have a spare set of clothes in the trunk of my patrol cruiser, warm thermal stuff. I'll go get it," Marshal Wyatt said as he backed away from the group.

Carl nodded in thanks as he held the Russian steady. Marshal Wyatt ran towards the entrance of the ship, leaving Dwyane and Carl to continue holding onto the man's trembling arms. A few seconds passed and Carl could tell the cosmonaut was really feeling the cold now. His trembling increased rapidly.

The cosmonaut looked down at the two men and spoke once more. He gestured with his head and started to step out of the tank again. After a shaky step, he managed to put his foot on the metal riser, but quickly retracted it from the cold steel. Dwayne ensured Carl had a secure grasp on the Russian before he took off one of his jackets as well, placing it on the floor as a mat.

Carl waited for Dwayne to grab the cosmonaut's arm again before he removed his second jacket and draped it around the shivering man as a cloak. Carl was already feeling the nip of the air. While being mildly uncomfortable, he wasn't in danger of freezing to death like this old Russian was. The cosmonaut stepped forward again and onto the riser. He gained some balance and brought his other leg out. He was out of the tank, the place that had been his home for centuries.

"Old Reliable. Can you translate what he says?" Carl asked already knowing the answer.

"No, unfortunately I do not recognize this gentlemen's dialect. In offline mode I can only translate between Western Standard and East Asian Standard. For more languages and dialects, I would need to be connected to a central hub that has access to The Network," the robot said pleasantly.

Carl could tell that having Old Reliable speak was making the Cosmonaut uncomfortable. The man's eyes darted between Carl and the worker drone. He studied its hovering engines, its blue eyes, its various gadgets and tools. Carl in turn studied the man. He now noticed just how little muscle mass was on the old timer's body. He weighed next to nothing and looked dangerously frail. Something told Carl that a person was not meant to stay in those tanks for as long as this Russian had.

Marshal Wyatt returned a minute later with a set of baggy clothes. His sudden entrance visibly frightened the cosmonaut, but Carl and Dwayne had a firm grip on him so he didn't loose balance again. Wyatt carefully handed the Russian the winter clothes. A pair of pants, a sweater and a coat, followed by a pair of thermal boots. The boots were about three sizes too big but the Cosmonaut didn't appear to mind.

"Let's warm this ship up," Dwyane said as he looked to Marshal Wyatt. "If we run some extension cords from the tower building, we can plug in our mobile heaters. It should get this place to a reasonable temperature for our friend here."

Wyatt nodded and turned to leave when Carl said, "Lets move him out of here while it heats up. Let's take him up to the telecom room, should be a good temperature in there by now."

"Sounds like a plan to me," Dwyane said as he assisted the cosmonaut in putting on the sweater.

The three men grabbed onto the Russian and slowly escorted him out of the ship. Old Reliable beeped as they moved down the hall. The cosmonaut's eyes shifted from fear to curiosity. He was about to step out onto an alien world.

V.

The telecommunications bunker was warm by the time Carl and the cosmonaut arrived. The rest of the construction team took to the universe's oldest man in stride. There were a few gasps and murmurs but nothing obscene. Everyone helped the cosmonaut out of the hole first, with Carl, Dwayne, and Marshal Wyatt, exiting close behind. Carl assisted the Russian into the only chair in the bunker and covered him with another coat. The man was still shaking, no doubt having caught a chill from the ship and that green sludge. His lack of muscle mass or fat did not help matters.

A minute passed before Dwayne entered with a few items in his arms: notably a blanket, thermos, cups and several protein bars. He placed them down in a pile on a nearby table and asked, "So, what's the plan?"

Carl had been thinking about this since the moment they had exited the ship. "London-Constantinople is out of our small weather satellite's range, right?"

"I don't know, you're the telecom guy. You tell me," Dwyane said as he chewed on one of the protein bars.

"Well it is. I was more talking to myself, but here's what I'm thinking. If your boys uncover the rest of that ship, we might be able to use its antenna and contact the fellas on the next colony over. Wherever our Ruskey was supposed to go was obviously far from home. His antenna should reach the next planet over without much difficulty."

"How old did you say that ship was again?"

"Three hundred and ninety years or so, give or take," Carl answered as he handed a protein bar to the Cosmonaut who delicately accepted it.

"So, you're telling me a four-hundred-year-old antenna on a ship that crash landed, is going to have a longer range than our satellite and com tower?" Dwyane asked as he poured the thermos full of coffee into several plastic cups.

"Ya, that's exactly what I'm saying. Our weather satellite isn't meant to talk to anyone else other than us, and the tower is still unfinished. The Ulysses was our main communication source but no one expected the Scourge to blow through again so soon."

Carl handed the cup of coffee to the Russian, who gazed at it, not knowing what it was. He didn't fully trust "future" drinks, least of all hot brown ones. Carl grabbed a cup for himself and took a sip. Upon seeing this, the cosmonaut followed suit and took a swig from his own cup.

Recognizing the taste immediately, his eyes lit up. He nodded and smiled to Carl and Dwayne with a big toothy grin. The Russian took a second sip, bigger than the first and looked content. Coffee hadn't changed much in four hundred years, it seemed.

Carl looked back to Dwyane and continued. "If our satellite network and tower was finished, then of course we could broadcast to London-Constantinople, no problem. The Ulysses was carrying antennas and radio packs that can broadcast all the way to the Capital Rim. Those are still sitting in its cargo hold; they never unloaded them before tearing off after the uglies. Which leaves us with our current problem. No communications with anyone else. But if his antenna works, then our problem is solved.

Dwyane nodded and replied, "All right, I'll have the fellas start trying to dig out the rest of that ship. It's going to take a while. Anything we can do with our friend here?"

"Nothing right now. I doubt he will want to get into a truck with someone he doesn't know, plus he seems pretty happy here with his coffee. I'll try to explain my idea with drawings to him, but that's the best I can do."

Dwyane took a sip of coffee before wiping his mouth. He adjusted his scarf and turned to leave when Carl asked, "How did you guys find it anyways?"

"Seismic graph. We were looking for boulders or gas pockets. Any crap that might get in the way of our new trench lines. When the readings came back, hell, we didn't know what it was. Someone suggested it was metal and had the looks of a satellite or something. We called the marshal's office in case they were interested and then started digging."

Carl shook his head. "I can't believe no one saw it when they picked the site for the tower or bunker."

"No one was looking there. It's a massive field. Our Russian friend should count his lucky stars that we were lookin' at that spot at all. He might never have been found otherwise." Dwayne looked to the cosmonaut who had started to eat the protein bar.

The Russian chewed for a moment before grimacing and flipping his tongue in an attempt to get the taste out of his mouth. It looked like he found the bar to be disgusting. A man after Carl's own heart.

"Oh, he's appreciative. I can tell," Carl said as he topped off the cosmonaut's coffee.

Dwayne filled his own cup with a second round, tightened his gloves and went out to instruct his crew about digging for the craft's long buried antenna. Carl watched the foreman leave and wondered how on God's green Earth he was going to explain to this Russian that he needed the Soviet ship's antenna to boost their signal to call for help.

VI.

It actually went surprisingly well. Carl wasn't sure if it was his drawing skills or if the Russian was just really good at puzzle games. Carl was thankful that back in this old timer's day it was the best and brightest that went into space. Not like how it was now, in this new age of space exploration.

The cosmonaut drew a few pictures of his own by sketching a quick doodle of his ship. It showed the antenna as being smack dab in the middle of the vessel. He had labelled everything as well, but it was in Russian. Carl mostly understood the gist all the same.

The cosmonaut warmed up to Old Reliable a bit more with every hour that passed. At first, he flinched every time the worker drone hovered by, but now he seemed intrigued by it. He watched it float around and studied its design. Carl had thought it funny that a twenty-year-old construction bot was keeping this top-of-his-class cosmonaut entertained for such a long period of time.

Three hours went by before Foxford entered the bunker and informed them that the crew had uncovered the antenna. It was right where the cosmonaut's drawing said it would be. The group went outside into the sub-zero temperatures and passed by the row of digging equipment.

Dwayne was leaning against the tires of a backhoe attempting to light a cigarette, shielding the lighter from the harsh winds. The weather was continuing to get worse and now the surrounding hills were invisible, lost behind a wall of white.

The cosmonaut watched Dwayne for a moment before approaching. Upon reaching the foreman, he began to speak in Russian and pointed at the cigarette. Dwayne picked up what he was asking for and handed the comrade one from the pack. The cosmonaut said what Carl assumed to be a thank you, and Dwayne lit the cigarette for him. The Russian inhaled and then immediately went into a coughing fit for a good thirty seconds. He collected his breath and straightened up, nodding at Dwyane before taking another puff.

"Four-hundred-year-old lungs there, bucko. Gotta pace yourself," Dwayne said as he took a drag from his own cigarette and blew the smoke into the air.

The cosmonaut turned and walked to the edge of the hole, smoke in hand. He looked to several members of the construction crew and nodded in approval. The young labourers were still sweating, their coveralls caked in dirt. Carl wasn't sure if the cosmonaut was happy with the progress made on the uncovering of his ship, or if it he was impressed with how relatively intact his vessel had remained after all these years.

Carl looked to Dwayne and said, "Thanks guys. I'll take our weary traveler here and see if he can help me find a terminal to plug this in." As he spoke, he lifted his tablet and terminal cables into the air.

Dwayne nodded and Carl gestured for the Cosmonaut to follow him down into the ship. Together they slid down the hole. Carl maintained a slow pace and helped the Russian as needed. Old Reliable puttered behind them, his hover jets whirling away as he descended the excavation with ease. As Carl neared the bottom of the hole, he could see the finer details of the antenna. A metallic disk that was folded inward against the hull of the ship. It looked to be in nearly pristine condition, no signs of damage from the crash.

Now that more of the vessel had been revealed, Carl could see several deflated orange pontoons sitting underneath the ship. A mix of wires and fabric had wrapped themselves around the hull. No doubt left over from parachutes when the craft had entered the atmosphere and made its hard landing. These Russians knew how to build a spaceship, even with its out-of-date technology, Carl was impressed by the designs and craftsmanship.

The spacecrafts of today's day and age paled in comparison. The most cost-effective materials were used, assembled by the lowest bidder. No heart or soul was put into the vessels. Just steel held together with shoddy parts, always desperately in need of repairs.

The cosmonaut spoke a great deal as the two men entered the ship, most likely due to nerves. Now that the Soviet had been awake for several hours and was not in a state of panic, he could study the inside of his vessel. Carl just nodded whenever the cosmonaut spoke and followed him through the craft.

They headed past the hibernation drums and deeper into the craft before arriving at a sealed door that sat on the right side of the hall. Carl could see that the dark passageway continued onward, long into the distance. Multiple hatches lined the corridor, each labelled in Russian. The cosmonaut punched in a series of codes on the door, but the metal bulkhead refused to budge. He mumbled something at it and then turned and spoke to Carl. As he spoke, he smacked the door and made a cutting motion.

Carl turned to his worker drone and said, "Old Reliable, cut here for me. Level four for steel." As he spoke, he drew lines on the bulkhead with his finger to confirm the area he wanted the robot to cut.

The droid spooled up its laser and after a quick minute, the door was lifted into the air and out of the way. The cosmonaut nodded in thanks and tapped Old Reliable on one of its robotic arms. He spoke to the droid as he did so. Whatever he was saying sounded positive to Carl's ears.

The cosmonaut entered the unsealed room and gestured to be followed. As Carl entered, he saw what looked to be a communications station. Various monitors littered the walls and computer consoles were bolted to the floor. The Soviet looked at the largest of the consoles and then pointed at it repeatedly until Carl approached it. Carl grabbed his tablet and put it on the counter beside the terminal. He then grabbed his cables and searched for a jack in the computer to insert them.

After a moment, he realized just how foolish this notion was. He of course would have to strip the cables and attach them to the central motherboard of the console itself. No way a modern-day cable jack would fit into a socket from that era.

The cosmonaut was already two steps ahead and was getting to work taking off the protective panel near the foot of the terminal. Carl was impressed by just how on the ball this cosmonaut was. Not bad for a guy that had just spent nearly four hundred years frozen in slush.

VII.

"All hooked up," Dwayne said, as he leaned against the door of the communications room. He lit a cigarette and offered one to the cosmonaut, who took it with grace, sounding appreciative as he accepted it.

Dwyane again helped him light it and looked to Carl as he did so. "You give us the signal and we'll give this ship a boost like it's never seen," Dwyane said.

Carl studied the stripped leads that led into the motherboard of the computer and replied, "And you connected everything to the power outputs at the base of the com tower, right?"

"Ya ya, I got our electrician to do it. He installed the thing so I trust he knows its workings."

"Right. Well I'm ready whenever you are."

"How about you comrade? You ready?" Dwayne looked to the Russian and gave a thumbs up as he addressed him.

The cosmonaut exhaled a puff of smoke and despite his confused face, he raised his hand, giving a thumbs up in return.

Dwayne smiled and chuckled to himself. "I like this guy. A space cowboy after my own heart."

Carl smiled but was too focused on the ship's communications dish to laugh. He needed the craft to receive enough power for the antenna to be able to align properly. Then, God willing, it would be able to send and receive data. This was assuming that these terminals hadn't suffered from some unseen damage caused by the crash, or perhaps even before, when this Russian had been touring the stars.

Dwyane exited the room and Carl could hear him yell out to the team stationed up top. A small amount of time passed before various lights flashed around the telecommunications room. The cosmonaut cheered and patted Carl on the back. He then took the smoke from the corner of his mouth and gestured for Old Reliable to follow him, speaking a string of sentences as he did so.

The worker drone turned to look at the two men for a moment before saying, "Carl. I still do not understand his peculiar dialect."

"I know, just follow him. Help him with anything he needs," Carl responded with fingers crossed as he watched the monitors begin their boot-up sequence.

"That might be difficult, considering I don't—"

"You're going to have to figure it out," Carl said, interrupting the old droid.

The robot beeped and left the room. Carl sighed and ran a hand through his hair. He felt guilty for talking to his metallic companion the way he had. The drone could only follow its coding, something he tended to forget. He dismissed the thought and turned his attention back to his tablet.

The device was now flashing with hundreds of lines of code. Carl punched a few commands onto the screen and watched as the raw code was filtered through a series of programs to make the wealth of data more streamlined. The dish was receiving, loud and clear. It picked up all sorts of readings: the com tower, the weather satellite over head, the radio signals from the atmospheric processor.

Carl tweaked the settings of the antenna with the tablet. He changed the parameters so that the ship could begin broadcasting on public colony channels in this sector. Carl flicked over to London-Constantinople's unsecure emergency frequency. He remembered it with ease. After all, he had helped build their entire telecom network.

Carl ensured the antenna was aligned once again before typing a message. He looked at the screen and read it to ensure he was clear and concise: THIS IS CARL DOYLE, LNJ TELECOMMUNICATIONS TECHNICIAN AT THE COLONY OF TOKYO-MIAMI. I NEED ACCESS TO A CODED FREQUENCY SO I CAN RELAY INFORMATION TO YOU. INFORMATION IS CLASSIFIED. I WILL BE LISTENING TO UN-CODED FREQUENCY 1299.8, WAITING FOR YOUR REPLY. AGAIN, THIS INFORMATION IS CONFIDENTIAL AND I MUST COMMUNICATE ON A SECURE CHANNEL. PLEASE HURRY.

Carl looked to the blinking grey cursor that sat at the end of his paragraph. He read his message once more before pressing the "Enter" key on his tablet. He knew the message would take several minutes to reach its destination and even then, someone would have to be physically at the workstation to read it. This same person would then run Carl's name to ensure the message wasn't a trick or scam of some sort. Upon finding him on the roster, they would send a reply. This would in turn take additional time to be received by the ancient Russian dish.

Carl heard the sound of steel hitting the floor and got up from his post. He popped his head into the hallway and noticed that the door at the head of the ship had been cut open. Its steel bulkhead lay to the side—no doubt Old Reliable's handy work. The cosmonaut was already inside working vigorously on some task.

Carl could tell that the room must be the ship's bridge or a control room of sorts. Windows sat to the front of the flight deck, but with the blast shields down only a view of grey steel could be seen. A single chair was bolted to the floor in front of multiple control panels.

The cosmonaut moved like he was on cloud nine. He walked around the bridge, pressing buttons and watching the lights that flashed around the cockpit. He sat in his command chair and pressed a series of commands. A view screen activated and a sequence of Russian letters and numbers filled it. The cosmonaut scrolled through the data and added more strings of text to the screen.

The notion of going over to check on what the Soviet was doing had crossed Carl's mind, but he decided against it. It's not like he could carry on a conversation even if the Russian tried to explain the process to him.

Eighteen minutes later the communications terminal came to life. A disembodied voice echoed through the radio's speakers, filling the small room. The voice sounded like it belonged to an older gentleman, perhaps the manager on duty for the station.

"This is colony London-Constantinople replying to the written message left by Carl Doyle. Please respond."

The sudden voice had startled Carl and made him nearly spill the coffee that Marshall Wyatt and Foxford had brought down for them while they waited.

Carl folded up the various manuals and logbooks and moved over to the radio. He had been attempting to figure out the ship's archaic systems despite everything being in a language he couldn't understand. The pictures weren't of much help either and offered little assistance.

Carl was surprised by the radio call. Not only did his message get through, but they were replying in record time. Carl grabbed the pair of headphones he had found in a near by drawer and plugged them in.

He leaned forward to the microphone he had set up and said, "Yes, hello. Hello, London-Constantinople, I read you."

There was an agonizing delay between when he spoke and when the duty manager replied to him. While he waited, Carl could hear his voice echo off into the distance, hurling far off into the solar system beyond.

"Good morning. What can we do for you on this hot and scorching day?" The voice on the other end sounded chipper.

"I need you to either encrypt this channel or tell me which channel to switch over to. I have confidential information. I can give a company clearance code if you need it, and am fully aware of the repercussions of misuse of company recourses. This is a serious request."

A longer delay this time, then the eager voice came back. "Frequency has been encrypted. Is everyone okay? What's going on over there?"

Carl took a deep breath knowing just how stupid this question would sound. He cleared his throat and said, "Do you have anyone over there that speaks Russian?"

As he waited for a response, lights slowly began to flicker in the hallway outside. Keys and buttons illuminated along the walls with lines of code filling various monitors. There was the clicking of computers warming up, fan belts swirling, blowing air through the ship. The cosmonaut was rebooting his dormant vessel.

The voice in Carl's headset spoke again. It was obvious the duty manager was trying to suppress laughter. "Ya, right. Might as well ask me if I got a guy that speaks Latin around here too."

Carl rolled his eyes but was relieved none-the-less. This answer was tame compared to what he would have answered with if he had been on the receiving end of the wire and asked such a ridiculous question.

Carl cleared his throat and said as calmly as he could, "I am aware of just how crazy this sounds, but I need your help with something."

Carl went on to give his employee number and then told

the duty manager of London-Constantinople about the crashed ship, the frozen cosmonaut encased in the green slush, and the enormous language barrier that existed between them. He tried to be direct but also gave the next colony over enough information to avoid any undo questions.

The delay after he told his tale was excruciating. It was so long in fact, that Carl assumed they hung up and considered this to be the wildest, but well thought-up story they'd ever heard.

Eventually the silence came to an end and the voice said, "All right. I could spend the rest of the day doubting you and picking apart your story. But with these time delays? That would be an annoying process, and a huge waste of time. My time. Your time. Everybody's time. I hope this isn't some sort of joke or you'll make us both look like asses."

"How's everything going in there?" Dwayne called from the entrance to the ship, causing Carl to jump in his seat.

"Great, really good," Carl tried not to sound short, but he was focused on talking with the other colony; unnecessary delays like this one were cutting into his progress.

"Just making sure we haven't overloaded anything. Our friend from the motherland here has been turning everything on. He might cause a burn out."

"Nope, it's all okay in here," Carl said. He had always struggled with multitasking and having two conversations at once.

He waited a moment to ensure Dwayne wouldn't say anything else and thumbed the communications key. He was about to speak when the voice spoke through his head set once more.

"One more thing. We have an old guy on staff who speaks pretty good Mandarin supposedly. Does that help?"

Carl wanted to snap and reply with a rude remark but contained himself. The technicians at the other colony were no doubt just as stressed as he was. They were just shot-gunning ideas to try and work the situation.

Carl thumbed the speak button once more. "We have no access to The Galactic Network out here. Our satellite wasn't built for it and as you know, our assigned ship, the C.D.V. Ulysses, took off a few months ago. She was our primary source of communications. I need you guys to go digging in The Network to see if you can find an Old Russian translation software for me. The old Network was probably lousy with applications like that so it shouldn't be impossible to find one. The only problem is getting it to translate to Western Standard."

"Ya we were thinking the same thing. I'm sure we'll find it. You know what they say, once it goes on The Network, it's there forever. Don't worry Doyle, me and the fellas are on this."

Carl replied, thanking the voice and wishing them good luck. He knew it would take them hours, possibly days to complete the task he had asked of them.

He thumbed the communicator again. "I know this will take awhile. We should notify the Colonial Expansion Initiative of our findings."

"Oh, don't worry buddy. I sent off some info to headquarters and they said they got the memo. They are very intrigued in this case. Who wouldn't be right? They even got their techs looking into a translation software for you as well."

VIII.

The construction crew had gone home for the evening by the time London-Constantinople reported back. The cosmonaut had managed to get his ship back online for the most part, with Old Reliable having done most of the heavy lifting. The worker drone was doing a great job at following orders in a language he didn't understand. Carl had checked up on the two of them several times and was impressed with their progress. *Clever little bot,* Carl had thought numerous times throughout the day.

During the hours spent waiting to receive the call back, Carl had wandered over to the bridge on multiple occasions. The last time he had ventured over to the cockpit he had found that a large amount of the floor panels had been removed or outright cut open. Wires were spliced together, cables had been removed, and burned-out fuses littered the floor. This cosmonaut was something of an electrician himself. Old Reliable just hummed quietly to himself until the Soviet would point at something and then make a cutting motion usually followed by some Russian. The two were quickly becoming best friends.

Shortly before the construction crew had left the site, a few of them wished to shake the Russian's hand once more. Despite the cosmonaut not understanding them he still smiled and replied in a positive-sounding tone. Even with the language barrier, this ancient man had quite the personality. Carl was impressed with how well he was adapting to everything. The cold, the language, the crashed ship. He was able to take to any situation thrown at him. The Soviets had chosen their cosmonauts well.

"Carl, you still there?" the voice rang out in Carl's headphones.

He had been dozing off. "Yup, still here. Any luck?"

"Lots of luck, bud. We found a few Russian translator apps in the archives, a lot of missing data, though. The C.E.I. techs spliced two or three of them together. We aren't experts on the language by any means, but it looks to me like its eighty to ninety percent accurate. When we fed it a few test paragraphs it came out okay. Getting it to translate to Western Standard didn't take that much time, actually."

Carl's face glowed with excitement. He would finally be

able to talk with the last cosmonaut in the universe. But there was still much work to be done. He was well aware of the problems that arose with having to use London-Constantinople as a middleman through the translation process. The time delay between transmissions would take a great amount of time. Making carrying on a conversation much more difficult than it otherwise should be.

While the techs at London-Constantinople had been busy finding a solution to the language barrier issue, Carl had come up with a plan of his own. He would request for the colony to send the translation software data in a packet directly to the Russian ship. Old Reliable would be plugged directly into the vessel and when the information was broadcast, he would then download the data packet.

It would take a while to send an entire language worth of data, complete with its Western Standard meanings from one colony to another. But in the end, that would be faster and less infuriating than the alternative.

Carl thumbed the radio key and proposed his strategy to the colony. The voice on the other end sounded receptive to the idea and said that they would get to work on transmitting the data to their satellite network immediately. Carl answered that he would advise them when Old Reliable was plugged into the ship and ready to go.

Carl left the communications room and headed down the hall. He stepped into the bridge and immediately noticed Old Reliable was folded up in the corner. The old worker bot had gone into rest mode to save power. His ion cells weren't what they used to be, and the day's activities had been taxing for the little hover droid.

The cosmonaut lay on his back under a series of floor panels, a wrench placed firmly in his mouth. He let out several grunts and harsh sounding words as he fought with a set of bolts that held a fuse box closed above him. The Russian had been busy collecting all sorts of tools from around the ship. A container of frayed wire ends, copper casings and new fuses sat next to Old Reliable's sleeping body.

The cosmonaut noticed that Carl was standing over him and ceased fumbling with the fuse box. He reached into his pocket and offered up a cigarette through the open panel. Dwayne had finally surrendered and given the old timer the whole pack. Carl shook his head *no*, the Russian shrugged. He took the wrench from his mouth and replaced it with a fresh cigarette but didn't light it. Instead it just sat there, bobbing around his mouth while he wrestled with the bolts.

Carl walked over to Old Reliable and activated him. The robot booted up after a moment. It opened its blue "eyes" and looked around.

Carl patted the drone on its metallic body and said, "Old Reliable. I need to hook you up to the ship. Any idea which one of these consoles should do the trick?"

The worker drone scanned the room and activated its hover drive. He puttered over to the computer in front of the command chair, the same one the cosmonaut had spent most of the day in.

The droid extended a claw as it said, "This is where the man with the strange dialect likes to type instructions."

Carl nodded in thanks. The cosmonaut sat up, watching the two of them converse. He cocked his head, wondering what they were attempting to do. Carl noticed this and gestured to Old Reliable. He then held up two cables and pretended to plug them into the ships main console. The Russian nodded in agreement and quickly lit his smoke.

"Da," he said quietly to himself.

Carl was starting to assume that this word meant yes. The cosmonaut continued to speak but Carl only understood the one word. The Russian stood up and hurried over to his box of odds and ends. He grabbed two cables and stripped the ends down to the bare copper. Carl watched for a moment before he unscrewed the coverings on Old Reliable's circuit board. He placed the metallic cover against the wall and looked at the motherboard inside.

Carl looked at the cosmonaut and saw that he had attached the copper ends into the command console's data board. The Russian looked over and gave a thumbs up to Carl, smoke still hanging from his mouth. Carl grabbed the other ends of the cables and inserted them into Old Reliable's circuits.

"Okay. Once you see that the new data packet is received by the ship, you download it," Carl said as he tapped the drone on the shoulder.

"Yes, Carl. I am most certainly plugged in. The ship's computer is currently informing me in binary of how much damage it has received."

"Ignore that for now. Just focus on intercepting the information." Carl paused. He felt like he was being too curt with the droid. Despite being a collection of steel and circuits, it was preforming wonderfully under the circumstances. Carl knew he would be completely lost if it wasn't for his robotic companion. "You're doing a great job, Old Reliable. Thank you."

"You're most welcome, Carl. Thank you for giving me such a positive rating. I have learned from the best."

The worker droid beeped and Carl could tell it was scanning the incoming broadcasts with keen interest. Carl ran back to his communications console and thumbed the mic.

"London-Constantinople, how's it going over there?"

"We were about to call you and ask the same thing," the voice laughed after the familiar pause of the communications delay. The manager then continued, "Packet is up and into our satellites. Waiting to broadcast it to your location."

"Roger. Send it off, we're ready here."

IX.

It took nearly three hours for Old Reliable to receive the entirety of the information and download it. The cosmonaut hadn't slept one bit in that time—four hundred years of sleep will do that to a person. The Russian had kept himself busy by continuing to repair his ship and running calibrations to assess the damage. He was probably trying to keep his mind off the many questions he undoubtably had. Both Carl and the Russian had hundreds of them, but no way to receive answers. Not yet anyway.

Carl sat next to Old Reliable and watched as the last of the progress bar on the back of the drone's head went from *99%* to the full *100%*. The last twenty percent had seemed to take the longest. For some reason, the progress bar had gotten stuck at *82%* for some time. He prayed that the information upload hadn't fried the little droid's brain.

It seems his prayers were answered when the number continued to count up a little while later. With the packet having finally been downloaded into the bot's memory, Carl asked, "Well, how does it look?"

Old Reliable beeped cheerfully and activated his hover jets. He turned to face Carl and answered. Carl straightened his back and stiffened his neck in surprise. When the robot spoke, it was in Russian.

Carl ground his teeth. A whirlwind of fear and anxieties overcame him. Had the software overridden Old Reliable's language settings and deleted the Western Standard? His pulse elevated and he felt noticeably lightheaded. If that was the case, not only would he have a cosmonaut he couldn't understand, but also a worker drone as well. The Soviet and the droid would of course be able to communicate perfectly, but that didn't help Carl in the slightest.

Upon hearing the robot speak in his mother tongue, the Russian sprang up and cheered. He began speaking to Old

Reliable and hugged the drone. Carl had never seen a man so happy. The droid answered the cosmonaut's pleasantries and gestured with his claws at the central console. The Soviet nodded and relied back, the two of them were having a grand old time.

"Old Reliable. Override code One. One. Seven. Nine," Carl said, the fear was plain in his voice.

The worker drone stopped speaking and hovered silently for a moment. The Russian glanced at Carl, a look of concern filling his face. Carl held up his hand to signal, "one moment," and continued to watch the droid. The cosmonaut licked his lips and lit a fresh cigarette. He took a step back and sat in his command chair. No doubt he was eager to begin asking the droid copious amounts of questions.

Old Reliable beeped several times, the hard reboot code for the worker drone seemed to work. Luckily, the new software download hadn't removed its understanding of Western Standard, so the override codes still worked.

"System rebooted. Good evening, Carl," Old Reliable said in his normal monotone.

"Skip introduction," Carl said, secretly thanking a higher power that the droid was speaking normally again. The drone beeped and hummed, acknowledging the request. Carl patted the metallic body of the drone and then continued, "Old Reliable. Are you able to translate for me?"

The droid computed the request and replied, "I believe so, Carl."

"Excellent," Carl replied. He paused, his mind spinning with what he should ask as his first question. He had thought about this moment the entire day, but now that he was here and ready with a translator, he couldn't think of what to say. Which question was the most pressing? Which answer did he need the most?

He cleared his throat and said simply, "My friend. I am Carl Doyle. What is your name?" Old Reliable translated what was said immediately into Russian as he looked at the Soviet.

As the worker drone finished speaking, Carl held out his hand. The Cosmonaut listened to Old Reliable with a gleeful smile on his face. He stood up with a youthful energy and shook Carl's hand. The Soviet began to speak and Old Reliable translated again, this time turning the Russian words into Western Standard.

"Carl, I'm glad to finally know your name and am honoured to call you a friend as well. I am Fyodor Petrov, Cosmonaut and citizen of the Soviet Union. Pleased to make your acquaintance. You are a cosmonaut too, yes?"

Fyodor released Carl's hand, patted him on the shoulder and sat back down in the chair.

"Well, technically yes," Carl stammered. "But my official title is telecommunications technician."

Fyodor nodded as Old Reliable finished speaking. A look of seriousness filled his face as he said, "May I ask what year it is?"

"Well that's hard to answer. Years on this planet are measured a tad differently, but for Earth it's the year Two Thousand Three Hundred and Eighty-Nine. New Years was just a few weeks ago, actually."

The Russian swore, but Old Reliable didn't translate it. Either because this word was missing from its software and wouldn't translate properly, or the settings told him to omit curse words. Fyodor sighed and took a long drag from his cigarette. He savoured the taste before exhaling and admiring the smoke.

"That's a long time." He looked at the blast shields that hung outside of the cockpit's windows for a moment before continuing. "I guess that makes me a hell of a lot older than you," he chuckled.

Carl laughed as well. "That's one way to put it."

The cosmonaut grabbed the cup of coffee from the top of

a nearby monitor. It was his eighth portion of the day and had gone cold long ago. He took a sip and said, "So, we aren't on Earth. I figured as much. Where are we?"

"A colony on the outer rim: Tokyo-Miami. It's in the Scion Nebula.

"I don't know that system. Are we still in our home— Earth's galaxy?" His eyes were overcome with a mix of wonder and fear.

"It's on the far side of the Milky Way. Completely different spiral arm actually," Carl said as he exhaled. He thought of the sheer size of the black expanse between them and earth. "We are far, *far* away from our home."

"How did I end up on the far side?" Fyodor asked, as he ran a hand through his hair. A look of shock crept across his pale face.

"I've been racking my brain trying to answer that myself. Your ship's engines clearly aren't hyper capable. A worm hole maybe? or some other cosmic event that we haven't discovered. It's anyone's guess really. Maybe your ship's flight recorder would tell us more?"

"I doubt that." Fyodor answered as he leaned forward in his chair and adjusted the cigarette in his mouth. "I had to turn it off before the long sleep."

"Well, regardless of how it happened, you were lucky that we found you."

"Beyond lucky, I would say, all things considered," Fyodor answered as he sipped his coffee. His tone was distant and his face was blank as he stared at the steel walls of the control room. He was clearly trying to digest the wealth of information that had just been sprung on him. After a moment he blinked and swallowed hard as he asked, "Tell me, what remains of the Motherland? Is she okay?"

Carl sighed. How could he put this delicately? "Russia as you knew it? Well, it's different now. Moscow and St. Petersburg still exist but the people there aren't traditionally from Russia."

"What happened? Did we fight a war with America? Did they win? We didn't use the bombs, did we?"

"No, no bombs, thank God," Carl said. "As far as I know, Russia and America never fought—well, apart from a few pissing matches here and there. But after a couple of global depressions, a set of border wars, and other cultures having more children than the traditional Russian families were having . . . Well, a couple hundred years of that sort of thing and what was traditional Russia ceased to exist. It's a collection of micro-countries, or single state areas now."

Fyodor looked down at his boots. He looked depressed and despondent with the news.

Carl quickly added, "Same thing happened to America, more or less. The Washington Free States are a thing, but they don't carry any real weight in global affairs."

The comment did nothing to cure Fyodor's obvious sadness. The cosmonaut took a long time to answer and when he finally did, his voice was distant, "I guess that's just the way the world goes. When I put myself to sleep, I knew the chances of ever waking up again were small. Incalculably small, in fact, less than a fraction of a percent. I knew if I ever did wake up, the Earth would be different. I knew this, but it doesn't make it any easier. Does anyone speak Russian anymore?"

"Maybe in Siberia or remote towns, but it's not a major language."

There was a long pause in the conversation as Fyodor took several drags from his cigarette, mulling over the news he had just received. Carl felt tremendous sympathy for the man. While these events had been ancient history for every other living being in the universe, this was all new to him. An old man who had just been informed that his home was gone—

and had been for many generations—was not an easy thing to hear.

Fyodor sighed and nodded, trying to force a smile and change the conversation, "You don't speak what I would know as English. Did the same thing happen to that language?"

"Pretty much. The four big European and Latin American languages amalgamated into one. It just kind of happened over the course of time. It wasn't planned. It just did, I guess. Asia did the same thing. They have three main dialects now. Eastern, Western, and Central Asian Standard." Carl paused, he realized he was digressing. While he liked filling Fyodor in on nearly four hundred years of human history, he had questions of his own, questions that were burning a hole in his mind and needed to be answered.

"What year did you take off?" he asked, his tone full of intrigue, and sounded more aggressive than he wanted.

The cosmonaut finished his cigarette and crushed the butt into the bottom of an empty cup that served as a makeshift ashtray. He fished out a fresh one from the package and lit it as he spoke. He sighed once more and said, "Nineteen Eighty-Three."

"What was your mission?" Carl was failing to keep his curiosity under control, no doubt Fyodor would become annoyed with this onslaught of questions.

To Carl's surprise, the Russian laughed for a moment before saying, "I was expecting that one. Normally, I would have said it's confidential. But considering the same people that assigned me to this journey are long dead and the government to which I swore allegiance a distant memory, I guess it doesn't matter." He took a sip of coffee and continued, "Mars. That's where I was headed. That was our mission."

"You just said 'our' mission, but you are alone, right? Did we miss one of your crew members and leave them in a tank?" Carl asked as he looked to the entrance of the flight deck.

His eyes wandered down the hallway and over to the row of life pods that lay quietly on their risers. The cosmonaut took another drag from his smoke, his eyebrows lifted as Old Reliable translated what Carl had said.

"No, its just me. No need for alarm," Fyodor replied and held out a hand to calm Carl down who had begun to stand. "I am the second ship of our operation. Stage one, the first ship, consisted of a crew of nine. They launched three months before me, Christmas Day of Nineteen Eighty-Two and off they went to Mars." Fyodor paused again, remembering each of their faces, his fellow teammates.

He must've realized that they were all dead from the passing of time. His expression dropped once more. The Soviet sighed before speaking again.

"They had the brunt of the work. Their assignment was to land, set up a base, collect samples, preform expeditions, things like that.

"Stage two—me, was to land three months after they had arrived. This went against what the original plan had been when we were recruited for the mission. Originally, all of us were meant to depart on the same day, in one *N2* class rocket. However, it was decided mid-way through construction of our vessel, the '*Laika*,' that the original plan would not be possible.

"Many issues arose regarding just one craft being used. Namely, weight and room for resources. Between all the oxygen we would need to bring for the journey, recycler units, rations, expedition equipment and then finally the sleep capsules and their required life support items, well the ship would weigh too much.

"The science team came back with two alternatives: either they go back to the drawing board and come up with an entirely new ship with a brand-new engine, or, they send two ships. The first being the *Laika*, or '*Laika One*' as we called it. And the second being '*Laika Two*.' I'll give you three guesses which option they chose." Fyodor laughed and patted the hull of the ship delicately. "Yes beautiful little pup they created here, and on such short notice. Held together pretty well, too. Even after the accident."

"What happened, what accident? Why didn't you make it?" Carl asked. He was in shock.

Even just the idea that the Soviet Union had tried for Mars, way back then, so many years before anyone else ever had struck up the nerve to do so, was fascinating.

"The accident," Fyodor repeated, "Happened when I was about halfway to the red planet. I was slightly off course and adjusted my heading with the thrusters. One of the coordinated engines on the old girl misfired and blew me off into nowhere. I tried to correct it but just made everything even worse. I had lost navigational control and the rear engines no longer responded. I was lucky I had only been using the thrusters and not the full engine's power. A blow out like that would have eviscerated me.

"A quick assessment of the damage and I knew I was going to overshoot Mars by quite a bit with no way to correct this problem. In fact, I was on a completely different heading, not a chance I was making it to the red planet. I knew this. My antenna still worked though, so I was able to advise command of the situation. They weren't much help," Fyodor paused. He shook his head as he relived the memories.

"They told me to go back to sleep in the pods," he continued. "Those orders broke my heart, but what could they do? Hundreds of thousands of miles away and I'm in a crippled ship. I knew I was done for, dead in the water, so to speak. I wasn't letting that take me out, not without a fight at least. I figured I might as well balance the odds in my favour even if it was just slightly.

"I drained the other tanks of their nutrients and plugged them all into mine. I then attached the ship's oxygen supplies and recyclers to feed directly into my pod. After all, I was carrying enough for a whole colony of ten to survive for a few years—" Fyodor stopped. "I should elaborate." He thought for a moment, trying to put years worth of planning into a few sentences was no easy task.

"Ideally, once stage one of the operation had been completed and I had arrived, all of us would sleep in the life tanks for a year. When that time had passed, we would then wake up and check with Moscow on how progress on the new *N3* rocket was coming. This was the rocket that would serve as our relief. Either it would bring the first wave of colonists, or it would be our ship to return home. Like I said, that was the plan anyway. They had given us more supplies than they expected us to use. You know in case the *N3* was not ready on time.

"Anyway, I attached all the oxygen reserves and the other pod's nutrients into my tank. I knew that when a person was asleep inside it, the machine slowed down all your vitals considerably. I would need much less oxygen and supplements than normal to stay alive. The science team had said they built these pods to last. I guess they were right." He patted the side of the ship once more.

"I turned off all the ship's systems—well, except for the ones keeping my tank active. I needed to conserve all the power I could. The only other thing I left active was the emergency landing equipment. It must have worked," Fyodor smiled for a moment and continued to speak. "A combination of parachutes, reserve chutes, steel wind breakers and pontoons to absorb the blow. They tested these systems a great deal in Siberia, very fitting in a twisted way I suppose. The engineers said the landing equipment should work, even with no reverse thrusters. I think the science team knew about the *N2*'s history of engine problems and designed the emergency landing gear to work no matter what.

"Sorry, I realize I'm babbling but, one thing I noticed when you woke me up. My tank's life-support gel had turned green. It was blue when I filled it. I must have been running out of supplies. Good thing you found me when you did."

Carl looked at Old Reliable for a long time. It was a lot to process all at once, both for Carl and the aging robot. The cosmonaut noticed the delay in questions and quickly asked, "Did the rest of my team get the colony started?"

Carl bit the side of his cheek. The precursor to the Colonial Expansion Initiative had explored Mars thoroughly nearly two centuries ago. No sign of any colonies or research equipment when the first ships landed. When the Soviet Union collapsed in 1999, there had been no records of any such mission. The project must have been so heavily botched that the communists destroyed all documents eluding to it out of sheer embarrassment.

Carl thought of a hundred ways the cosmonaut team could have failed. Crash-landed on the surface, with the Martian weather taking care of the debris. Broke up upon entry, caused by more $N2$ engine trouble. Shooting off course just like their comrade in *Laika Two* had.

He swallowed and said, "They set up their equipment and got everything started. They completed their mission."

Fyodor lit up upon hearing the news. It pained Carl to lie but he didn't want this cosmonaut to think of his teammates as failures, his memories of them tarnished. Carl wanted more than anything to give this Russian a small sliver of happiness in the bleak world he had woken up to.

"So, we got to Mars before the Americans," Fyodor said. "First satellite in orbit. First man in space. First woman in space. First space walk, and now the first ones to Mars. The Americans may have gotten to the moon, but we got the real prize." He stopped speaking for a moment, remembering one face in particular. "I knew Kotov would get them there. You would have liked her. Heart of a lion that one. She was the best cosmonaut we had. Top of her class. Leadership ability, problem solving skills, and always calm, never stressed. If I had a drink in my hand, I would put forward a toast to Masha Kotov and to the other eight of my brothers and sisters. Absolutely fearless, the entire lot of them. Gagarin, Leonov, Tereshkova, they would have been so proud of Kotov and her crew. I just wish I could have been there to see them again."

"Fyodor. Why did they send you alone, why not with another crew member?" Carl asked. He wanted to change the subject, and this question was eating away at him.

"They thought sending me alone would be fine. Once I got to Mars, I would then be in the company of the other nine cosmonauts. They kept saying Gagarin went alone, so why not I? Our moon landers had been designed for one person. Moscow thought it would all work out. I was expected to be asleep in the pod most of the journey, and Moscow could control the wake-up time remotely if need be. There was resistance from much of the science team regarding sending me alone, but the higher ups eventually decided that it was the best option.

"The other nine cosmonauts all served an important function on building the research base. To now train an eleventh cosmonaut for the mission to go with me would take time, and more importantly, take up more resources. This would add more weight to the already heavy rocket. Besides, who was I to argue? I'm just a pilot and they said I would be a hero of the Soviet Union upon my landing."

"Why Mars? That's such an ambitious project for your government to undertake," Carl said as he looked around the aging vessel.

"Early prototypes of the *N2* rocket were already being tested when the Americans started building their permanent moon research base in February of Nineteen-Eighty. Moscow had a conniption about that. They ordered the production of the *N2* rocket to be moved ahead by a great margin. Years ahead of the planned schedule. All the focus of sending a manned mission to the moon was switched to Mars. If we couldn't build the first base on the moon, then we would be the first to build one on Mars. The space race had entered a new phase.

"I remember, mere days before *Laika One* was set to launch, there was talk about cancelling the program entirely. Funding was grinding to a halt and a military coup from some of the Baltic States was on the horizon. Our head of operations, Vasily Kornilov, decided to go ahead and clear the rocket for launch anyway. He said to the chiefs, 'the ships are already built, everything is already paid for. My cosmonauts are ready. Ready to be heroes. Ready to do their duty.' He kept repeating his hope, 'These missions will reunite the country. A country in danger of collapse.' It was a great speech."

Carl wanted to avoid bringing up Fyodor's old comrades once again and so he redirected the conversation. "Listen, Fyodor. Let's go to my apartment, get you some decent food and out of the cold. No use sticking around this old ship. We can talk more there. No doubt you must be starving."

Fyodor nodded and finished his smoke. "And the robot?"

"Oh, he'll come with us. He can translate at will now. He doesn't need to be connected to the vessel anymore."

Carl finished speaking and stood up from the console he was leaning against. He unplugged Old Reliable and secured the protective metal cover on his companion. Carl then walked down the hall and entered the communications room.

He thumbed the microphone. "Good news. The translation software was downloaded by my bot, it works great. I'm going to get our friend a meal and I'll be back tomorrow at about six-thirty A.M. local time, in case your superiors have any questions for me then."

Carl waited for the response. The voice that answered after the delay was different from the one before. They must have sent the first duty manager home; it had been a long day for him.

This new person sounded much younger and more tired.

"Rodger that. We'll still be here on the midnight shift awaiting your call. Good luck. Oh ya, the C.E.I. headquarters advised us that they are sending a military destroyer-class vessel to pick the Russian up. They said it's departing from Navtica Station and should arrive on your location in about eight days. Keep him safe for us until then. Goodnight fellas. London-Constantinople clear."

Carl took off the headphones. The Expansion Initiative must not have trusted regular civilians to transport the cosmonaut around. They weren't taking any chances on this one. No doubt they would want to talk with Fyodor in great detail upon meeting him. And they should, he had quite the story to tell.

X.

The next seven days flew by. Carl tried to feed the cosmonaut as much as possible in an attempt to return some of his lost body mass. The first day was the worst for Fyodor though, just as the cosmonaut had predicted the night before. He had woken up the next morning with what could only be described simply as the worst hangover imaginable. This side effect was something the science teams had warned him would happen if he were to stay in the life pod for too long.

Fyodor was displaying all the *fun* symptoms you wouldn't wish upon your worst enemy. He couldn't keep anything down and was so lightheaded he couldn't stand. Fyodor had mentioned that this should have happened sooner, but the adrenaline and hard work had kept it at bay, at least temporarily.

Carl had wanted to stay home for the day and ensure the Russian was able to take care of himself, but the cosmonaut had insisted he go.

Fyodor had said, "I lasted four hundred years on my own. I think I can manage twelve hours."

When Carl headed to work, he left Old Reliable in the apartment so that Fyodor had someone to talk to and to help him complete basic tasks. Carl had joked that there wouldn't be any need for Fyodor to use the cutting laser on anything today. The Soviet laughed and said he would still try to find some application for it.

The second day was the same as the first but by then the old timer could keep down liquids. Word had spread across the colony by this point and Carl was getting calls and messages for people wanting to come out and see the cosmonaut, the living wonder of the world. Carl continuously warned them that the man was too sick for visitors, and they should come by when he was feeling up to it.

Day three was different. When Carl awoke to the sound of his alarm clock at 4:30 in the morning, he found Fyodor in the living room, completing a set of push ups. Not many of course, but still a few. He also switched to a plank and held it for a time that was impressive, considering his lack of muscle mass.

Fyodor asked if he could join Carl at work as the two finished sipping their coffees. Carl was opposed to the idea at first but Fyodor insisted. He wanted to keep busy and contribute. He also personally wanted to thank all the people that had found him. That had saved him. Carl saw no harm in this and relented.

That day on the construction site no actual work was completed, everyone was to enthralled with Fyodor. The cosmonaut shook everyone's hand. Signed countless autographs and posed for no less than a thousand pictures. Some with the construction crews, some with Old Reliable, some in front of the ship, some in his command chair. Carl would have been annoyed if it had been him in that position, but Fyodor? He smiled the entire time. In fact, it was his idea to put on one of his flight suits and pose for a few extra photos. He was enjoying his new celebrity life. People drove from all across the colony, construction crews, plumbers, demolition teams, processor engineers, everyone wanted to meet the hero, Fyodor Petrov.

During the next four days Fyodor helped Carl and the construction crews complete various tasks around the site. He wanted to learn and was keen to lend a hand in the colony's construction. Fyodor kept saying he was, "helping to build the future."

The cosmonaut assisted with the unrolling of cables, cleaning equipment, picking up scrap, and shovelling snow. He just continued to work, only asking to be paid in coffee and cigarettes. He was the cheapest labourer the universe had ever seen. If he kept this up, he would be I.N.J.'s favourite employee and he wasn't even on their pay roll.

By the seventh day, the construction crew had completely uncovered the rest of *Laika Two*. The Russian pointed out several design details about the ship and asked questions of his own concerning modern-day starship assembly. Carl and his peers had no answer for the majority of the questions put forward. Like most technology, the inner workings of which were a complete mystery to the average citizen.

Fyodor's Western Standard had also improved greatly. He was able to utter a few basic phrases and a string of common words. Old Reliable was finally able to get some relief from having to be a translator. The droid never complained though, he just beeped happily whenever he was asked to assist.

Halfway through the seventh day, the destroyer contacted the colony by way of *Laika Two's* antenna and stated they were less than a day away. They wanted to know where to make landfall. Carl was the one to speak to the ship's communications officer. He notified the lieutenant that the cosmonaut could be found at the crashed vessel, next to the unfinished tower.

The eighth day came, and Fyodor knew he had to leave. Carl had given him items for the voyage home, mostly clothing he didn't mind parting with, but nothing too ratty. He wanted Fyodor to look presentable when the military arrived. Earlier in the week, the cosmonaut had retrieved a bag of his own clothing from his vessel and had insisted on wearing these ancient items when he met the landing party. Fyodor didn't want to trouble anyone with constantly borrowing other people's belongings. Carl assured him that it was not an inconvenience in the slightest and insisted Fyodor keep his twentieth century clothing tucked away safely. The fashion of yesteryear did not exist in any capacity, and these fabrics would fetch a pretty penny to a museum eagerly awaiting to complete their collections.

The dropships from the destroyer flew over the hills at 9:37 A.M. Three of them in total. Their sleek designs were more impressive than any ship Carl had ridden in. Fyodor was in the middle of the field helping unspool cables. He studied the ships as they ripped overhead, seemingly in awe of how they handled, and the glow of their ion engines. The pilot in him could hardly wait to fly one for himself.

The Russian finished unwinding the spool and ran over to Carl. Old Reliable beeped and puttered close behind. The dropships hovered overhead for a moment before one descended, landing on the snow-covered roadway. Fyodor looked at the construction crews and thanked them once more before looking to Carl.

The dropship's doors opened and a group of men exited: an officer in the lead with two medics moving behind. The officer carried no rifle, only his holstered sidearm at his hip. Carl assumed the military didn't wish to spook Fyodor by parading unneeded weapons around.

The officer walked down the snow shovelled path to the communications tower and approached the crew. He removed his field cap and nodded at both Carl and Fyodor as he stood before them. The officer handed Fyodor a small microphone and pointed to his own neck. Carl could see a microphone was attached to the lapel of his uniform. The man waited for Fyodor to attach the device to his coat before speaking.

As he spoke, the microphone translated the Western Standard to Russian instantaneously. Old Reliable began to translate but stopped when he heard it wasn't necessary.

"I am Major Jorge Carson," the officer said as he held out a hand to shake.

Fyodor shook Major Carson's hand and the officer continued. "You must be Fyodor. We've heard a lot about you. All good things, of course."

Fyodor smiled as he spoke. "It is nice to meet you, Sir. Where are we going?" He looked impressed when his microphone took his Russian and translated it immediately.

"To the Capital Rim. A lot of very important people want to meet you. Presidents, ministers, generals, admirals, you name it. Many curious CEO's from our space programs want nothing more than to have pictures taken with you."

Fyodor smiled again and looked to Carl for reassurance that this was real. Carl nodded. "Now, I'll tell you what's next Fyodor," Major Carson continued. "These medics here will examine you. Once you're cleared in the shuttle, we will fly you up to our ship, the C.D.V. Hermes. Then it's back home. Back to Earth. It's changed a little since you've been there."

"I know. Carl here has told me so."

"I'm glad he did. Less of a shock when we get there. Some changes for the better, some for the worse. But that's life I suppose."

"What about my ship, major?" Fyodor asked as he gestured to the four-hundred-year-old beast of a vessel that sat in the hole.

"It's coming with us. Those two dropships over there are going to hoist it up. First, we will make sure the heat shields are intact and repair them if necessary. Then it will be loaded in the destroyer. It's a piece of history; we can't leave it behind." The major paused and fumbled in his breast pocket for a moment before pulling out a felt case. He continued once the case was firmly in hand, "I'm getting ahead of myself, though." He cleared his throat, "Fyodor Petrov. On behalf of the Colonial Expansion Initiative, Earth, and all her colonies, I present you, a medal." He opened the case, revealing a gold star attached to red felt. "Hero of The Soviet Union."

Fyodor stood up straight as the medal gleamed in the sunlight. His eyes started to water. Major Carson took the medallion out of the case and pinned it on the cosmonaut's shirt. Fyodor was happier and prouder than any man alive. The major finished securing the medal and took a step back.

"We found pictures of it in the archives. Our armours on board made it. Does it look accurate to how you remember it?"

"Yes, exactly as I remember it." Fyodor said as he looked at the shining medal on his chest, his voice trembled as memories of a life-long past flooded his mind.

"I'm glad to hear it. If you have any belongings to bring, now's the time."

Fyodor nodded and saluted the major. Once the officer returned the salute he ran over to the bunker and grabbed the only three things he had taken from his ship in preparation for the military's landing: his flight suit, his bag of clothing and his Soviet Union flag, possibly the last flag of its kind still in existence.

Fyodor returned to the major and the two medics approached. One grabbed his flight suit and then offered to take the flag but Fyodor shook his head that he wished to hold onto it for himself.

Major Carson smiled. "Time to go home."

The major pivoted and started toward the landed drop-ship, the medics following close behind. Fyodor took a step forward, then hesitated. He turned around and hugged Carl.

"Thank you for everything," he said as his voice quivered.

"It was nothing. I'm glad we found you," Carl replied as sadness crept over him; he was sorry to see his new friend go.

Fyodor smiled and he reached into his pocket. "I have something for you," he said as he extended his hand towards Carl.

Fyodor opened his hand revealing a circular patch. The artwork and stitching were of the absolute highest quality. The design depicted a portion of Mars at the bottom of the artwork with white Russian lettering etched across the red planet. Jutting up into the dark sky were two ships, similar designs for both. Both had the letters *C.C.C.P.* written vertically down their hulls in red, the same tone as the Martian surface. Ten stars hovered over the planet, arching across the horizon. One for each cosmonaut. Earth sat as a small sphere of blues and greens to the far right of the image, placed above the glowing stars.

"Our mission's patch. 'Operation Worker's Paradise.' That's what it says at the bottom," Fyodor said as he pointed to the white writing.

"Fyodor this is amazing. I don't know what to say," Carl said, as he looked at the patch in his hand. It was absolutely beautiful.

"I believe it is customary to say thank you, or have customs changed so greatly in the last few centuries?" he laughed and nudged Carl with his elbow.

The historian in Carl was thrilled to be holding this piece of forgotten history. Long removed from the annals of time, but for no longer. Now, with Fyodor's help, these untold events, and the names of the overlooked cosmonauts who had made the ultimate sacrifice, would be returned to their rightful place in history. They had earned a spot, and for their stories to be told.

"Thank you, this means a lot."

"Now we both have one. I had a couple extras and wanted

to give you something to remember our operation by. I have one on the arm of my flight suit as well."

The two men smiled, but quickly they faded, as it was time to say goodbye. Fyodor hugged Carl for a long time before letting go and moving over to Old Reliable. He hugged its cold steel body and patted the old worker drone on the head, thanking it for all its service. Fyodor stood up and turned back to Carl. "If your company ever wants to sell this robot, you tell me. I'll buy it. I know I have no money, but I'm sure I will get some soon."

Carl grabbed a card from his wallet and handed it to Fyodor. "This is my personal contact number, work number and mail code. I know you don't know how to use these yet, but you will. Stay in touch."

Fyodor looked to Old Reliable as he translated what Carl said. He looked at the card for a moment before putting it delicately in his pocket. He inhaled and tried to hold back his obvious sadness. He shook Carl's hand one last time before heading to the dropship where Major Carson and the medics were waiting.

He trudged up to the top of the ramp and turned to face the work crew that had gathered around the construction site. Fyodor waved one last time before entering the dropship. His medal hung handsomely on his shirt, and the Soviet flag dangled in his left hand.

Carl noticed one of the other dropships ceased hovering and landed next to Fyodor's vessel. A team of nine technicians exited. Shovels, picks, and chains in hand. They scaled *Laika Two* and began to get her ready be raised up out of that hole so the repairs could commence.

Carl stood with Old Reliable and waited for Fyodor's dropship to lift off. After several minutes, it did just that. Fyodor Petrov had been cleared by the medics of any contaminants and was given the green light to be airborne once more. Beautiful words to any pilot. Carl watched the ship take flight and fly over the hills. Fyodor had quite the life ahead of him and would do well for himself.

He would write a series of books, go on speaking tours across a hundred worlds, and be the subject of multiple documentaries. Everyone would want to meet and have their picture taken with The Oldest Man, The Last Cosmonaut, The Final Soviet, Comrade Fyodor, and whatever other titles people could come up with for him. Fyodor would have a very comfortable life ahead, and he deserved it. It was not only a miracle that his ship had survived the crash, but that he had been found at all. Pure luck, or fate, or divine intervention, that he would be marooned on the spot where colonists would one day decide to place a communications tower.

As the dropship disappeared behind the hills, Carl had a sudden and intriguing thought. Fyodor had more flight hours than all the American astronauts combined. He had flown farther than any person from his era and was the first man to land on an interstellar world. He had even contributed to the construction of Tokyo-Miami. Fyodor would be remembered in the coming history, alongside greats like, Yuri Gagarin, Neil Armstrong, and Buzz Aldrin. The Russians had won the space race after all.

APPENDICES

APPENDIX A:

NEXT GENERATION IN MOTOR SPORTS: SEASON TWENTY-EIGHT:
CHAMPIONSHIP RACE FIVE: HELIX MINING COLONY: MARTIAN TRACK

ALL INFORMATION CONTAINED IN THIS DOCUMENT IS SUBJECT TO COPYRIGHT AND IS OWNED IN FULL, OR IN PARTNERSHIP BY THE N.G.M.S. AND ITS RESPECTIVE OWNERS OR STAKEHOLDERS. DISTRIBUTION OR REPRODUCTION OF ANY PART OR PIECE OF THIS DOCUMENT WITHOUT WRITTEN AUTHORIZATION FROM THE N.G.M.S WILL RESULT IN LEGAL ACTION.

OFFICIAL RESULTS:

1ST SVETLANA KRAVCHENKO—NOVA MOTORSPORTS
2ND ADRIAN "TITAN" JACOBSON—WRAITH CYCLE SYSTEMS
3RD ALBERTO CASTILLO CABRERA—STAR BLITZ RACERS
4TH JAFARI "TIGER" ACHEBE—PACIFIC SPEED ASSOCIATION
5TH JACQUE "HOPPER" GOLSON—E.W.P. RACING
6TH KWAITO "ARISAKA" SAITO—HEXWAY BIKES

7*TH* ISMAIL KOTH—LIGHTNING M.C.A.

8*TH* KRISTEN "AVENGER" SINGER—TURBO C.A.S. LIMITED

9*TH* TALLI "APACHE" DAWSON—N.A.R.A. MOTORCYCLES

10*TH* JENNA "NILE" CRISTELLI—RAVEN MOTORS

11*TH* SASHA LINDELL—UNITED METAL WORKS

12*TH* WANG FANG CHOE—FREE FORM INDUSTRIES

13*TH* JAMES FURLONG—INDEPENDENT MOTORSPORTS

14*TH* SEO YOON—UNITED KOREAN RACING LTD.

15*TH* JANICE "MOTOR CITY" WILDMAN—FLASH ENGINES INC.

16*TH* NANCY "SAPPHIRE" ZONG—FALCON INDUSTRIES

17*TH* KEVIN MCMANTIS—NEW YORK CYCLES LTD.

18*TH* FONTANE "FURY"—ROCKET RACER INDUSTRIES

19*TH* VERONICA "VENGEANCE" SILVERMAN—S.A.R.A.D. CYCLE AND
SPORTS

20*TH* GUNTHER HESS—DRAGON MOTORS

21*ST* LLOYD CLARKE—SUPERSONIC RACERS

22*ND* JASON CARRINGTON—VULTURE MOTORCYCLE ASSOCIATION

DID NOT FINISH RESULTS:

D.N.F. LOUIS "EMPIRE" MARQUEE—FORTIFIED SYSTEMS- K.I.A.

D.N.F. PEARCY BALDWOODS—BLOODSPORT BIKES- K.I.A.

D.N.F. MATHIAS "CYCLONE" JORIG—ORION MOTORSPORTS-
SURVIVED

D.N.F. ELENA ORTEGA—LATIN PROUD SPORT BIKES- K.I.A.

D.N.F. OTHELLO NACKSAR—BANE MOTORS- SURVIVED

D.N.F. VINCENT "DRAX" WINDSOR—MARAUDER MOTORCYCLES-
SURVIVED

D.N.F. HARVEY ALI—SKY LIMIT INDUSTRIES- K.I.A.

D.N.F. HANZ "GUS" AXELSON—WARBIRD MOTORSPORTS- K.I.A.

D.N.F. FERNANDA "SUERTE" GOMEZ—LATINA MOTORSPORTS- K.I.A.

D.N.F. AIMI "RISING SUN" YAMAMOTO—C67 900 MECHANIX
ASSOCIATED- K.I.A.

D.N.F. JACK "SAINT" FORD—RAZOR MOTORS- SURVIVED

D.N.F. KYLE "NOMAD" ST. JOHN——LAWSON-SOKO LTD.- K.I.A.

D.N.F. AARON LEE——SPEEDWING CORP.- K.I.A.

D.N.F. RALPH "RANGER" POSSEBON——POSSEBON AND SONS RACING

INC.- K.I.A.

D.N.F. LILLY CARPENTER——SOUNDWAVE DESIGNS- SURVIVED

APPENDIX B:

Korean Steel Setlist- Friday September 16th 1988

(Last full show before the events of Saturday September 17th 1988)

LIVE SET:

ACE IN THE HOLE——WITH OVERWHELMING FORCE

FASHIONABLE ECSTASY——NIGHT DANGER

LEAVE 'EM FOR DEAD——BREAK AND ENTER

---BAND INTRODUCTIONS---

32-32——TASTE THE STEEL

BOMBS OVER BROOKLYN——BOMBS OVER BROOKLYN

L.A. RIDERS——LIV LIVE

FLYING BLIND——INDICTABLE OFFENCE

TAILLIGHT FEVER——BREAK AND ENTER

FOREIGN POLICY——NIGHT DANGER

LOVE ME——LOVE HER DEADLY

RED LIGHTNING——BOMBS OVER BROOKLYN

---GUITAR SOLOS---
BACK OFF——BOMBS OVER BROOKLYN
DEVASTATE AND DEVIATE——NIGHT DANGER
GODSPEED (HIGH-STRUNG)——INDICTABLE OFFENCE
SOCIOLOGICAL INMATE——LOVE HER DEADLY
HUNTER FOR LOVE——BREAK AND ENTER
HOLD ME CLOSE——WITH OVERWHELMING FORCE
MUSKETS OF THE RHINE——BOMBS OVER BROOKLYN

ENCORE:

FOR KING AND COUNTRY——INDICTABLE OFFENCE
LIGHTS OUT (FOR YOU)——BREAK AND ENTER

NUMBER OF TRACKS PREFORMED FROM EACH ALBUM:

TASTE THE STEEL (1980): 1 TRACK
BREAK AND ENTER (1981): 4 TRACKS
NIGHT DANGER (1982): 3 TRACKS
INDICTABLE OFFENCE (1983): 3 TRACKS
BOMBS OVER BROOKLYN (1984): 4 TRACKS
LIV LIVE (1985): 1 TRACK
LOVE HER DEADLY (1986): 2 TRACKS
WITH OVERWHELMING FORCE (1988): 2 TRACKS

A CALL TO ACTION

Thank you for reading my debut anthology. If you enjoyed this book, please leave a kind review on Amazon or Goodreads. Not only do reviews help with sales immensely, but it also provides feedback for me as a writer to know what I'm doing well.

To learn more about what I'm working on next, you can follow me on Goodreads or like my Facebook page: "The Works of Robert J. Bradshaw." I also publish a monthly newsletter where I not only share the latest news on my current projects, but also reveal developments and updates on future titles. Links to subscribe to the newsletter can be found through my Facebook page.

ACKNOWLEDGMENTS

I would like to say a very special thank you to all of those who helped make this collection possible:

Colleen and Dennis Atkinson, Veronica Martinez Soto, Nathan Olmstead, Adam Kudryk, Gabriela Hernandez Maltos, Kyle Mencfeld, Emily Chabot from One Tree Quill Publishing for all her hard work and Ronnie at *"Tegnemaskin.no"* for his amazing cover art on this second edition.

From the bottom of my heart, thank you.

-Robert J. Bradshaw,
May 2022

ALSO BY ROBERT J. BRADSHAW

SHADOWS AT MIDNIGHT:

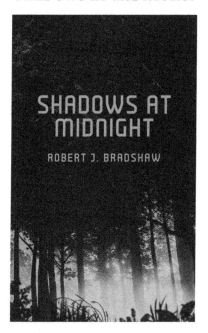

A Mayan ruin with a long-forgotten secret, a cult that is attempting to bridge the gap between worlds, and a beast that lurks inside the phone lines… In this collection of tales, the mysteries only get darker.

Stories of stunning science fiction, otherworldly horrors, and pulse pounding thrills, coming together to create an anthology you won't be forgetting anytime soon.

Get your copy, today!

A MONARCH AMONG KINGS:

Far off in the Andromeda Galaxy, thousands of colonists have carved out a life for themselves on the remote world of Seryhenya.

However, as a young officer in the Colonial Guard Corps will soon discover, the planet might just hold more life than expected...

Follow multiple viewpoints as each character struggles to navigate the unfolding crisis. Some want to destroy this potential threat before it can fester; others want to live and let live. It is up for debate who is correct in their assessment of the situation.

But keeping an eye on the horizon might not be the only thing the colonists have to worry about...

Get your copy, today!

ABOUT THE AUTHOR

Robert J. Bradshaw was born and raised in St. Catharines, Ontario, Canada. He relocated to British Columbia, seeking adventure. He currently lives in the Fraser Valley region.

Science fiction and horror are genres that have gripped him his entire life and, in his opinion, are at their best when they blend together, complimenting each other perfectly.

Songs of the Abyss is but the first of two pulse pounding anthologies unleashed on the world. His second collection, *Shadows At Midnight*, was released in October of 2021.

Bradshaw is currently hard at work on his debut novel as well as another gathering of tales.

Printed in Great Britain
by Amazon

25379087R00166